DOROTHY LAMBERT
MUCH DITHERING

DOROTHY Lambert was born Alicia Dorothea Irwin on 17 February 1884 in County Cork, Ireland. Until her marriage she lived with her family in 'Roskeen', a Georgian country house near Mallow.

In 1906 she married Eric Lambert, a solicitor. Soon after their marriage the couple sailed to Bombay, where their daughter, Eileen (known by her middle name 'Audrey') was born in 1908. Dorothy returned to Cork for the birth in July 1913 of their son, Thomas, who only lived for a few months. The Lamberts were both back in India at the outbreak of the First World War, during which Eric served in the army, but after the war they returned to England, where Eric became a partner in a firm of Dover solicitors, and was later Dover's coroner.

The Lamberts lived in Shepherdswell, a few miles outside Dover, where Dorothy and her family immersed themselves in the social and cultural life of the village. This included numerous theatrical entertainments, some of the plays written by Dorothy herself.

Her novel-writing career began at the age of 43, and ultimately included twenty-seven novels, the last published in 1953. Dorothy Lambert died in a nursing home near Dover in 1967, having outlived Eric by nine years.

S0-ABB-078

NOVELS BY DOROTHY LAMBERT

DOROTHY LAMBERT

MUCH DITHERING

With an introduction by
Elizabeth Crawford

DEAN STREET PRESS

A Furrowed Middlebrow Book

FM49

Published by Dean Street Press 2020

Copyright © 1938 Dorothy Lambert

Introduction © 2020 Elizabeth Crawford

All Rights Reserved

Published by licence, issued under the UK Orphan Works
Licensing Scheme

First published in 1938 by Collins

Cover by DSP

ISBN 978 1 913527 33 4

www.deanstreetpress.co.uk

INTRODUCTION

'AN EXCELLENT evening's entertainment' reported the *Dover Express* (3 January 1934) of two plays staged a couple of days earlier by the Shepherdswell Village Players. The reviewer gave full details of the event, mentioning that the second of the plays, 'Christmas Party', written and produced by Mrs. Dorothy Lambert, 'contained many amusing and delicate scenes'. Among the play's characters were a 'Jocelyn', a 'Mrs. Goodbun', and a 'Colonel Tidmarsh', all of whom re-appeared four years later, their parts expanded in a full-length novel, *Much Dithering*. Given by 'Jocelyn', catered for by the obliging 'Mrs. Goodbun', and attended by, among others, 'Colonel Tidmarsh', a Christmas Day party does, indeed, feature in the novel, at the centre of the action a chimney fire, the reactions to which sort the Much Dithering sheep from the Much Dithering goats. An exceedingly prolific writer, having published eight novels between 1929 and 1934, Dorothy Lambert clearly held a medley of plots, characters, and scenes in her imagination, ready to revive them whenever the opportunity arose. Between the staging of 'Christmas Party' and the publication of *Much Dithering* she wrote eight novels; Jocelyn and her companions had had to wait their turn before fulfilling their destinies.

Dorothy Lambert was 45 years old when Mills and Boon published her first novel. *Redferne M.F.H.* (1929) was 'a tale of Irish hunting life', which also featured 'raids and fights between Free State and Republic'. As the reviewer in the *Aberdeen Press and Journal* (21 February 1929) commented, 'the author obviously knows Ireland'. Indeed, she did, for she was born Alicia Dorothea Irwin on 17 February 1884 in Co. Cork and, until her marriage, lived with her family in Roskeen, a Georgian country house close to Kanturk, near Mallow. Her father, Arthur Irwin (1849-1919), was a civil engineer whose family came from Co. Tyrone in the north of Ireland and her mother, Alice Louisa Power (1857-1934), was the daughter of John Power of Roskeen, whose family had held land in that area of Cork since the early

18th century. Dorothy, therefore, grew up as a member of the Anglo-Irish landed gentry and it is this milieu that features in many of her earlier novels.

We know nothing of Dorothy's life with her parents, sister, one surviving brother and three servants in the 'big house' of Roskeen, nor anything of her education. However, from her Irish novels one might deduce that she relished an outdoor life, felt comfortable with neighbours from all levels of society, and had a hearty appetite for life's possibilities. In 1906 she married Eric Tom Lambert (1878-1958) at the Church of Ireland church at Kanturk. He was a Cambridge-educated solicitor, son of the head of a long-established firm of Nottingham lace manufacturers, hardly a natural denizen of the wilds of Cork. The story behind his meeting with Dorothy must stem from a romance of their elders for, in 1899, two years after the death of Eric's mother, his father had married Eloise Power, a cousin of Dorothy's mother. It is not difficult to imagine love blossoming between members of the younger generation during holiday visits to Roskeen. Indeed it is just such a theme, the introduction of an attractive outsider into a close-knit community, that is central to many of Dorothy Lambert's novels, both those set in Ireland and those, such as *Much Dithering*, in England.

Soon after their marriage Dorothy and Eric set out for Bombay, where their daughter, Audrey, was born in 1908. Dorothy returned to Cork for the birth in July 1913 of their son, Thomas, who only lived for a few months. The Lamberts were in India at the outbreak of the First World War, during which Eric served as a major in the Bombay Brigade of the Royal Artillery, but after the war returned to England, where he became a partner in a firm of Dover solicitors, Knocker, Elwin and Lambert and, from 1923 until 1948, Dover's coroner.

The Lamberts lived at Sheep's Close in Shepherdswell, a few miles outside Dover, where, as the local paper shows, Dorothy immersed herself in the social and cultural life of the village. She was at one time secretary to the local Women's Institute, a soloist in the flourishing Musical Society, and, as we have seen, a leading light in the Shepherdswell Village Players. Press reports of her activities suggest that Dorothy was lively, warm-hearted, and gregarious. She embedded herself in the life of the village, drawing names for her characters from people she encountered on her daily round. For instance, the Dover firm of Hedgecock and Warner supplied props for at least one of her plays and 'Joe Hedgecock' turns up as mine host of Much Dithering's Roebuck Inn. In turn, Wilfred Roebuck was an actor in Dorothy's production of *Two Birds and a Stone*. For, as Much Dithering offered its inhabitants 'classes for handicrafts, country dancing, glee-singing and study circles', so newcomers such as Dorothy saw that the tiny village of Shepherdswell kept itself well amused.

In fact, all three Lamberts played their parts in fund-raising entertainments. For instance, Audrey took a leading role in *Two Birds and a Stone*, a play written by her mother and staged in Dover in 1939, and Eric played 'Rupert Earle' in 'Christmas Party', surely the love interest (renamed 'Gervase Blythe' for *Much Dithering*). He also took the lead in a production of 'Widows are Wonderful', another of Dorothy's plays. This received the accolade of being adjudicated by actor Robert Newton, who 'gave careful and encouraging criticism, both on the play and its players'. (*Dover Express*, 21 February 1936).

In setting her scenes in *Much Dithering* Dorothy Lambert drew on a lifetime of experience in matters great and small, from life in the Indian army to costume making for amateur dramatic productions. She knows The Priory, the Honourable Augusta Renshawe's 'big house', Jocelyn's 'Dower House', with its 'oak panelling and Jacobean cretonnes', and the Roebuck Inn where 'the bar-parlour was warm and comfortably old-fashioned, gleaming with pewter and copper'. She knows Gervase, the 'rolling stone' who awakens Jocelyn, Much Dithering's Sleeping Beauty, Ambrose Tidmarsh, the dull colonel returned from India on the lookout for a wife to administer to his old-age needs, Ermyntrude Lascelles, recently widowed for a second time and determined to capture a husband whose career might do her justice, and Mrs. Pomfret, who knows that 'burglars don't sing the Messiah'. She also colludes with her readers, most of whom would be reading a library copy, in voicing the thoughts of Mrs. Faggot, Much Dithering's post mistress, who 'was astute enough (for she read all the sensational fiction that her branch of a circulating library could supply) to realise that the chief ingredients for a good two-penno'orth of village scandal existed, or were about to exist, in the hitherto blameless village outside her window'.

However, Art did not imitate Life and, while creating 'Jocelyn Renshawe', 'a rather pathetic slave to duty', admired for her 'charming Victorian dignity', at home Dorothy Lambert encouraged her daughter's developing career. Although much the same age as *Much Dithering*'s heroine, Audrey had already acquired a University of London degree, published two novels, one of which was set in Ireland, and qualified as a solicitor. She later became senior partner in her father's firm and married the senior partner of Dover's other law practice. Although Mrs. Pomfret declares that 'We've always been old-fashioned here in Much Dithering and I hope we always will be', in real life Dorothy Lambert was not one to inhibit progress. She carried on writing, publishing another ten novels after *Much Dithering*, before her death in 1967.

Elizabeth Crawford

CHAPTER ONE

ERMYNTRUDE Lascelles, widowed for the second time, felt that Fate had treated her shabbily in removing her George just as he was about to get command of his regiment. The rôle of a colonel's wife would have suited her admirably, and twice it had been almost within reach and then snatched away: once in India when Dick Pallfrey had been killed on the Frontier; and then, *most* annoyingly, just when the regiment was going to Egypt, George Lascelles was inconsiderate enough to contract measles—measles, of all things! So like George, who made a point of contracting every possible disease and was really a very tiresome, fussy little man, only bearable because he had a little money and would one day be a colonel, being a sound if uninspired soldier, and might even have gone as far as a brigadier. But no! Being George, within sight of achieving his wife's ambition, he contracted measles, which led to pneumonia, and so Ermyntrude was a widow who lived in a private hotel in South Kensington and visited her friends with unfailing regularity.

With her daughter at Much Dithering, Ermyntrude spent as little time as possible. She disliked her sister-in-law and despised her daughter for her lack of initiative and fondness for good works. Jocelyn's marriage, too, had been such a dreary failure. If only she had been able to keep her husband alive a year longer! But there again Fate had been unkindly freakish, and Lancelot Renshawe died of a chill a few months before his father, so Jocelyn had not achieved what all her relatives had so ardently desired for her. The property that had for centuries belonged to the Renshawes had passed her by and had been inherited by a nephew of whom no one knew anything, and Jocelyn, instead of being the Lady of the Manor and a daughter of whom Ermyntrude could be proud (as well as being able to provide a pleasant country house in which to stay), was still a person of no importance, living in a small, old-fashioned and inconvenient dower house, and even that only until the new owner should return. The Dower House was part of the Priory, and would pass to the new owner of the property in time, and then presumably Jocelyn would take a small house in Much Dithering near her aunt and would continue to do good works and to be as stodgy and unenterprising in her middle age as she had been in her youth. Youth? No, Jocelyn had never had any youth. She was dull and stupid and existed as a species of doormat to her mother-in-law and aunt, and her house had no gas or electric light, and the bath water was very seldom hot, and it was sheer purgatory to be forced to go and spend a few weeks in it when funds were low and it was imperative to live cheaply in order to save money for spring clothes.

No wonder Ermyntrude had a grievance—several grievances, in fact. She was still young and extremely decorative, even if she was unfortunately "outsize" and had to choose clothes with slimming lines. Her hair was auburn, her eyes dark blue and heavily lashed, and her complexion a credit to the "little place" just off Gloucester Road from which it came. If only George had lived she would have been a credit to the regiment and a menace to the peace of mind of its junior officers, for she was a practised and voracious "baby snatcher."

Her latest victim (a willing one) had been Adrian Murchison-Bellaby, a subaltern in the regiment she had so nearly commanded, and she was surprised and delighted when Adrian told her of the country place his people (rich purveyors of potted meat) had taken. Dithering Place? But how extraordinary! And Adrian was going to spend some weeks there on leave during the winter for the hunting and shooting, and in Much Dithering there would be absolutely no one for the poor boy to talk to, and he would be bored to tears, and the Murchison-Bellabys kept a *chef*. It was a pity about Jocelyn's bath-water, but it couldn't be helped. She would insist on a constant supply of hot water in kettles, or even goad Jocelyn into putting in a new boiler. After all, Adrian was a good catch and desirous of climbing higher in the social scale. Ermyntrude was still in the forties and looked in the thirties (or imagined that she did!), and even if there were a few years' difference in their ages it really wouldn't matter. He liked a good time, and she was the right sort of wife to guide him on the right lines, and if he were eventually to leave the Army and settle down as a country gentleman and stand for Parliament, as his mother ardently desired, she would be eminently the right woman for the position. Yes, she must certainly keep her eye on Adrian, and a visit to Much Dithering would be an excellent idea.

It was very odd the way Fate worked. Who would ever have imagined that Much Dithering would prove a battle-ground in which to pit her wits against those of Adrian's mother, who would be sure to object to her age? Ermyntrude felt convinced, however, that her own experience of the world and superior social standing and quality would prove victorious in any encounter with Mrs. Murchison-Bellaby. Of her success with Adrian she had no doubt whatever. He was completely subjugated, and his capture was so certain that she passed that part over with indifference. He was merely the stepping-stone to the country house she desired and the position of wife to the local Member of Parliament. She would soon be the chief lady of the Ditherings, and oust that abominable woman, the Honourable Mrs. Renshawe. Jocelyn must be brought out—or no, on the whole Jocelyn must be kept in the background, for a daughter who was twenty-five and entirely given over to good works would never fit into her scheme. A widowed daughter of that age was all very well so long as she was tucked away where no one was likely to come across her, but it would be difficult to spring her on Adrian, who up till now had heard vaguely of "my little girl" or "my child," who was very shy and delicate and had to live a quiet life in the country. Ermyntrude would have to impress upon Jocelyn that the Murchison-Bellabys were *not* her sort of people and prevent her coming into contact with them if possible. And yet, if Jocelyn did not call and make their acquaintance, how could she in her turn get to know them? The point was exasperating. At all events, Adrian must not meet Jocelyn until he was safely booked to be her stepfather. He was going to Much Dithering for Christmas, she knew, so she would have to go down a week or so before he was due for his leave and make it clear to Jocelyn that her part would be to remain strictly in the background where the Murchison-Bellabys were concerned and to stick dutifully to her good works, in which sphere she would certainly not be likely to meet the Murchison-Bellabys, who would, of course, be busy entertaining a smart—well, not so very *smart*, perhaps, but at any rate a rich—party of friends for Christmas, and would not be bothering about a dull little village and its doings. She might even (and this was a very bright idea) say that Jocelyn was her stepdaughter, or at any rate give that impression, and if Jocelyn would remember to call her "Ermyntrude" and not "Mummy," it would not call attention to any particular relationship at all.

Decidedly she must go to Much Dithering and get her plans laid. The explanations would be a little tiresome, but she was sure that Jocelyn would be reasonable and dutiful. And her sister-in-law and that odious woman, the Honourable Augusta? They disliked her and might make it awkward if they said stupid things, but they were not the sort of people to attract the Murchison-Bellabys, and very probably they would never get the chance to discuss her. Anyhow, all these were risks that had to be taken, so there was no use worrying; they had to be faced and defeated. She would order some new frocks at once and go to Much Dithering immediately. There was no time like the present.

CHAPTER TWO

A FEW days after Ermyntrude's arrival in Much Dithering Mrs. Pomfret, the vicar's wife, was receiving Mrs. Murchison-Bellaby's call in return for the one she had paid some weeks previously. Mrs. Pomfret's drawing-room was not so much a drawing-room as a species of clearing-house for lost belongings connected with her parish activities. With the festivities of the Christmas season looming in the immediate future, things were in even worse confusion than usual, but Mrs. Pomfret, a genial person whose soul was above such commonplaces as an untidy drawing-room, received her visitors with her usual exuberance, cleared off the pile of music from one chair and some yards of coloured muslin, destined for dresses for the Band of Hope Infant's Entertainment, from another, and seated herself on the piano stool, twirling it to face Mrs. Murchison-Bellaby and her daughter Jasmine.

"We're really beginning to feel settled in at last," explained Mrs. Murchison-Bellaby graciously, "and I must apologise for not returning your call sooner, but we've been so busy. We felt we must be settled in by Christmas. Didn't we, Jasmine?"

Mrs. Murchison-Bellaby was very large and artificial-looking and wore a magnificent fur coat, but she was really quite an ordinary kind-hearted person with an ambition to be treated nicely and allowed to take an active part in the life of this comic little village where she had come to live and in which she hoped to make a niche for herself and her family. She liked the look of Mrs. Pomfret, and she smiled ingratiatingly at her.

Her daughter Jasmine was a handsome girl of about twenty, dark-eyed, full-lipped, with a sulky droop to her red mouth. She was not inclined to follow her mother's lead of affability towards a woman who lived in what appeared to be a second-hand store, and wore a tartan skirt with a green knitted jumper, and whose untidy hair, dressed in a loose coil, was in imminent danger of descending. Indeed, Mrs. Pomfret seemed to realise this, and was at the moment engaged in re-inserting a large tortoiseshell pin into the perilous structure that was slipping towards the nape of her neck.

Jasmine made an inaudible reply to her mother's query and continued to make an inventory of the strange contents of the room. A grand piano bore several pyramids of music, an Aladdin lamp, a work-basket, a copper pot full of preserved beech-leaves, and several tin boxes full of unspecified junk. The chairs were a poor lot, and the battered chesterfield obviously had broken springs, which after all hardly mattered, since it was quite impossible to sit on it, as it was covered with rolls of white cotton-wool in red baize, out of which Mrs. Pomfret had been engaged in cutting large letters to form the text: "Christ is born in Bethlehem" to form part of her Christmas decorations in church.

"You are wondering what that is?" Mrs. Pomfret said in her direct manner, noticing the speculation in Jasmine's eyes. "It's the text I put round the chancel walls for Christmas. I've had to replace the old one—moths or mice, or both, ruined the letters; I was very annoyed. Talking of decorations, Mrs. Murchison-Bellaby, I wonder—"

"Oh, anything!" promised Mrs. Murchison-Bellaby with enthusiasm. "Just say what you'd like us to send."

"That's very kind of you," said Mrs. Pomfret, her eyes shining with pleasure. "How splendid of you to want to be one of our little band of workers. We were afraid that, being new and coming from London, you wouldn't want to have anything to do with ordinary village life and our little doings. This is a *great* relief. I'm sure Percival will be delighted. He likes the better-class people to set a good example to the village. It's so necessary, Mrs. Murchison-Bellaby. We want to bring it home to our young people that our church is the greatest thing we possess, and that all classes must meet on common ground and—"

"I'll tell Leopold," Mrs. Murchison-Bellaby assured her. "We'll be sure to come regularly, and our young people, too. I have great hopes that my son will like the place, and that some day he will leave the Army and marry and settle here and stand for Parliament. That's my ambition."

"And very suitable, too," agreed Mrs. Pomfret.

"Tell me," said Jasmine suddenly, "what sort of people live here? I mean decent people that one wants to know."

"Now let me see—" Mrs. Pomfret looked thoughtful.

"Of course there's the Honourable Augusta at the Priory. She's the widow of our late lamented Lord of the Manor and a bit antiquated in her views, I fear."

"In fact, a frump," broke in Jasmine rudely. "No good! Go on—who else?"

"Then there's Miss Pallfrey at Green Gates—a dear; but you'll call her a frump, too, I'm afraid. And then there's her niece Jocelyn Renshawe. She's quite young and my right hand in the parish. I'd be lost without her. You'll love her—every one does—and you'll be very good for her." She paused and looked Jasmine over. "Yes, you'll be very good for her. She's almost too good, though I, the vicar's wife, say so. She's young in years, but she has never been allowed to enjoy her youth. Her aunt brought her up, and she was married off at eighteen to young Lancelot Renshawe, who was—well, to be blunt, not quite mental, but *soft*. Then he died some time ago, and she is still ordered about by her aunt and mother-in-law. I'd like to see Jocelyn *young*. You must shake her up."

"She sounds like a stained-glass window," said Jasmine, looking bored; "but I'll see what I can do. My brother Adrian might cheer things up for her, only he'd probably shock her."

Mrs. Murchison-Bellaby leaned forward. "Is she pretty?" she asked anxiously.

"Oh, *very* pretty," replied Mrs. Pomfret; "and as good as she is pretty."

"What an unusual combination!" yawned Jasmine. "I believe she called the other day. We seem to have missed something."

"We must return her call at once," declared Mrs. Murchison-Bellaby.

"Is there no one else?!' asked Jasmine impatiently. "It doesn't sound very promising so far."

"There is Colonel Tidmarsh, a retired Army man—very pleasant, but a little gloomy, poor fellow. He is a widower, and I fear has never got over the death of his wife."

"How tiresome!"

Mrs. Pomfret put a finger to her lip. "Ah, but I think he is on the mend. I'm sure he admires Jocelyn Renshawe, and I think it would be quite a good thing for her, if nothing else turned up—not *lively*, of course—but she won't expect liveliness—and it would be a comfort to her aunt to leave her in safe hands when she dies."

"It sounds a pretty poor idea to me," scoffed Jasmine, "to be left in *safe hands*. Heavens, give me a spice of danger! I want to be *alive*. Safety doesn't appeal to me."

"I dare say not, but every one has her own point of view. I'm glad to say Jocelyn is full of common sense and is never likely to seek for excitement or danger."

"Well, she can keep Colonel Titmouse, or whatever his name is," said Jasmine. "Is that really all? No one else at all?"

"Oh, just a few—General and Mrs. Wingham and a few people in Little Dithering and beyond that near Totterford."

"Well, *I* think Much Dithering is a marvellous place to be *buried* in," said Jasmine bitterly; "but as long as I'm alive I shan't spend much of my time in it, and I'd hate to be a menace to the peace of mind of either your Titmouse or the stained-glass saint. Neither is quite in my line."

"You do talk such silly nonsense," complained Mrs. Murchison-Bellaby. "You and Adrian will drive me crazy one of these days." She turned to Mrs. Pomfret and began to talk about village affairs with eager curiosity, Mrs. Pomfret entering with immense enthusiasm into a discussion so near her heart, while Jasmine, bored beyond expression, sat and looked out into the untidy garden and speculated lazily as to what life in a place of this sort could possibly bring one. No adventure, certainly, which was her idea of life; but, from all she had seen and heard of Much Dithering in her short sojourn in her new home, every one and everything in the whole place was just dead and mouldering. Really, she couldn't do anything about it!

CHAPTER THREE

IT WAS a pity that the second Wednesdays were invariably wet. Jocelyn Renshawe, a rather pathetic slave to duty, always visited the almshouses and took out the Parish Magazines on the second Wednesdays, and as her mother-in-law pointed out, what was put off to another day always interfered with something else, and anyhow if one got into the habit of considering the English climate or of allowing it to interfere with one's arrangements, one might just as well hibernate, or whatever were the seasonable equivalents, during the rest of the year. Fine-weather people were fine-weather sportsmen, fine-weather friends, and in every way to be despised.

Without actually agreeing with the Honourable Augusta, Jocelyn's aunt, Miss Mellicent Pallfrey, held that duty was duty, so into the depressing gloom of a particularly unpleasant

December afternoon went Jocelyn for her two-mile walk to Little Dithering. Her car was unfortunately out of action and in the hands of the local motor mechanic, who had promised faithfully that it would be ready in time; but the Fates were against it, and therefore Jocelyn, her Burberry buttoned close and a small felt hat pulled low to keep the driving mist out of her eyes, tramped along the narrow road with a neat American-cloth satchel full of improving literature for her old ladies at the almshouses.

There was a bundle of notices, too, about the annual meeting of the Women's Institute, for Jocelyn was a conscientious secretary and delivered important notices by hand if the baker was unable to do it. In the case of Little Dithering she did it herself when she went to the almshouses, as it was all in the same lane, and she might as well stop at the crossroads and hand it out at the cluster of cottages.

Little Dithering was off the map as far as local transport was concerned. No bus called at the small picturesque hamlet, and if one wanted to get there, one walked if one hadn't a car. It was quite a pleasant walk on a fine day, for the country round the Ditherings was pretty in its rural seclusion, and one rarely met any traffic to disturb the peace of one's progress along the narrow winding lanes. Only on fine Saturday afternoons or on Sundays small cars filled to overflowing with family outings were to be met with, drifting round the uncharted country in a semi-demented fashion, the drivers, if they were not used to the locality, having completely lost their way, owing to the numerous little roads running round corners in all directions and separating at crossroads which had no signposts or else bore confusing names that no one had ever heard of and which were not to be discovered on road maps. The inhabitants of the Ditherings certainly believed in keeping themselves to themselves so far as directions to assist strangers to find their way were concerned.

The chief landowner in the neighbourhood was the Honourable Mrs. Renshawe, the widow of the late Rupert Renshawe, whose family had owned extensive property there for more than two centuries. The Honourable Augusta held the reins of government in her territory in very firm hands and maintained an almost feudal autocracy, refusing to move with the times or grant reasonably modern conveniences to her tenants and dependants. She looked after her estate very efficiently, keeping everything under her personal supervision, spending several hours every day with her agent, tramping or riding over her farms or through her woods, which she regarded with immense pride, for forestry was her chief hobby, and most of her time was spent in superintending the care of the big tracts of woodland that surrounded the property.

Being so busy in these directions, she naturally had no time for interesting herself in the social welfare of the people in the villages of Much and Little Dithering. Beyond an occasional edict telling them not to, if she thought they were displaying troublesome tendencies, she left them pretty much to themselves, delegating any duties of visiting and maintaining personal contact to her daughter-in-law Jocelyn, the widow of her only son, who had died nearly a year before his father. Jocelyn was very useful, and fortunately had a strong sense of duty and was content to act under orders. Indeed she had never done anything else as long as she could remember, and could hardly imagine any other existence than the one she had. It had always been the same, and she had never looked into a future that promised change. Nothing in the Ditherings ever changed; they just went on. No one new ever came to live in the neighbourhood (except some odd people who had recently taken a large house close to Much Dithering that had been empty for some years since an elderly Renshawe relation had died), so life flowed on uneventfully. Summer fêtes in aid of the day schools or the church, village concerts, Women's Institute meetings, and the annual garden party at the Priory—such were the events of the year. No wonder that Jocelyn was a specimen of human cabbage, and fitted into her surroundings so completely that she was hardly noticeable. She was always there when wanted, and she was always taken for granted. She took herself for granted and had never thought of herself as an individual with a personality of her own to develop. Her looks were an accident—a lucky accident, for she herself was unaware of her possibilities, and merely accepted herself as God had made her, as she had been brought up to do by her old-fashioned aunt during the years she had spent in her care when her parents were abroad with the Regiment. Later, when her father had been killed and her mother had married again, she had still gone on living with her aunt, for her mother had no desire to be hampered with the care of a growing-up daughter who was in such excellent hands and being so well looked after—so why worry? Ermyntrude Lascelles never believed in worrying over things that might possibly be regarded as responsibilities if taken seriously, so Jocelyn grew up a product of the peaceful cabbagery that Miss Pallfrey inhabited in Much Dithering behind the thick yew hedges of Green Gates, the little house in the village in which she had lived ever since her father, the late Vicar of Dithering, had died and she had had to leave the Vicarage.

There in the course of the peaceful years Jocelyn had grown up and been selected by the Honourable Augusta as the bride for her delicate son, who had, like Jocelyn, been educated at home with a tutor. Indeed Jocelyn had shared the tutor for the studies that were considered necessary for her education but beyond the capacity for imparting instruction possessed by her aunt. It was inevitable that Lancelot Renshawe should imagine himself in love with the pretty, gentle girl beside whom he had grown up. His parents were delighted. Lancelot must marry, of course, but his delicate health had always prevented his going out into the world and choosing a wife, even if he had wished to do so. His own inclinations were those of a recluse, and the idea of marrying Jocelyn, whose ideas of life appeared to be practically identical, was far more to his taste than the suggestion of adventure in the choice of someone he had known only for a short time.

Jocelyn naturally felt that to marry Lancelot was her destiny. Marriage to the heir of all the Ditherings was regarded as the peak of achievement in her daughter's hitherto obscure career by Jocelyn's mother, who was relieved that a married daughter, who would undoubtedly have "dated" her had she ever appeared in the wider world, would still remain buried in Much Dithering.

It suited her admirably. The romance, in fact, was encouraged by every one concerned, and its course was not so much smoothed as steam-rolled. It was "roses, roses all the way," and the happy couple were established in the charming Dower House sheltering behind high redbrick walls mellow with age, just inside Priory Park, close to the village.

Lancelot was interested in his stamp collection and in the cultivation of expensive bulbs. Catalogues of both his hobbies were his favourite reading matter. His intellect was not his strong point, and he took absolutely no interest in outdoor life. Not even the heritage to which he would one day succeed evoked any interest in sport, farming, or any of the usual happenings of country life. His father was bitterly disappointed in his heir, but the Honourable Augusta had a fiercely protective passion for her weakling son and spent her energy in efforts to make up for his deficiencies, taking the place that should have been his in helping her husband in his schemes for farming and forestry, hoping that one day she would succeed in awakening an interest in his heritage in Lancelot's lethargic mind, and if she herself should not be able to achieve her purpose, then Jocelyn must be rallied to the cause and spend her energies, too, in the vain endeavour. Better still, Jocelyn must produce a son to carry on the family and prove a better man for the job than his father.

There, alas! was another disappointment. Jocelyn had no child, and Lancelot succumbed to a chill caught on a wet afternoon when planting a row of tulips in a herbaceous border. So here were the two widowed ladies of Dithering Priory, each in her own way contributing her time and energies to the well-being of their possessions and dependants, and life flowed by as it had always done and presumably would always continue to do in the Ditherings.

The most striking thing about Much Dithering was its peacefulness. The few people who saw it from charabancs on morning or evening or circular drives said: "Isn't it *peaceful*?" or "Isn't it *quiet*?" And some said they thought it was a lovely place to be *buried* in, but while they were alive they preferred a place with more *life*, if you knew what they meant. Its charms even impressed themselves on motorists, since, the street being full of odd corners and sharp turns, it was necessary to slow down and observe the 30-mile limit, which gave them a little time to look about and observe the antiquity of the cottages, the fine church encircled by its centuries-old yews, the quaintness of the square where the few shops displayed their wares, the narrow bumpiness of the bridge across the slow-flowing river that meandered down the valley, and the fine sweep of the beech-woods that crowned the hills and helped to give the impression of isolation to the little village straggling along its one street in the bottom of the valley.

There were pleasant "residences," too, tucked away behind high red-brick walls or thick yew hedges in austere withdrawal from the gaze of charabanc-riders. Much Dithering was "different," and its "difference" attracted would-be inhabitants, but the number of residences was small, and there was no land available for building. Nevertheless, the select circle had been penetrated once or twice by outsiders, who inserted themselves into the places left by the death of the original owners, or even entered into possession by right of inheritance, in which case, of course, they were admitted to have a certain right to existence and were cautiously accepted. In the case of blatant butting-in, however, Much Dithering opinion was very reserved and not to be purchased by display of the interloper's wealth.

The most painful "insertion" was that of the Murchison-Bellabys—London people who had recently taken Dithering Place, which had been empty since old Miss Renshawe died some years earlier, while a less noticeable newcomer was Colonel Tidmarsh at The Brook, but he was in the right tradition, for his predecessor had also been a retired Army man and a prop and stay to Church and State in Much Dithering. Mrs. Pomfret at the Vicarage said she hoped the new people would be regular church-goers and would sing in the choir and take an interest in the choral society, which was short of voices. The vicar said he hoped they would all be good parishioners and would take an interest in the cricket club, which badly needed patching up and pulling together, as well as a new roller and repairs to the pavilion. Miss Pallfrey said they would never be the same as the predecessors, and left it at that, and the Honourable Augusta Renshawe was rude and ignored them.

CHAPTER FOUR

JOCELYN, her last notice and magazine delivered, set out for home in the gloomy drizzle which every now and then developed into a solid downpour. She left Little Dithering behind and came to the cross-roads by the bridge, where a two-seater car was drawn up by the roadside, while its owner stood on the bridge, lighting a pipe and looking about him with interest, in spite of the heavy rain which was now sweeping down over the woods on the hillside beyond the little river. As Jocelyn was crossing the bridge the stranger turned from his contemplation of the landscape and addressed her.

"I beg your pardon, but can you tell me just where I am? I've lost my way completely, and there's no signpost. I want to go to a place called Much Dithering."

Jocelyn's eyes, wide-set and very dark blue, looked back at the stranger with surprised interest. "You are quite close to Much Dithering," she told him in rather a distant tone that indicated quite plainly that she never spoke to strange men on a lonely road. "It's just down this road, a mile or two on."

The stranger was not in the least abashed by her chilly reply. He looked up at the low drift of dark cloud that had come over the hill and turned up his coat-collar against the deluge that suddenly descended in a splashing downpour. "If you're going there yourself," he suggested with a matter-of-fact heartiness, "you'd better let me drive you. It's too wet for any one to walk in such a storm."

The rain was stinging Jocelyn's cheeks to a fine glow and running off her Burberry in streams. She looked, and was, exceedingly wet, but she disdained such a suggestion, deciding that he was certainly not to be encouraged. "Oh, no, thank you," she replied distantly. "I like walking in the rain, and it isn't far."

She set off at a smart pace through the splashing torrent with a resolute air of independence. There was a vivid flame of lightning and sudden crash of thunder. She gasped. A thunderstorm was even worse than a strange man who spoke to her on a lonely road on a wet day. Two miles to Much Dithering in a thunderstorm, all alone! She looked desperately over her shoulder and saw that the stranger was still on the bridge, looking after her. It was growing uncannily dark as the black cloud spread lower and the rain was like a waterspout. Jocelyn's courage failed her. She ran back to the bridge, crying out: "Don't go away! Don't leave me alone, *please*. I'm simply terrified of thunderstorms."

"So am I," the stranger returned cheerfully. "There's a bit of shelter in the car. Let's get in, shall we?"

"Oh, yes." Jocelyn was shaking all over. "Quick! And don't go to Much Dithering yet. There are trees by the roadside all the way."

"No, we'll just stay here till the worst is over. I'm afraid you're awfully wet."

"Ye-es, but it ca-an't be helped," returned Jocelyn with chattering teeth as another blue flame of lightning danced along the telegraph wires a little way from the car, and the thunder crashed again.

He looked down into her frightened face with a friendly smile. "Don't be frightened. The next one will be farther off—you'll see. I saw the first flash strike a big willow a hundred yards upstream, so the storm must be passing down the valley."

The hiss and splash of the rain was lessening already and the cloud was passing. Jocelyn shook a small deluge of water from the brim of her hat and looked less scared. She strove to achieve a semblance of courage, but she was still shaking all over, a ridiculous effect that a thunderstorm always had on her.

"You're very cold, I'm afraid," said the stranger in a tone of concern. "Let me give you a drop of brandy. I always carry a flask with me in case of emergency, and this is certainly one."

"Oh, but *really*—" began Jocelyn; but he produced a silver flask from a pocket in the car and gave her a stiff dose which ran warmly through her chilled veins and made her feel better. Her teeth stopped chattering and she achieved a smile.

"Better?"

"Oh, yes, thank you. Much better."

"Good! There, did you see that flash? Quite a long way off, and the rain is clearing. Shall we go on? Where do you live? I'll drive you there."

"I live in Much Dithering, but—Oh, I don't think—" She had a picture of her arrival in the village, stepping out of a strange man's car, and wilted under the gleam of amusement in the "strange man's" twinkling blue eyes. She stiffened slightly and sat very straight, looking at him with serious eyes. "Thank you very much for being so kind to me, but I think it is quite fine enough to walk home, and I shall be nice and warm again."

"Yes, I see. Well, if you'd really rather—" He got out and opened the door for her. "Good-bye."

"Good-bye, and thank you." She held out her hand in token of her gratitude. He shook it warmly, still with a hint of a joke lurking in his eyes, and watched her walk away, a slim, straight figure in a dripping Burberry and a wet felt hat which, as he watched her, she pulled off and shook out, revealing a small head sleek with the dampness of the close-fitting hat, her hair parted and dressed in a coil low on her neck.

"'But she is too young to be taken from her Mammy,'" hummed the stranger with a laugh as he got back into his car. His eyes fell on the satchel of American cloth on the floor and he picked it up. "Now let me see if I can discover any indication of the shy lady's degree or address." There was a black note-book containing neat records of notes and meetings, and it contained a visiting card in one of the pockets, which he had no hesitation in exploring: "Mrs. Lancelot Renshawe, Dower House, Much Dithering." So that was who she was! He replaced the card and drove after her. How annoyed she would be at his speaking to her again!

Jocelyn *was* annoyed, very annoyed indeed, when the car passed her slowly and drew up. As a matter of fact, it would have stopped in any case, for an immense willow tree had crashed across the road, completely blocking it.

"And now?" inquired the annoying man, getting out of the car as Jocelyn approached and stood looking at the fallen tree.

"Now?" she echoed.

"Is there another road to Much Dithering?"

"Oh, yes, but it's a long way round and a very bad road."

"Get in and we'll get there as quickly as possible. No arguing, please."

"But I think I can climb over somehow."

"I haven't time to wait until you satisfy yourself that it is really impossible. Please get in."

Jocelyn felt trapped. The rain was beginning again and the evening was exceedingly dark and depressing. Besides, the storm was still carrying on quite heartily not so very far away, and storms had a nasty way of returning on their tracks. She got in meekly enough, and the car backed up the narrow road to the cross-ways, where she pointed out the alternative route, and they set off in the gathering dusk.

"Please don't be so worried," he begged. "I know you think I'm a fearful ruffian, but I'm respectable enough, really, and it is out of the question to allow you to walk back to Much Dithering when it is so very simple to drive you there."

"It is more than kind of you," Jocelyn responded primly, "and I am very grateful indeed. It would have taken me some time to walk back, and it would certainly have been dark long before I reached home."

"Where are we?" he asked as the road wound up a steep hillside under high banks of trees. "This part of the country is new to me. Hallo, is this a gate?"

"Yes," answered Jocelyn, "the first of five. I'll get out and open them. They have awkward catches, I know." She got out of the car as she spoke.

"These are the High Woods of Dithering Priory," she explained, getting in when she had carefully closed and latched the gate behind the car. "This is really a sort of private road through the estate, and Mrs. Renshawe is very particular that no one must leave the gates open."

"Who is Mrs. Renshawe?"

"She lives at the Priory."

"I see—the local tin god?"

"Well, yes, I think that describes her rather nicely." Jocelyn laughed suddenly. "But she wouldn't like to hear you say it!" She got out to open the next gate.

Conversation was somewhat disjointed owing to the number of gates and Jocelyn's corresponding exits and entrances, but presently, after a tiresome drive, the lights of the village twinkled round a bend in the road. They had arrived.

"I live here," Jocelyn told him, indicating a white gate in a high red-brick wall.

"Another gate?"

"The last," she laughed; "and I really do thank you. Er—won't you come in and have some tea and—and meet my mother?"

"It is very kind of you," he returned, "but I don't feel like meeting any one's mother this evening. I must get on. Good-bye again, and thank you for your company and for opening all those gates. I should never have found my way if you hadn't accompanied me on this adventurous journey."

"May I know your name?" asked Jocelyn shyly, standing by the car. "I would like to tell my mother. I mean, you've been so kind—"

He paused a moment. "My name is Blythe. Goodbye."

"Good-bye."

Jocelyn stood in the rain and watched the car disappear round the next bend in the road before she unlatched the white gate and went up the short drive to the house, where a gleam of light shone through the hall window and shed a welcoming ray to guide her through the wet darkness.

CHAPTER FIVE

ERMYNTRUDE Lascelles hated thunderstorms, and felt aggrieved that her inconsiderate daughter should have gone jaunting off to Little Dithering on an afternoon when it was perfectly obvious that something was going to happen. It had been black and overcast all day; and why Jocelyn should have insisted on going out, except that she was obstinate and imbecile and had absolutely no sense and *deserved* to get wet (only that she would probably get a bad cold, or more likely a chill, and would need nursing, but being a *fool* she wouldn't think of such eventualities; she only consulted her own pleasures), was beyond Mrs. Lascelles' comprehension. Really, to go off and leave her nerve-ridden mother all alone in a bad thunderstorm passed all limits. Ermyntrude rang the bell violently.

"Bertha," she said peevishly, "draw the curtains and light the lamp at once. Why haven't you done so before? Bring tea immediately, and plenty of hot toast. Mrs. Renshawe ought to be in directly." She poked the fire and threw on some logs. "I'm frozen, Bertha, and I'm really feeling very upset with this dreadful storm. *Why* did Mrs. Renshawe go out?"

Bertha vouchsafed no reply. She merely shrugged her shoulders as she drew down the blinds and jerked the curtains together.

"Bertha, don't be so rough!" snapped Ermyntrude. "I shall complain to Mrs. Renshawe of your bad manners."

Bertha flounced out of the room with a toss of her flaxen head, and Ermyntrude flung another log on the fire with an expression of exasperation. "That girl!"

Bertha opened the door a few minutes later and announced: "Miss Pallfrey, madam."

"Oh, my dear!" wailed Mellicent Pallfrey, hurrying in. "What an afternoon! Poor, *poor* Jocelyn, she'll be drowned, if nothing worse. I *flew* round to see if she had come back yet. I was so uneasy. I remembered it was the second Wednesday just as the storm broke, and I said, 'Good gracious, Jocelyn will be out in all this! I must go and see if she has come back safely.' So here I am, dear. Oh, Bertha, take my mackintosh. It's very wet. Thank you, Bertha. What nice manners Bertha has. She was always a sweet girl. She used to be in my Sunday School class, and she always won prizes. Her mother is an excellent woman, and has brought up her girls so sensibly."

A crash of thunder shook the room.

"Oh, dear!" exclaimed Miss Pallfrey. "What will happen to our darling Jocelyn?"

"She should never have gone out," snapped Ermyntrude, "but she never *thinks*. Since you're here, Mellicent, you'd better stay and have tea. I'm thankful to have someone for company. I was feeling quite *ill*. I can never stand thunderstorms, and Jocelyn ought to know it."

"But she couldn't possibly have imagined that there was going to be thunder in December—so very unusual; and, after all, it is the second Wednesday, and dear Jocelyn never misses her old ladies. She has a strong sense of duty."

"Towards other people. She never considers her duty to *me*."

"Oh, my dear Ermyntrude, I think you are quite wrong. Jocelyn is a devoted daughter. You feel upset by the storm or you would never say that. You'll feel better when you've had some tea."

Ermyntrude poured out tea resentfully, but her appetite did not appear to suffer to any great extent, in spite of her recent alarm. Indeed her sister-in-law seemed surprised at the rapid disappearance of a dish of hot buttered toast and plate of sandwiches.

"I thought you were dieting, Ermyntrude," she said a little doubtfully.

"So I am. I have to take the greatest care," returned Ermyntrude, leaning back with a sigh of repletion and lighting a Turkish cigarette.

"Jocelyn says—" began Miss Pallfrey.

"For goodness' sake don't begin worrying me with what Jocelyn says," retorted Ermyntrude. "She's out of the way and can't nag. She gives me no peace. I'm simply *starved* when she's here to tell me I mustn't. I was absolutely *weak*, what with the thunderstorm and anxiety for Jocelyn—so unfeeling of her."

"She ought to have been back long before this," broke in Miss Pallfrey in a tone of genuine anxiety—an anxiety that became acute as the time passed and Jocelyn still did not appear. Ermyntrude railed bitterly at her daughter's lack of feeling in thus absenting herself and causing her such acute misery, but Mellicent was seriously alarmed. It was quite dark and Jocelyn ought to have been back nearly an hour ago. The storm had really been a very bad one. What could have happened? Poor Miss Mellicent was feeling very upset altogether when the door opened and Jocelyn put her head into the room.

"I'm very wet and I'm going to have a hot bath straight away. Please order hot tea and plenty of toast. I'm starving."

The door closed on her mother's shrill demand as to the reason for her delayed return and her aunt's relieved duckings. She preferred to postpone her explanations until she was warm and dry.

"I was on my way home and found a big willow tree had been split by a flash of lightning and lay across the road not far from the bridge," she explained later, pouring out tea and helping herself to toast. She had a bright spot of colour in her usually pale cheeks, and her eyes were very blue and sparkling. Her aunt diagnosed a chill and feverish symptoms, but Ermyntrude never diagnosed illness in any one but herself, and was unaware of any unusual symptoms in her daughter. "And while I was wondering how on earth I should get home," Jocelyn went on rapidly, "a car came along and a—a man asked me how he could get to Much Dithering. He was a stranger and did not know the country, and—and he very kindly indeed gave me a lift home. We had to come home the high road by the woods, of course, and there are five gates, and I had to open and close them, so it took a long time, and—"

"Was he a *gentleman*?" inquired Miss Pallfrey anxiously.

"He behaved like one," replied Jocelyn with a quiver of a smile.

"A stranger? What did he want to come here for?" asked Ermyntrude.

"I didn't ask him."

"Didn't he tell you?"

"No."

"How very odd," commented Miss Pallfrey uncertainly.

"It was perfectly natural," retorted Jocelyn. "It would have been much odder to expect me to walk all that way alone in the dark. I simply couldn't have faced it."

"No, dear, of course not. It really was most fortunate. I only meant that it was odd not to tell you why he was coming here."

"What is his name?" inquired Ermyntrude. "I suppose he told you that?"

"Yes, but it didn't really seem to matter much. It was Bligh or Blythe. I couldn't quite catch it; but, as I say, it doesn't seem to matter."

"What did he look like?" Ermyntrude's curiosity was thoroughly aroused.

"It was getting dark and he had a coat-collar turned up. I really can't tell you very much."

"I simply can't understand you, Jocelyn! You go through life with your eyes and ears shut. How do you expect to get *any*where?"

Jocelyn looked at her mother in astonishment. "Where exactly should I have got to?" she asked after a pause.

"You should have brought him in to tea; then we could have seen for ourselves."

"Yes, dear," added Miss Pallfrey; "and then we could have judged better if he was the—the sort of man—I mean, dear, it was not very *wise*—you ran a risk—"

"Yes," agreed Jocelyn, pouring out another cup of tea; "but it would have been too late to tell me not to. Anyhow, I did ask him in, but he declined very firmly and drove away into the dark. The adventure is now over and all is well."

"You left the notices of the annual meeting?" asked Miss Pallfrey.

Jocelyn gave a faint sigh. "Oh, yes, I left the notices."

Miss Pallfrey got up to leave a little later. She still felt uneasy about the unwonted colour in her niece's cheeks, and the feverish symptoms which were, if anything, more marked. "I think, dear child," she advised, "that you should take two or three aspirins and a hot drink, and go to bed early with two hot-water bottles. You are in for a bad chill, if I'm not mistaken."

"A chill?" echoed Jocelyn. "Oh, no, Aunt Mellicent, I never felt better in my life."

"By the way," interrupted her mother, remembering something that had entirely slipped her mind till that moment, "Colonel Tidmarsh called this afternoon just after you had gone out."

"Oh, did he?" The total lack of interest in Jocelyn's tone annoyed Ermyntrude. "He was *extremely* disappointed at missing you," she said irritably. "Jocelyn, I do wish you'd show some symptoms of being human."

"Colonel Tidmarsh doesn't exactly inspire one to any particular display of humanity," returned Jocelyn, stifling a yawn as she became aware that she was suddenly exceedingly tired and that the room was hot and unbearably stuffy. "In fact," she added, "he bores me to the point of tears."

Just then she became aware of the sound of someone arriving in the hall, and Mrs. Pomfret came in in her usual hurry.

"Oh, Jocelyn," she exclaimed, "I'm so worried. Yes, it's the anthem. We seem to have *no* voices that can sing B flat, and the basses are a poor lot. The railway porter from Eden Hill hasn't a bad voice—for a porter, I mean. I've had him singing tenor, but I think I'll put him with the basses: he is rather growly. Oh, good-afternoon, Mrs. Lascelles. What a dreadful storm! Awful weather we're having altogether, in fact, aren't we? And there are such a lot of colds about. Percival went to ask how the General is. He was coughing such a lot on Sunday, poor man! Yes, sugar and milk, please. What nice scones you always have, Jocelyn."

There was a brief pause while Mrs. Pomfret took a bite; but almost immediately she was cleared for action, as it were. "I depend on you, my dear, to keep the altos straight; and I mean to ask Colonel Tidmarsh to help us, too."

"Does he sing?" Jocelyn inquired a little doubtfully.

"Well, no, not exactly, but I thought it might cheer him up. He's so dreary, poor man!" She took another bite.

"But quite charming," said Miss Pallfrey, "and such a *gentleman*. I wonder why he has come to live here."

"Well, he lost his wife some years ago," explained Mrs. Pomfret, "and has been travelling about a good deal; and one day he came through here on a bus drive from Totterford, where he was staying at the Hydro, and he liked it because it was so peaceful, and it just happened that The Brook was to let and he was able to get it."

"Much Dithering isn't what it was," sighed Miss Pallfrey. "So many of the old people have died or lost their money, and these new people creep in, and will soon overrun the place. These Montague-Blobbses, or whatever they call themselves, for instance."

"The Murchison-Bellabys, I suppose you mean," corrected Mrs. Pomfret with her mouth full. "Yes, please, dearie, another cup."

"The same thing." Miss Pallfrey shrugged her thin shoulders as if the name of such impossible people was of no account. "Vulgar nobodies splashing their horrible money about. I have not called, and I do not intend to."

"It takes all sorts to make the population, you know, said Mrs. Pomfret charitably—"the rich as well as the poor. Have you called, Jocelyn?"

"As a matter of fact, I did," confessed Jocelyn. "My mother was very insistent that I should. She knows their son, and felt that I really ought to call and be neighbourly."

"I think Mrs. Murchison-Bellaby is quite a decent sort," declared Mrs. Pomfret. "She came to see me yesterday, and we got on very well. She is anxious to do anything she can to help in village affairs."

"Impertinent interference!" fumed Miss Pallfrey. "This village has got on very well for centuries without the help of Murchison-Bellabys or any other Jewish profiteers."

"Well," laughed Mrs. Pomfret, "we can always do with subscriptions, even from Jews. Everything in the parish screams for subscriptions and donations, and money gets scarcer and scarcer."

"Mrs. Renshawe says—" began Miss Pallfrey.

"I can't help what Mrs. Renshawe says," broke in Mrs. Pomfret. "She knows the subscriptions aren't all they might be these days, and we must make up deficits somehow. I called some time ago, of course, but so far she hasn't taken any notice of them. I think she's wrong. Well, Jocelyn, I must be going. Oh, and by the way, dear, the Murchison-Bellaby girl will be an excellent tonic for you; she'll shake you up. I don't *like* her; but, you know, tonics aren't always *nice*—in fact, they're sometimes very nasty, but they have an invigorating effect, all the same. I like the mother; she's quite a dear. Well, bye-bye, duckie, and don't forget to come and practise the anthem—to-morrow afternoon."

Jocelyn accompanied Mrs. Pomfret to the hall door and Ermyntrude turned to her sister-in-law with a flabbergasted expression. "Fancy the Murchison-Bellabys going in for helping in village affairs! I *am* surprised."

"It's a pose, of course." Miss Pallfrey looked equally disgusted. "Rich Londoners wanting to buy local popularity and do the right thing. It won't last."

"No, it won't last, of course," agreed Ermyntrude absently and thought in dismay: "But the damage will be done if they come across Jocelyn and she gives me away."

She sat lost in disturbing thoughts till Jocelyn, having seen Mrs. Pomfret out, and also her aunt, returned to the room. *"Jocelyn,"* she said in an urgent tone, "I want to impress on you that you are *not* to call me or allude to me as 'mother,' especially when talking to the Murchison-Bellabys. A grown-up married daughter dates one so abominably, and I have no desire to pose as a middle-aged matron finished with all that makes life endurable. Please regard this as confidential and obey my wishes."

Jocelyn looked a little surprised. "Certainly, if you wish it."

"I do wish it," said Ermyntrude very firmly.

CHAPTER SIX

GERVASE Blythe, having dropped Jocelyn at the gate of the Dower House, drove into the village in search of an inn.

The Roebuck, standing back from the Green, glowed cheerfully in the wet gloom and promised comfort, so at The Roebuck he pulled into the gravelled yard and got out of the car. The bar-parlour was warm and comfortably old-fashioned, gleaming with pewter and copper, with a log fire burning on a basket-grate in an open fireplace.

A girl was sitting in a corner of the oak settle, knitting and reading. She laid down her work as Gervase came in and stood looking about him.

"Yes, sir, what did you want?" She broke off and looked interrogatively at him, a dark, handsome young woman, rather a surprise in an English inn with her big black eyes, olive-tinted skin and gleaming black hair parted in the middle of a low, broad forehead and dressed low on her neck—a young woman, too, well aware of her unusual looks and possessed of a poise that was refreshing, but on the other hand she was disturbing in her still, dark beauty, and Gervase unhesitatingly labelled her as "dangerous."

"I want some tea and toast at the moment, and, if possible, a bed for the night."

"Certainly, sir." Her eyes travelled over him with interest. "You are very wet. Won't you hang your coat up? Let me take it. I think it should be dried." Without any fuss she made him at home by the fire and went to bring him his tea.

"No, sir," Joe Hedgecock said in reply to Gervase's inquiry later that evening when, after a well-cooked steak and a most surprising sweet omelette for a country inn, he went to the private bar at his landlord's invitation for a glass of a special liqueur brandy for which The Roebuck was famed, "we haven't got a squire here—not since Mr. Renshawe died a year or two ago. He was a fine old gentleman—not many of his sort left these days. His lady lives at the Priory, and a holy terror she is—

holds on to everything like grim death and won't move with the times. Why, would you believe it? She won't allow me to have a petrol pump! Won't allow one in the whole village. Says it would attract motorists, and she wants to keep 'em away—not sense, it isn't, but she won't listen to reason and just goes her own way."

Gervase smoked in silence for a little. "Funny you should mention that—about petrol pumps, I mean, for that's my line of business. I had heard that there were no pumps here, and as I was in this part of the country I thought I'd look into the matter."

"You'll get no satisfaction out of the Honourable! It's all down in the leases of the houses on this estate—nothing *she* don't approve of."

"She's within her rights, I suppose? No one can find any flaw?"

"Not that I know of; but she's only there on sufferance now, as you might say."

"No children?"

"A son; but he was a poor soft sort of fool, and he died before the old man. Funny, *he* left a widow, too. There's just the pair of women left now."

"Yes, funny! And afterwards—isn't there any heir?"

"Should be, but he seems to have disappeared, for all one hears of him. A wild chap—no good to any one, so it's said; but I wish he'd turn up, just to give the Honourable a bit of a shock and let her see she isn't the only one."

"Another spot of brandy," suggested Gervase. "On me, this time."

"Thank you, sir."

"You said the son married? Any children? No, I suppose not, if the next heir is this fellow you've just spoken of."

"No, there were no children there, and a good job, too. Young Lancelot was barmy. They married him off to the old vicar's granddaughter, a quiet sort of girl that hadn't no spirit— all squeezed out of her by her old aunt and then the Honourable, but a nice young lady if she ever got a chance."

"H'm!" Gervase laughed. "I shouldn't think this can be exactly a gay place—not much excitement to be had. Does any one else live here?"

"There's a queer crowd come to live at The Place—not much breeding, but plenty of cash. They're trying to make their way, but it'll be uphill work if the Honourable don't approve—and she don't! I don't know that she's wrong. There's money *and* money—and, in spite of all, I'm one as holds that good blood tells. You can't get away from that when you see the goings-on of them as has money and no blood. Still, they'll learn—in time. The old birds are pretty quaint, but the son is a fair caution. In the Army, he is, and the girl—" He broke off and shrugged. "Well, she might amuse you, or again she might not. A man's children are sometimes worth bringing up, and some-times they just aren't." He jerked a thumb towards the door. "There's my girl in there. Got a good education and grows up a proper lady in looks and style, but the country wasn't what she wanted. A mannequin in London—that's what she is—all for clothes and dressing up, and, my lad, he plays in a Dago dance band up in London—no good to any one. It's the mixed blood. I married an Italian, you see—a maid of the Honourable's, she was; and she didn't half make a row about it. She's had it in for me ever since."

"I must certainly go and see this redoubtable lady to-mor-row," decided Gervase. "You whet my curiosity enormously."

"You'll get no change," Joe Hedgecock told him with an air of finality. "Waste of time, and don't say I didn't warn you. She never sees any one on business—tells 'em to go to her agent, and he has orders to send 'em packing. What I thinks myself is she's frightened that some day the chap that's come in for the prop-erty will turn up from the back of beyond."

"Where is he now?" asked Gervase.

"His whereabouts aren't known, or at least they aren't published. A bad hat, they say, a rolling stone and no credit to the family, so they've always kept quiet about him."

"Who did you say he was?"

"A nephew of the old squire's. They wanted him to go into the Church, so Louisa told me—but that was long before young Lancelot went and died on them, and he didn't fancy the Church, so he ran away and enlisted—a bright lad he was, from all accounts. The Honourable couldn't bear him because he was strong and rough and worth a dozen of her half-baked kid—never had a good word for him."

"H'm! And you don't think I can sell her anything—farm tractors, steam ploughs, motor-cars? They're all in my line. I'm travelling for a big firm of engineers."

"Not a bit of use, sir. Horses, she uses, and she's no time for new-fangled ideas. Waste of time your going to see her, that's all it is."

"I dare say you're right." Gervase filled a pipe reflectively and lit it. "In that case I'll go on in the morning. I'm interested in a new garage in Totterford. I wish I could do something about it with you. Well, perhaps I'll have another try later, when you've got a new landlord."

"If you'll leave me your card," suggested Mr. Hedgecock.

"I'll send you one when I get back to London. I haven't got one on me this evening. Good-night, landlord. I'll certainly be back one of these days."

"Good-night, sir. Always glad to see you."

The next morning Gervase strolled out to have a look at the village. On the bridge over the little River Waver he came upon a gloomy-looking middle-aged man who had just emerged from the gate of a small house that stood by the river, tucked away behind the thick yew hedges which appeared to be a feature of Much Dithering gardens and gave a somewhat sombre aspect to the village on this grey December morning. Gervase looked a second time, a half-roused memory crossing his mind. He knew he had seen that long, sand-coloured, mule-like face before and disliked it then, as now. Sand and mules were also part of the memory. India—the Frontier—rocks—sand—mules—kites—and, yes, surely—Ambrose Tidmarsh, the unpopular major in the I.M.S. attached to the fort in which Gervase had spent some months with his regiment. What an odd coincidence meeting him here of all places!

"Surely you are Tidmarsh, Ambrose Tidmarsh?" he said, halting in front of the approaching gentleman, who appeared to be excessively astonished but admitted that he was indeed Ambrose Tidmarsh, though his manner implied that he considered it no business of the stranger—who apparently wished to claim acquaintance. "You wouldn't remember me, I expect," went on Gervase. "But I was with the Pioneers on the Frontier when you were the M.O. You took a bullet out of my shoulder when I was sniped. I still have the mark."

"Oh—er—yes, let me see. The name? I can't put a name to you, but you are vaguely familiar."

"Blythe—Gervase Blythe. No, of course you wouldn't remember."

"And—er—what brings you *here*?"

"Well"—Gervase laughed and had an inspiration that tickled him—"I'm just passing through. The storm held me up last evening, and it was a damned unpleasant night, so when I stopped here for tea and found I'd struck a good pub, I just stayed."

Colonel Tidmarsh had a sudden gleam of recollection. "You—er—left us rather suddenly, if I'm not mistaken—Landi Kotal, I mean. I forget the—er—details. Forgive me if I—er—stir up an old tale."

Gervase grinned. "Oh, not at all. You mean when I had to clear out in a hurry because that old ruffian of a moneylender was out for my blood. Yes, I had a narrow shave. I got down to Karachi and got on board an Arab *dhow* that was trading along the coast to Bombay, and there I took a boat to Australia and made a small fortune in a racing stable, quite honestly—well, comparatively honestly. I'm one of those blokes that money sticks to. I'm very lucky with my investments. I'm in on a big scheme now. Ought to make anything up to £50,000 on the deal. It's funny, isn't it, when you remember how completely broke I was in the past?"

"It's perfectly amazing!" exclaimed Colonel Tidmarsh warmly. "My dear fellow, I congratulate you."

Gervase smiled blandly. "Yes, I think I may say that I'm a successful example of a self-made man. Dead pasts and wild oats are safely behind me, and I ride calmly at anchor in a harbour of prosperity and respectability. Queer, isn't it?"

"Very praiseworthy indeed." Colonel Tidmarsh thawed visibly. "You have certainly changed a good deal from the old days if you are now a rich man."

"And a respectable one," Gervase reminded him.

"Yes, yes; but what I mean is—well, I dare say you've had luck—"

"Oh, I'm lucky. I've got the flair. I just *know*. Everything I've touched for the last ten years has just turned to money—perfectly extraordinary. A fortune-teller in Lahore once told me I'd end up by being a millionaire, and I believe he's right."

Colonel Tidmarsh's rather hollow eyes gleamed as he laid his hand on Gervase's arm. "This is really most interesting. Look here, Blythe, I live here—this is my little place just here. Come in and have a glass of sherry. I'd like a chat—old days, and all that."

"I'm sorry," returned Gervase regretfully, "but I must be getting on. I have an appointment with my stockbroker in town this afternoon."

"Come and spend a day or two—any time you like. I live alone. I'd be delighted—a lonely man, you know. My poor wife—a sad story. A good yarn over the old days would cheer me up. You must come and stay—*any* time—" He was walking beside Gervase towards The Roebuck, and was a little incoherent in his anxiety to persuade him to accept his hospitality.

"Do you really mean it?" Gervase asked abruptly. "If I said I'd simply love to come back for a night or two? I too, live alone. I've no fixed abode. I move about at present, but I'm looking for a nice place to settle in. Can I come next week? I expect to go abroad early in January—Paris, Monte Carlo, winter sports."

"What about Christmas?" suggested Colonel Tidmarsh. "Yes, let's say Christmas for old times' sake. We once spent Christmas together in that God-forsaken fort. Let this be a happier one."

"It might easily be that," remarked Gervase. "That was a peculiarly blightsome occasion. We ran out of drinks, and most of us were on the sick list. Thank you, Tidmarsh, I'll come with pleasure. I'll turn up on Christmas Eve about tea-time. So-long!"

"Splendid!" rejoined Colonel Tidmarsh. "I shall look forward to your visit with pleasure. I warn you, I live very plainly—hard times, and so on. No luxury or—or—"

"*That's* all right." Gervase got into his car. "'Kind hearts are more than coronets,' as Tennyson said. And isn't there something about stalled oxen and dinners of herbs—or is that Shakespeare? As a matter of fact, luxury rather appals me; I've lived too long in wild places, and I'm rather a savage at heart."

He drove away, leaving Colonel Tidmarsh staring after him and muttering: "A millionaire? Dear me, I hope I'll get something out of him in return for my hospitality. A good tip, now—"

"Poor old Tidmarsh!" thought Gervase. "The meanest man on this earth, and he's out to pick up tips for making easy money and hopes I'll put him on to a good thing or two and make his fortune. It suits me very well, though, to stay with him. As a friend of a respectable inhabitant I shall slip into Much Dithering in a perfectly natural way that couldn't be done just staying at the pub. My luck is certainly in just now, even if I've told a mouthful of lies as bait for the old shark."

CHAPTER SEVEN

"Good-Morning, Mrs. Goodbun," Jocelyn said cheerfully. One was always offensively cheerful in greeting Mrs. Goodbun. It was an involuntary barrage behind which one took refuge from the slings and arrows of Mrs. Goodbun's outrageous fortune. One said, "Good-morning!" cheerfully, but feared the worst.

Mrs. Goodbun gave a loud sniffle and a hollow cough. "Good-morning, madam, and I 'opes as 'ow I finds you better'n wot I am, for sure, and father—oh, father ain't 'alf cheerful this morning, neither, with 'is lumbago. Workin' up for a merry Christmas, *we* are, and that's the truth."

"1 lb. ground almonds, 1 lb. icing sugar," wrote Jocelyn rapidly, "glacé cherries, dates, figs, crystallised fruit." She mustn't forget anything! "Now for common or garden needs. Oh—er—Mrs. Goodbun—"

"Sn'f! Yes, madam?" Mrs. Goodbun, wiping her hands on a kitchen-rubber, came out of the scullery and stood regarding her "lady" with woebegone resignation.

"Oh—er—Mrs. Goodbun, I was thinking of having a little party on Christmas Day, if it would be quite convenient—"

"Sn'f! Oh, yes, madam. I says, to Goodbun: 'Father,' I says, 'Mrs. Renshawe'll spring a shock on me,' I says. 'Visitors and such-like.' But you must please yourself, madam, I'm sure."

"Well, you see," began Jocelyn apologetically.

"Oh, that's all right, madam. Sn'f! I shall be 'appy to oblige, only I likes to 'ave *warning*, that's all. Sn'f!"

"Yes, Mrs. Goodbun; but, after all, it's a week to Christmas still, and I thought—"

"Sn'f! Very good, madam. I'll make a note," conceded Mrs. Goodbun, "if the Colonel don't 'appen to want me that night. 'E did appear to mention something about a friend, but I didn't rightly understand 'im, and any'ow, you've spoke for me first, and 'im being a newcomer, 'e must go to the wall. Sn'f!"

"Oh, dear!" said Jocelyn. "I don't really like to interfere with his arrangements, and only for my mother I wouldn't dream of asking you at all; but, you see, she's very particular—"

"She's one wot would be used to good living," interrupted Mrs. Goodbun, "and one wot likes the best. Sn'f! Well, madam, I'll oblige if I can bring father along to 'elp me clear up and p'raps 'ave a bit of good cheer."

"Oh, yes, certainly." Jocelyn was relieved to find the matter so simple, and duly grateful for Mrs. Goodbun's willingness to oblige. The only snag was Colonel Tidmarsh. She felt guilty about that. Suppose he had counted on Mrs. Goodbun?

"My dear!" exclaimed Ermyntrude irritably, when she mentioned the matter to her later. "If you weren't so stupid you'd see at once that the solution of your problem is to ask him, too. He'll be delighted, I'm sure. You've no sense at all, Jocelyn."

"He's not very lively," began Jocelyn.

"Rubbish! He's quite anxious to make a good impression and may be worth encouraging."

"Encouraging?" Jocelyn sighed.

Ermyntrude felt she could have shaken her. To marry off her unwanted daughter again would be a solution to one of her own problems. She had a premonition that Adrian might be troublesome, and a desire to place Jocelyn out of his reach suddenly took form in her scheming mind. When Ermyntrude had an idea of that sort she allowed it to obsess her and grow to dominate all her thoughts. Now this idea so suddenly conceived became her chief preoccupation. If Jocelyn could be neatly polished off to this elderly admirer (if Mrs. Pomfret was to be believed), what a good settlement it would be, and there would be no fear of any entanglement as far as Adrian was concerned.

"Yes, Jocelyn, ask Colonel Tidmarsh to come to dinner. I should like to know him better."

Jocelyn drew on her gloves and stood a moment, studying her shopping list. "Oh, very well, if it will please you," she agreed with a faint smile. "I've asked the Pomfrets and Aunt Mellicent, too."

"So long as you don't ask that awful mother-in-law of yours. I couldn't bear that!"

Jocelyn made no reply. It was unnecessary to point out that her mother-in-law couldn't bear Ermyntrude.

She went out into the cold grey morning and walked briskly into the village square, where the post office and two or three shops represented the commercial centre. The slow river was crossed by a quaint old bridge, and just beyond stood the handsome church surrounded by tall trees, an avenue of yews leading to its wide porch. Here also was the church hall, the centre of the social activities encouraged by the enterprising wife of the vicar, who held the hopeful view that if one gave the local boys and girls plenty of good, honest fun in the spirit of "Merrie England," they would be content to remain in the village and cease to yearn for the gayer and more dubious forms of amusement to be had in the cinemas of Totterford.

At the moment there was a heartening array of notices on the board by the front door, and it was easily to be gathered that no one need suffer from dull moments in Much Dithering if only they were members of the various classes for handicrafts, country dancing, glee-singing and study circles. It appeared that social evenings were of fortnightly occurrence, and practice dances held on Thursdays only. There were extras from time to time—Conservative Association meetings and entertainments, or Grand Concerts arranged by Mrs. Pomfret when she felt more than usually enthusiastic about her glee-singers and determined to exploit local talent. Besides, the prospect of a Grand Concert now and then kept up the interest of the classes and acted as a tonic—or so she believed. The Christmas season promised to be a heavy strain on local enterprise and talent, as Jocelyn knew very well, for she was on the committees of all Mrs. Pomfret's festive productions.

On the bridge just outside his own gate Jocelyn met the subject of her vexed thoughts, and took the opportunity to invite him to dine with her on Christmas Day.

"I shall be delighted, dear lady," Colonel Tidmarsh assured her. "How exceedingly kind of you! Yes, our Mrs. Goodbun had mentioned that she might not be able to oblige that evening, and it really was rather an inconvenience—" He broke off and looked dismayed. "Oh, dear! I had quite forgotten—how very annoying! Oh, really, that is exceedingly unfortunate! I had forgotten just for the moment that I had met an old friend the other day and asked him to spend Christmas. I never thought—I mean, Mrs. Renshawe, your invitation is such a delightful surprise—I never anticipated—Oh, I *am* put out."

Jocelyn hesitated. It was an excellent opportunity to escape from what she felt was an obligation to make up to Colonel Tidmarsh for the inconvenience she was causing him by demanding that Mrs. Goodbun should cook for her on Christmas Day. The fault, of course, was her mother's, for without Ermyntrude she could have spent Christmas at the Priory as usual, but the Honourable Augusta loathed Ermyntrude and Ermyntrude despised Miss Pallfrey, and therefore both houses were closed, as it were. But now she had done what she could for Colonel Tidmarsh and need feel no further compunction. Feebly, for she hated to appear glad to back out of her invitation, she inquired with tepid interest: "Oh, I—I see. Yes! Who is your friend?"

"A man named Blythe whom I once knew in India. I met him here, actually on this bridge. He was passing through—a most extraordinary thing. I'd forgotten all about him, but he remembered me at once—yes, most flattering in a way, I suppose, and then we got talking and recalling old days on the Frontier. I once saved his life—a very ticklish operation. He had been sniped, and the bullet missed his lung and was embedded in the shoulder-muscles. Yes, he remembered it very clearly, and was—*is*, I hope—grateful to me. He is a very rich man, and I—well, he confessed that he was a lonely man, like myself, so I—I asked him for the sake of our old acquaintance. Most unfortunate—oh, most unfortunate, Mrs. Renshawe, since it means that I must decline your kind invitation."

Jocelyn looked at him with limpid blue eyes. A faint flush was in her cheeks and she had a suggestion of elation, a gleam of some suppressed excitement that seemed to be expressed in a glow of vitality that had been absent when she had first spoken to him. There was a little quiver of excitement in her voice when she said diffidently: "Oh, but, Colonel Tidmarsh, why should that prevent you coming to dinner? Couldn't you bring him, too?" And she added: "You see, there's my Ermyntrude, and I've asked the Pomfrets. So wouldn't it be a pity to—I mean, not to—I mean, won't you both come?"

"I—oh, really, Mrs. Renshawe, this is very good of you. I never dreamt—I hardly know if I dare take the responsibility of introducing a man of whom I know so little, and that little not at all to his credit. He was a—well, distinctly scapegrace fellow when I knew him, but he assures me he is a reformed character these days. I've no real knowledge of what he is. It seems a risk to introduce him into your house. You mustn't blame me if he isn't quite—quite all I should like a man to be."

Jocelyn smiled radiantly. "There's always Ermyntrude," she said. "I'm sure she would greatly enjoy him, so do bring him. It will be most interesting." She nodded in a friendly way, quite different from her usual cool unawareness of his desire to be better acquainted. She always gave him the impression of keeping him at a respectful distance, which depressed him, for he cherished a growing admiration for her charming appearance and serene disposition, which he felt were greatly to be desired in a young widow with enough money to be an asset while not sufficient to render her liable to be termed "a rich widow," which sounded rather "obvious," if not precisely vulgar. Jocelyn, indeed, attracted him more every time he came across her, and this grey morning on the bridge her suggestion of shy elusiveness, the unexpected glow of warmth in her blue eyes and delicate flicker of colour in her cheeks, the quiver of a smile in her unexpected dimple made her appear so extraordinarily lovely that he regarded her from a new standpoint and realised that he was actually in love with her—a disturbing thought, but a peculiarly attractive one. He had admired her for some time, but this was no mere admiration—it was the love of a strong, silent man. He regarded her as his future wife with a feeling of perfect assurance; there could be no doubt whatever of the future. He watched her walk away with her light-footed grace with a glow of possessive pride before he turned back to his house. He wanted to shut himself up in his study and reflect on the strange occurrence and make plans for the future.

He was deeply touched by this instance of her thoughtfulness in realising that she would be depriving him of the assistance of Mrs. Goodbun, whose services as cook were in urgent demand in Much Dithering on the occasion of the not very frequent "little dinners" in the modest establishments like his own where the "extras" demanded on such occasions were beyond the capacity of (in his own case) the one manservant, an excellent fellow, but not quite up to the mark in savouries or anything a little out of the ordinary. It appeared that Mrs. Renshawe's Bertha also needed the assistance of Mrs. Goodbun, and as she had "stood in" for Mrs. Renshawe and Miss Pallfrey for many years, Mrs. Renshawe had established a prior claim on her services, and he would have been greatly inconvenienced if she had not been so kind and anxious that he should not suffer by her having need of Mrs. Goodbun on the same night as himself—an odd coincidence, he thought, that they should share the same little domestic difficulties, and that she should make this graceful gesture of helping him out of what might have been an awkward position. Few women would have been so thoughtful!

Her consideration for his feelings and her desire to do what she could to atone for the inconvenience she was causing him was most charming and, he dared to think, encouraging, for if she were quite indifferent to his comfort she could easily have ignored the situation and allowed him to cope with it as best he might. Now he could look forward to a delightful evening. He had not often been in her house, and the last time she had not been at home and he had been received by a most disagreeable and undesirable person who (so Mrs. Pomfret had informed him later) was, most unfortunately, her mother. Still, if things went in the right direction, as he now began to entertain the most ardent hopes that they would, he would certainly see that Mrs. Lascelles was not encouraged to pay visits to the Dower House. He felt sure that Jocelyn had a sweet, pliable disposition and would make a loving, dutiful wife without any tiresome "modern" views, and would be content to be guided by him in matters that were outside her experience. If this man Blythe could be persuaded to put him on to a "good thing" and help him to make money, what an excellent thing it would be!

Really, at the moment his future looked uncommonly rosy. The very pattern that seemed to interweave itself in such a strange series of coincidences pointed to an unusual climax. If he hadn't met Gervase Blythe he would not have had a visitor for Christmas and therefore would not have required Mrs. Goodbun to cook his dinner, in which case Mrs. Renshawe would never have thought of asking him to her house and paving the way for a closer acquaintance and a chance for him to follow up the advantage he would thus enjoy and which would lead to their ultimate happiness. He also hoped very much that the coincidence connected with Gervase Blythe would lead to sound investments and satisfactory dividends. He trusted that Gervase would prove the sort of guest one could safely produce in decent society, but he really knew very little about him. It was so many years since they had met, until he had miraculously turned up here in Much Dithering. Fate must certainly have some good reason for its odd jests just now, and he wished he knew what the stars had in store for him. It seemed incredible that Mrs. Goodbun should have been the medium selected to bring about momentous happenings and turning-points in his life and Jocelyn's!

CHAPTER EIGHT

CHRISTMAS morning was crisp and frosty with a faint mist over the low ground by the river rising into the pale clearness of the blue overhead. A powdering of hoar-frost sparkled in the sun, and the mellow old houses had a picturesque Christmas-card-like effect as Jocelyn walked briskly across the bridge and joined the church-goers. She was rather early, for she had a desire to be safely in her seat behind the choir-stalls before Colonel Tidmarsh arrived. Ermyntrude's remark about his desiring encouragement had alarmed her, though she felt it was absurd. She hardly knew him. Nobody really knew him. He lived to himself so much that as far as Much Dithering was concerned he might as well not have existed. Nevertheless she was a little nervous of meeting him this morning, and her usual serenity was shaken.

Miss Pallfrey was early, too, beaming with Christmas greetings for every one, and General Wingham, fussy as usual, and his wife, plaintive and suffering from a cold in the head. The Honourable Augusta put her hand on Jocelyn's arm as she passed her pew and pressed an envelope into her hand—her invariable Christmas gift of a £5 note. Mrs. Pomfret hurried in with expansive smiles and pods, and swept Jocelyn with her for a last-minute confabulation as to the alto line in the anthem and an alteration in the chant for the *Te Deum*. Then from her secluded corner Jocelyn saw Colonel Tidmarsh, accompanied by a stranger, her unknown friend of the thunderstorm, enter his usual pew, but a pillar concealed them from her view when they were seated, and she sat back with a feeling of shy reluctance. The Murchison-Bellabys came in late, as if they were determined to impress their arrival upon Much Dithering society. Mrs. Murchison-Bellaby, wrapped in expensive sables, was followed up the church by her son and daughter, and Mr. Murchison-Bellaby brought up the rear of the procession, looking as if he hoped that no one would blame *him* for being so late.

At the church gate after the service a few people lingered to exchange Christmas greetings, and Jocelyn was disturbed at seeing Colonel Tidmarsh and his friend obviously waiting till she came out with Mrs. Pomfret. Before he could seize upon her, however, Mrs. Murchison-Bellaby had swooped.

"Mrs. Renshawe, isn't it? I felt I must speak to you and thank you so much for calling on me the other day. Let me wish you a happy Christmas and all the usual things. Christmas morning is such a happy time, isn't it? And one feels one *must* be friendly in such an atmosphere of Peace and Goodwill. This is my daughter."

Jocelyn, engulfed by the Murchison-Bellabys, was borne on the wave of their progress down the path and into the square beyond the reach of Colonel Tidmarsh.

"My son Adrian, and my husband. Now we all know each other, don't we? And it will give us such pleasure if you will dine with us next Tuesday at eight o'clock."

Jocelyn was a little dazed. "Oh, thank you, but I'm afraid—I mean, I have my mother staying with me—"

(Oh, why had she said that?)

"Bring your mother, too," Mrs. Murchison-Bellaby said gushingly. "We shall be delighted—shan't we, Jasmine? Jasmine is my right hand," she explained; "arranges all our house-parties and entertainments—don't you, Jasmine?"

Jasmine paid no attention to her fond parent's burbling.

She was walking behind with Adrian, and Mr. Murchison-Bellaby, as usual, brought up the rear; it was his natural position, and he never sought to assert his authority or claim recognition as the head of the family. He was a meagre little man in a handsome fur-lined coat with an astrakhan collar out of which his ears emerged pinkly. He had short-sighted blue eyes behind thick glasses, and his round face was mildly benevolent.

"Can we drive you home?" Mrs. Murchison-Bellaby inquired, and Jocelyn, catching sight of Colonel Tidmarsh coming down the path behind them, seized the chance to escape thus thrust upon her. She disliked the idea of meeting Gervase Blythe before these strange people.

"Oh, thank you, yes. You pass my house, so it won't be taking you out of your way," she said gratefully, and followed Mrs. Murchison-Bellaby towards the large opulent Rolls Royce. She was at once aware of Adrian's critical, appraising scrutiny and Jasmine's hardly concealed opinion that she was really not worth her notice and that she thought the fuss her mother was making was quite unnecessary.

It was quite obvious that Adrian was very favourably impressed; his glance of admiration told Jocelyn so, and she was not displeased to think that she had aroused such an instant interest in a young man about whom she had heard a great deal from Ermyntrude as being quite the last word in smart young men. Adrian's interest in her was not the reason for the quick flush of colour that made her suddenly so vivid and attractive as she bowed shyly in response to Colonel Tidmarsh and his friend, who raised their hats politely as they passed the car; but he took the blush as a tribute to his power of attraction, and decided that this Mrs. Renshawe was worthy of his attention. Renshawe? The name had an association with someone. . . . Oh, Lord, yes—Ermyntrude, of course!

A hasty glance round showed him that Ermyntrude was not with Mrs. Renshawe, and he felt relieved, but his mind still dwelt on the possibility of a connection between the two, which was a disturbing thought. Ermyntrude had told him she was coming to Much Dithering for Christmas with a Mrs. Renshawe. Were there *two* Mrs. Renshawes? Oh, yes, of course—the haughty dowager at the Priory—that was it. This was the young widow his mother had mentioned—a mere girl, to judge by her sweet unaffected air and her readiness to blush when he looked at her, a charming survival of the old-fashioned, unsophisticated innocence of the Victorian age. She was lovely, unique. Even her unbecoming squirrel coat and her "worthy" velvet hat were unable to blight the loveliness of her perfect colouring and aristocratic features. Her eyes were genuinely violet, black-lashed and with a delightful transparency of expression that betrayed her feelings with an ingenuous charm that he found distracting. Her soft, sweet mouth made him want to kiss her straight away. She had a sedateness and sweet seriousness he had never before encountered, and she was slim and graceful, and her voice was gentle and low-pitched—what a woman! And she didn't know how lovely she was, and had no *idea* how to dress herself. She was a crime, and he'd fallen head over heels in love with her because of a little tendril of golden hair that curled round one ear. What a curse that Ermyntrude was staying down here. He was sick of the sight of her, and must get out of her clutches somehow and be free to follow up his new infatuation. Jocelyn was so enchanting, something completely beyond his experience. The world held no one else.

As they reached the gate of the Dower House he leapt out of the car to help her alight.

"That's all right," he told Jasmine. "I'll walk home." And he walked beside Jocelyn up the short drive. "You don't mind my coming with you?" he asked. "You know, a fellow does get fed up when his family is always on his heels. I was awfully bored at being dragged to church; but I'm glad I went now. I say, this is a jolly place—simply frightfully jolly."

Jocelyn was astonished at his obvious sincerity and desire to please her. Ermyntrude had mentioned Adrian so unceasingly, and had been so insistent that he wasn't at all the sort of man who would put up with being bored in Much Dithering, or be appreciated by its worthy inhabitants, that Jocelyn was rather awed by his condescension, even if, as was of course possible, he was so anxious to meet Ermyntrude again that he was prepared to put up with being bored by herself as one of the "worthy inhabitants." She also realised with a flash of dreadful compunction that in her unexpected meeting just now she had foolishly mentioned "her mother," who was staying with her, and she hoped that the slip had not been noticed. She felt it would be unwise to try to correct her statement in case Adrian had not heard her, and decided fatalistically to let it pass.

She glanced with some interest at Adrian as he walked beside her from the gate, a little amused by his anxiety to be "nice" to a person who would possibly have to put up with quite a lot of his company in her house when he came to see the lady on whom his affections were so firmly centred. He was a fine, upstanding young man, built on his mother's lines and rather overweight for his age. A touch of arrogance in his bearing lent him an air of being "someone." His dark hair was brushed very smooth, and he had a bristly red moustache, which she thought was rather a pity. On the whole, he was an important-looking young man who somehow failed to be quite *right*. She couldn't tell why, but she felt that he was like the cover of a cheap novel (not that she ever read cheap novels, but she disliked the people on the dust-covers, and classed Adrian with the type at first sight). She wondered what Ermyntrude could see in him.

Adrian went on talking, unaware of her wandering attention. "May I come in for a minute or two? That's awfully nice of you—simply topping."

He followed Jocelyn across the hall and into the drawing-room, feeling that he really had met the one woman in the world for him. A meeting outside the church on Christmas morning, love at first sight—had anything ever been so romantic? It was like a fairy tale. A fairy tale? Yes, and all the best traditions were being observed, for there, actually in the chimney-corner, sat the Wicked Fairy, without whom no fairy tale could ever be complete—Ermyntrude! Of all people in the world, why should it be Ermyntrude? The lovely old-world atmosphere and serenity of Jocelyn's home was shattered. As a fit setting for Jocelyn it was perfect, but Ermyntrude jarred horribly. She was out of place—cheap—commonplace. Adrian's fairy tale faded out.

Ermyntrude had only just risen and come downstairs. She was extremely surprised to see Adrian come in with Jocelyn. It had never occurred to her that going to church on Christmas morning would be in his line; but then she really knew nothing

of his habits when residing in the bosom of his family, especially in this new country place where they were endeavouring
to fulfil their obligations as landed gentry. Anyhow, here was
Adrian very unexpectedly, and, to tell the truth, very inoppor-
tunely, for she was not dressed just as she would have wished,
nor was her make-up as perfect as it would have been when
she was fully prepared to dazzle him. In fact, her acquaintance
with Adrian was so entirely artificial that it was a shock to meet
him in a natural, matter-of-course way now that he walked into
Jocelyn's drawing-room without previous warning. Ermyntrude liked plenty of warning, and hated to be taken unawares,
without time to execute repairs to her make-up. She was at a
disadvantage, she felt, and she resented it.

"Good gracious!" she exclaimed peevishly (she was invariably peevish until the afternoon), realising that her handbag was
upstairs and that she had no powder-puff and had not applied
any lipstick because Mellicent Pallfrey was coming to lunch and
had a marked aversion to painted faces.

Adrian was even more surprised to find Ermyntrude at this
moment. In a flash he realised just exactly what she stood for in
his silly, extravagant life—a woman older than himself (he had
always known that), but handsome and alluring enough to hold
him captive by her mature charm and her brilliant air of being
a woman of great importance in the social world, to which he
craved to belong. She flattered his vanity and made him think he
was in love with her. He liked being seen with her. The perfection of her turn-out and her superb arrogance dazzled him, and
he had been content to drift into a fatuous love affair that had
held enough attraction and danger to make it seem rather a
dashing adventure.

Now he saw Ermyntrude as she really was, and he hated her.
The attraction of his adventure had vanished; only the danger
remained, for he guessed that Ermyntrude superseded would
probably be nasty and make everything sordid. Jocelyn was
the one woman he wanted to marry, a woman so sweet and
unspoiled, so perfect in every way to be the wife he desired, only

till now he had never known it, for he had never before met any one like her.

His first sensation on meeting Ermyntrude was an outraged indignation that she had deceived him by pretending that she was so much younger and lovelier that she actually was, and a sudden suspicion that this was the *mother* whom Jocelyn had mentioned seemed to be the crowning outrage of her presence in Much Dithering at such a juncture. He stiffened visibly in an access of cold rage at Ermyntrude's startled greeting. Good manners were never his strong point, and Ermyntrude was familiar with his "difficult" moods and, realising that this was one of them, was convinced that he was angry at meeting her so unexpectedly in Jocelyn's presence, and of course he was also probably very much under the family influence and feeling "caged." Poor boy!

"Ermyntrude," said Jocelyn, beautifully unaware of the tension in the atmosphere, "here is Mr. Murchison-Bellaby. He brought me home from church. Will you excuse me a moment while I fetch some sherry? Bertha is probably rather busy just now. Aunt Mellicent is coming to lunch, you know, and that means a little extra to do." She went out of the room, leaving them together.

Adrian walked over to the window. "What amazing violets, and how wasted in an atmosphere of cheap tobacco and expensive scent! May I open the window?" He did so without waiting for Ermyntrude's permission, and sat on the window-ledge, surveying the room critically—a delightful room with its oak panelling and Jacobean cretonnes. There were old prints on the walls above the dark panelling, and some beautiful china in the cabinets, and on a table by the window where he sat a bowl of violets made a pool of purple. Without Ermyntrude it would have been perfect.

Ermyntrude glowered at him, her eyes full of resentment at his rudeness, but she decided that he was probably peeved at having run into Jocelyn when he had come just to see *her*. "How did you find your way here?" she asked, coming and seating herself beside him and laying her cheek against his shoulder.

"I came back from church with Mrs. Renshawe."

"Church, Adrian? What a reformed character already! Living in the country is evidently good for your soul."

"That's not very funny," he rejoined sulkily, "and I wish you wouldn't sit just here. Mrs. Renshawe might come in."

"That needn't worry you, darling," murmured Ermyntrude reassuringly. "I don't mean to worry about Jocelyn. After all, you'll be here often, and we must have an understanding of some sort."

He sprang up and went back to the fire, looking very angry. "You know, I've told you I can't have any—what you call 'understanding.' I'm dependent on my father, and if I marry against his wishes I might as well drown myself. It's all very well, Ermyntrude, but—"

"I don't think we'll discuss it just now, Adrian dear. As you say, Jocelyn may come in. She is very easily shocked, poor dear! Her Puritan upbringing has made her a perfect prig."

He flushed with anger. "Then we won't shock her," he said with a short laugh. "If I am to come and see you here, Ermyntrude, we must remember to behave nicely!" (There was that, of course. He had an excuse to come as often as he liked to see Ermyntrude, but he would have to go cautiously and keep on Ermyntrude's right side.)

"Darling," gushed Ermyntrude, "how sweet of you; and believe me, Adrian, once I've met your people they will realise how much I can help you in your career, and all will be well. I know it, darling. I have no fears."

Jocelyn came in before Adrian could reply. She had taken off her coat and hat, and as she knelt to make up the fire her golden head was smooth and burnished, but the tantalising tendril still curled round her ear, Adrian noticed, falling more abjectly in love than before. All the difficulties that loomed in his path made him more determined to set them aside. Jocelyn was an angel, so far above his commonplace love affair with Ermyntrude that he was suddenly sick with shame, and Ermyntrude wanted him to marry *her*, and could—and probably would—make it impossible for him ever to approach Jocelyn. Certainly his sins were coming home to roost, and he hated Ermyntrude, and could gladly have murdered her!

He got up, feeling that he could not stand her another moment. "I've just remembered that some friends of mine are coming down to lunch, and I ought to be there to meet them," he explained hurriedly. "Good-bye, Mrs. Renshawe. I'll look forward to seeing you on Tuesday night." He bowed perfunctorily to Ermyntrude and took his departure.

"What a dreadfully dull person you are, Jocelyn," complained her mother. "No wonder Adrian was bored. You had the effect of a wet blanket just now. He simply couldn't find a single word to say. I warned him you were easily shocked, and it appeared to have stunned him into a stony silence, poor boy! He's really most amusing—but in the right company, of course!"

Jocelyn flushed. "I thought he was a very rude young man. I'm sorry it was my fault."

"Well, it can't be helped, only do for heaven's sake try to be a little brighter this evening. Colonel Tidmarsh is more your style, and you can leave the other man to me. From what Colonel Tidmarsh has told you, I imagine he's a man of the world, and might be amusing. I like exploring the possibilities of new people. I shall wear my black and silver, I think. It's dashing and suits me, and it ought to cheer up your party. What will you wear? Your line should be something quiet and Quakerish. I'm sure Colonel Tidmarsh admires the quiet type; but, of course, you never know. He might even fall for *me* after a surfeit of the dull women in this awful village! I'll do my best, anyhow."

"Thank you," responded Jocelyn with a gleam of resentment in her eyes. "Well, you're welcome to Colonel Tidmarsh, Ermyntrude. I hope you'll find him better company than I do; but, as you so frequently point out, I am such a dull person that I fail to draw out the brighter side of people, so I probably miss that qualities that every one tells me Colonel Tidmarsh possesses. I must take lessons from you to-day."

"One was either born a fool or one wasn't," retorted Ermyntrude. "You were!"

CHAPTER NINE

As LUCK would have it, Jocelyn met Gervase in the hall as she came out of the kitchen, where she had been superintending the cooking of the Christmas dinner. Ermyntrude was in the drawing-room and Colonel Tidmarsh was in the porch, pulling off his goloshes, one of which had unaccountably got stuck.

She stopped in confusion and stood silent a moment.

"Mrs. Renshawe," Gervase said quickly, "I'm staying with Colonel Tidmarsh, an old acquaintance of mine, so it happens that I come to dine with you to-night."

Jocelyn came forward slowly and held out her hand. "I'm very glad."

"I hoped you wouldn't think I was thrusting myself on you."

"No, oh no, of course not," she answered hurriedly. "I—it's a funny coincidence, isn't it? But a very pleasant one. I haven't told any one I've met you before. Did you—I mean, does Colonel Tidmarsh know?"

Ambrose Tidmarsh, freed of his goloshes, came in fussily. "Oh, Mrs. Renshawe, I'm so sorry. One of my goloshes got stuck, most unaccountably, and delayed me. I see Blythe hasn't waited to be introduced. Really, Blythe, I think you might have waited for me. I do hope Mrs. Renshawe isn't very annoyed at your butting in like this."

Jocelyn, on the contrary, felt annoyed at his interference. "I think Mr. Blythe was quite right to come in from the porch. After all, he could hardly be expected to wait on your goloshes. Will you hang your coat in there," and she indicated the alcove behind the stairs. He made his way obediently across the hall.

"One moment," said Gervase as Jocelyn turned to the drawing-room door. "I'm a guilty secret, am I?"

She paused, and a glint of mischief lit her eyes. "Oh! Yes, I—I think you must be a guilty secret."

"I think so, too," he agreed, and for a moment they looked at each other with a sense of mischief shared. Then Ambrose joined them and they went into the room together. Ermyntrude greeted Ambrose effusively and Gervase rather guardedly. She had yet to take his measure, and a false start would be a mistake. She understood that he was merely a bird of passage; but, on the other hand, if he was rich and lived in London, he might prove a valuable acquaintance. Lunches or dinners now and then would be pleasant. He was good-looking and well turned out—obviously somebody—and he had charming manners. He looked her over with the air of a man who had an eye for details and missed nothing—evidently a man of understanding. Altogether his coming here to-night was rather lucky, and she determined to cultivate his acquaintance. One never knew when a spare man would be useful.

Jocelyn glanced uneasily at the clock and wondered where the Pomfrets were. It would be a pity if the dinner over which she and Bertha had taken so much trouble should be spoiled by too long a delay. Her anxiety was becoming acute when Bertha came in and handed her a scrawled note from Pomfret to say that the vicar had developed lumbago and they would be unable to come to dinner. She was disconcerted at realising that she was to be deprived of Mrs. Pomfret's genial support on which she had been unconsciously depending, for she dreaded Ermyntrude's ruthless criticisms and unpleasant little way of putting her completely on one side and taking charge, as if she were the hostess and not Jocelyn.

That was exactly what Ermyntrude decided to do. She imagined that Gervase would appreciate her brilliance and *savoir faire* and be a kindred spirit while Ambrose talked in his dull fashion to an equally dull and uninspired Jocelyn. As a matter of fact, this arrangement suited Ambrose admirably. He disliked Ermyntrude exceedingly, and had come on purpose to make himself agreeable to Jocelyn. At the same time, however, he resented Ermyntrude's unconcealed determination to exploit Gervase and encourage him to talk about himself. Gervase was an unopened oyster, and Ermyntrude was clever enough to realise that he had certainly acquired sufficient "past" to make him an interesting partner. Ambrose had not learned anything definite about Gervase's past, but he was convinced that it was far from being all that it ought to have been. He remembered that Gervase was an excellent talker and fond of a good story, and he feared that with Ermyntrude to encourage him he would soon get under way and take over the part of chief entertainer at Jocelyn's dinner and put every one else on one side.

It was soon clear that his fears were to be realised. Before long Gervase was fairly launched on a series of reminiscences which Ermyntrude found diverting, Jocelyn somewhat disconcerting, and Ambrose highly regrettable. Ermyntrude had demanded champagne—in fact, she had provided it—and she was having her money's worth, she considered. She was content to play second fiddle to Gervase, recognising that his talent was superior even to her own in the art of making a dull evening "go." Besides, it was extremely amusing to watch Ambrose grow angrier each moment and Jocelyn register astonishment and disapproval at the livelier episodes in Gervase's spirited recital. Not that he went beyond the limits imposed by the presence of ladies—even Ambrose admitted that—but he was such a new experience for Jocelyn that she found herself half-vexed, half-fascinated, and was not sure which feeling predominated. Unconsciously she ignored the angry Ambrose and listened to Gervase with an attention he found flattering, and he was careful not to exceed the speed limit in the restricted area of his hostess's transparent unsophistication.

After a while Jocelyn found herself enjoying the evening in a way she had never anticipated, and realised that Gervase was the good fairy who had taken charge. Ermyntrude was at the top of her form and forgot to be disagreeable. Colonel Tidmarsh alone was disgruntled and out of things, but she had no time to worry over that. She even forgot her own inability to "sparkle" and act the part of hostess (so frequently rubbed in by Ermyntrude) in her pleasure at realising that Gervase was her guest and that it was in order to make her party a success that he had stepped in to pull an obviously ill-assorted company together. He managed to convey this impression with an occasional glance that seemed to suggest that "his good intent was all for her delight," and that if he pleased her, the rest might go hang.

Ermyntrude naturally took it for granted that he was merely entertaining her, and Ambrose sought jealously to discover an opportunity to interrupt and rebuke him for his monopoly of the conversation, but Gervase blandly overrode any effort to stem the flow of his eloquence, and succeeded in placing Ambrose completely as an "also ran."

Jocelyn listened with a two-fold interest. She had a desire to know something about this man whose acquaintance she had made in such (to her) an unconventional way—who he was and what he did, but interesting and entertaining as he was, she realised that he was telling nothing of what she really wanted to know. There were no personal touches she could put together. He brought different parts of the world vividly before her. His experiences had been varied and full of incident. Racing in Australia, ranching in South America, something unspecified in Canada, something of financial importance in South Africa, here, there and everywhere on the Continent of Europe, and soldiering in India and Persia. Jocelyn was bewildered at the swiftness of it all, and unsatisfied at the end of it when, the dinner having come to a satisfactory conclusion, she and Ermyntrude went to the drawing-room, leaving Ambrose and Gervase to port and cigars.

"Heavens!" exclaimed Ermyntrude, powdering her nose and examining herself critically in the mirror of her handbag. "What a man! And what a good thing I was there. He'd have had a pretty thin time with only you and the Tiddler person. I flatter myself I was a success. I shall certainly follow up this good beginning and see something of him when I get back to London."

Jocelyn was silent and her mother glanced at her and laughed. "Oh, I could see you were shocked. That's the worst of being so 'worthy,' Jocelyn. It really is time you grew up. Oh, by the way, he doesn't know I'm your *mother*, does he?"

"Not from me, but possibly Colonel Tidmarsh told him—*he* knows."

Ermyntrude looked disgusted. "Well, it can't be helped, and anyhow I made the right impression. Besides, he isn't young himself—at least forty-five."

Jocelyn felt catty. "What about Adrian?"

Ermyntrude shrugged. "It will do him a lot of good to know that he isn't the only one."

Jocelyn poured out the coffee feeling resentful. That Ermyntrude should annex Gervase struck her as distinctly hard, but she could do nothing about it.

Ambrose and Gervase came in as she was wondering what to do about their coffee, and Ermyntrude made room on the settee. "Come and sit here, Mr. Blythe, and tell me a blue story—something really lurid, like blue lightning. I'm sure you can tell them magnificently."

"I don't tell blue stories," replied Gervase sedately. "Besides, my friend Colonel Tidmarsh wouldn't like it."

Ambrose, ever vigilant, turned quickly. "What is it that I wouldn't like?"

"A blue story? You don't like them, do you?"

"Blue stories—in Mrs. Renshawe's drawing-room? Certainly not!"

"Don't look so worried," Gervase said soothingly. "I shan't tell any. My behaviour in a lady's drawing-room is above reproach. I admit that I *can* tell a blue story in the congenial atmosphere of a camp-fire or the smoking-room of an ocean liner, or even in the bar of a pub, but I behave quite nicely according to my company." He made Jocelyn a little bow which brought a dancing gleam to her eyes. As it was quite impossible to evade Ambrose, and Ermyntrude made it clear that she intended him to continue his attention to her, he made the best of a bad job and sat down beside her, but he was able to exchange sympathetic glances with Jocelyn, who was now firmly barricaded in a big arm-chair with Ambrose seated close by, very much on guard.

"Tell me," Gervase said to Ermyntrude. "What do you do besides being rude to people in the country?"

"I live in town," replied Ermyntrude importantly, "and that I find is quite a full-time job when one lives a very social life as I do."

"I'm sure of that."

Ermyntrude looked at him a little doubtfully, not quite sure if she liked his tone. "Do tell me more about yourself," she said with an air of being intelligently interested. "You've been about the world such a lot, haven't you? I like meeting people who know their way about. I find people who have never been outside England so depressingly ignorant—raw, in fact."

"Raw?"

"Yes, raw and green. I tell Jocelyn that she should travel, but she is just a dormouse, completely immersed in the affairs of the parish."

"Intelligent little creature!" murmured Gervase gently. "I never knew quite what they did with themselves when they weren't hibernating."

Ermyntrude ignored that. "You live in town now, I think you said? We must meet—lunch or dine somewhere and do a show. I'm going back soon, but I believe Jocelyn has promised that we shall dine at the Murchison-Bellabys on Tuesday. How long are you staying here?"

"That depends on circumstances"—replied Gervase—"on how long Ambrose Tidmarsh will put up with me, for instance."

"I wonder how you can put up with him!" she retorted.

"You aren't attracted by him?"

"Attracted? Dear man, do I look like a woman likely to be attracted by a wet blanket? I like a man to be really a man."

"Something with a kick to it?"

"My idea exactly," agreed Ermyntrude. "Now I knew at once that *you* had a kick."

"Why is Ambrose here to-night?" asked Gervase suddenly.

Ermyntrude laughed. "Haven't you realised that he and Jocelyn—?"

"Oh, *that's* it?"

"They will be an ideal couple," said Ermyntrude indulgently. "He will take care of her and she will just go on being a—"

"A dormouse?"

"Exactly!" Ermyntrude lit a cigarette and settled herself among the cushions, pleasantly sleepy, her plump white arm outstretched on the couch, her hand almost touching his.

"Now tell me what you do," she murmured. "You interest me enormously."

But just at that moment there carne an interruption. Mrs. Goodbun opened the door and exclaimed in a state, of great agitation: "I beg parding, madam, but I think you'd better know that that there dratted kitchen chimbley 'as gone afire. It's burning something fierce. Me and Bertha and Goodbun 'as done our best, but you'd better come and 'ave a look."

Jocelyn sprang up in alarm. "Oh, I'm coming at once. Why didn't you tell me before? What set it alight at this hour?"

"Well, madam, I won't tell you a lie," said Mrs. Goodbun, who was swaying a little and speaking with peculiar carefulness. "It was Goodbun wot went and tipped the dripping-pan into the fire. Silly old geyser's what I say; but there, you can't never know what 'e'll be up to."

Jocelyn hurried out of the room, leaving Mrs. Goodbun still explaining.

"Woman, you're drunk!" cried Ermyntrude sharply. "Disgusting creature!"

"Oh, dear!" Colonel Tidmarsh looked very perturbed. "A fire? That is most unfortunate."

"Most unfortunate," agreed Gervase dryly, and went after Jocelyn.

"I have always had a perfect horror of fire," went on Ambrose nervously.

"Oh, heavens!" exclaimed Ermyntrude in a sudden panic. "My room is over the kitchen. I must get my things out. Come and help me. Come on—at once!" And she seized him by the arm and ran him out of the room before he could protest.

"Dis-disgusting creature!" said Mrs. Goodbun with immense scorn, and went back to the kitchen, where Jocelyn with Gervase and Bertha were dealing with the chimney, which was well alight and roaring with a most menacing sound.

"Where is the fire extinguisher?" cried Jocelyn. "Quick, Bertha!"

"Let me get it," said Gervase and went with Bertha.

"Salt on the fire," said Jocelyn, remembering all she knew about fires, "and stop the draught. But how? Oh, dear!"

"Stand clear and I'll see what I can do with this; but it's damned awkward." Gervase looked at the kitchen range and wondered how to get at the chimney.

"Buckets of water from the roof," suggested Jocelyn. "There's a ladder in the old coach-house. I'll show you."

Outside in the yard they could see smoke and red flames shooting high out of the tall old chimney and the burning soot was falling in glowing lumps all around them.

"Fetch Ambrose," said Gervase, "and I'll get the ladder up."

Jocelyn fled indoors and met Ambrose staggering down the stairs with Ermyntrude's suitcases, and Ermyntrude, wearing her fur coat, following just behind.

"I'm going to Colonel Tidmarsh's house," she explained. "I can't do any good here, and I'm simply terrified of fire, so the only thing I can do is to get out of the way. Colonel Tidmarsh will call the Fire Brigade and come back when he has taken me home."

"Yes, yes," agreed Ambrose, who looked quite as terrified as Ermyntrude. "I'll fetch the Fire Brigade. I shan't be long."

Jocelyn ran back to the yard. "He's taking Ermyntrude to his house and he'll send the Fire Brigade."

"That's kind of him." Gervase raised the long ladder and he and Jocelyn steadied it against the chimney-stack. "I hope he won't be too long about it. Have you a hosepipe, by any chance?"

"Only the garden hose—a long one."

"Good girl! Go and get it."

The hose was somewhat inadequate, but it was the best they could achieve for the moment, and once Gervase was on the roof he was able to direct a small but fairly steady flow into the chimney, which as a matter of fact had about burned itself out and began obligingly to yield to treatment. In fact, all was over except for a very considerable mess when Ambrose, looking very important in oilskins and rubber boots, led the Much Dithering Fire Brigade (or as much of it as he had been able to persuade to accompany him) to the scene of the scene of the fire.

Jocelyn and Gervase, looking very much the worse for their adventure, black-faced and dishevelled, were watching the smoke that still poured out of the chimney, smelling horribly of burning soot.

"Here we are!" called Ambrose. "Where is the fire hydrant? We'll run out the hose and soon have it out."

"Thanks," replied Gervase calmly, "we've done all that. You're a bit late, old chap; but you look very workmanlike, all the same."

The captain of the Fire Brigade, who had obviously been celebrating Christmas somewhat excessively, looked about him and said: "Hi, there! Where's the water?"

"You'll find some in a bucket over there, if you really want some," Gervase told him. "But really, you know, we've just about finished everything quite nicely."

"That's all very well," complained the captain. "But you can't 'ave no bloody fire without water! It ain't usual."

"I dare say you're right," agreed Gervase politely, "but we've not done so badly all the same. As you're here you can stand by for a bit and keep your eye on things. Come on, Mrs. Renshawe, you look as if you needed a wash; and a drink wouldn't do either of us any harm." He took Jocelyn's arm and led her into the house. In the hall he turned and looked at her. "You've a very black face and your lovely golden hair is covered with soot, but you manage to look—well, never mind. You must be awfully tired. I'd like to say, though, that you're the pluckiest girl I've ever met—and I've known a few. May I come and see you one day—without Ambrose?"

Jocelyn was at the end of her endurance, but she achieved a smile. She blushed, too, at his praise of her courage, but the flow of colour was concealed by the grime that overlaid her face. "Then you—you are staying?" she stammered.

"I shall stay as long as need be and come and see you—if I may?"

"Oh, do come," she said impulsively, and gave him her hand, smiling up at him.

Before Gervase could reply Ambrose came in, looking very bad-tempered. "I really do think, Blythe," he exclaimed, "that you should have taken care that Mrs. Renshawe wasn't worried by this affair. She must have been frightened to death, and has got herself into a terrible state. Mrs. Renshawe, I've been so worried about you. I do hope you are all right."

"Thanks to Mr. Blythe's splendid work, yes, Colonel Tidmarsh. He saved my house for me," replied Jocelyn with spirit. "I can never thank him enough. But I'm not going to try to-night; I'm far too tired and dirty." She smiled. "I hope the water will be really hot for a bath. It certainly ought to be! Good-night."

CHAPTER TEN

GERVASE satisfied himself that there was no further danger of the fire breaking out again before he went back to Colonel Tidmarsh's house. Ambrose's feelings had been so shattered that he had gone home without another word to Gervase. He had taken Ermyntrude to Miss Pallfrey's when she had insisted on leaving the Dower House with all her belongings, but unfortunately Miss Pallfrey was spending the evening with the Honourable Augusta and her house was shut up, so, Ermyntrude declaring that she would go to The Roebuck rather than risk her valuable possessions by returning to Jocelyn's house, to The Roebuck they went, and Ambrose left her to the care of the landlord's Italian wife while he went to change his evening clothes (being a careful man!) and then in search of the various members of the Fire Brigade.

Jocelyn's ingratitude for all he considered he had done stung him bitterly, and he vented his injured feelings on Gervase, who, he considered, had been unnecessarily officious. Even his desire to question him on the subject of investing money was banished by his ungovernable jealousy. He had a nasty black temper, which when roused took possession of him and rendered him unable to see things in proper perspective.

He spent a sleepless night (what was left of it!), nursed his injured feelings, and went to breakfast in a very bellicose mood, determined to tell his guest exactly what he thought of his mismanagement of Jocelyn's fire in order that he might exhibit himself in the absurd role of a hero and put him (Ambrose Tidmarsh) in an entirely false position, making him out a coward by suggesting that he had gone to fetch the Fire Brigade unnecessarily so as to keep out of the way. In these circumstances, therefore, he felt himself compelled to ask that Gervase should remove himself from Much Dithering at once, as his presence in the house was unendurable. He said a good deal more, too, for he had manufactured a first-glass grievance during his wakeful night, and it grew blacker and larger the more freely he expressed his outraged feelings.

Gervase heard him to the end. "All this is entirely in your own imagination; but I quite agree that the position is impossible, since you look at things from such a peculiar point of view. I shall leave your house at once. I'm sorry things have turned out like this."

Ambrose made no reply and Gervase left the room. He flung his things into has suitcase and went to find some breakfast at The Roebuck. As a matter of fact, it suited him very well, for he had always meant to go there when his short visit to Ambrose was over, and this abrupt departure saved him any explanation as to his reason for remaining in Much Dithering. It also meant that he was free to visit Jocelyn if he wished, without Ambrose interfering and being unpleasant, as he had been the night before. The situation was certainly piquant, and he derived a good deal of amusement from making his plans as he carried his suitcase to the inn.

Joe Hedgecock was glad to see him and was anxious for news of the fire. The lady was still asleep upstairs, he said. Quite a night of excitement it had been, and such stories about the house being burnt out, and so on.

Gervase engaged a room and had an excellent breakfast. He wondered what his next move should be. He had no intention of crossing Ermyntrude's path if it could be avoided, so he took a private sitting-room and retired there to read the papers in peace until it should be a reasonable hour to go and inquire how Jocelyn was this morning.

From his chair near the window he had a view of the Square and the bridge across which Ambrose must come if he, too, intended to call on Jocelyn, so he would be able to avoid an undesirable encounter. There was also a little comedy which amused him, for he saw a well-dressed young man drive up to the entrance to the inn and stay a moment to light a cigarette while he looked intently through the window of the private bar, which stood open. Presently the landlord's daughter appeared from behind the casement curtains and looked out casually, and the young man got out of his car and went up to the window with a glance round that suggested he was a little anxious. The lovely Lucia leaned out and smiled in an amused way, and the young man spoke to her in a low voice. She laughed indulgently once or twice and seemed to tell him something which alarmed him, for he cast a scared glance about him and, getting hastily into the car, drove away across the bridge and disappeared just as an imperious voice called: "Adrian! Stop! I want you."

Gervase saw Ermyntrude leaning out of an upstairs window, looking furiously after the rapidly disappearing car. She was clad (as far as he could judge) in a fluffy, feather-trimmed species of negligée, so he decided that she was not prepared to leave her bedroom just yet, and that if he were to hurry he might have the luck to find Jocelyn alone, but even as the idea came to him he saw a small car drive up to the door and Jocelyn herself got out. Ermyntrude's head had vanished and the landlord's daughter was ushering Jocelyn into the oak-panelled lounge-hall when he reached it.

"Good-morning," he said, smiling at her astonishment at his greeting. "I was coming to see you presently to make polite inquiries as to your welfare."

Jocelyn looked exceedingly surprised to see him. "But what are *you* doing here? I've come to fetch Ermyntrude, who spent the night here; but I hear she's not up yet. I must go and see—"

"She's quite all right; I've seen her looking out of her window, so do sit down and tell me how *you* got on. I would have gone to see you earlier, but I rather thought Ambrose might have gone, and I—well, I thought I'd wait till later."

She looked as if she wanted to ask a question, but decided not to and said with a quiver of a smile: "Yes, he did call, but I didn't see him. I wasn't quite dressed, so I told Bertha to say I was still in bed, feeling rather ill, and couldn't see any one. Then I came to fetch my—Ermyntrude."

"A bit of luck for me. I'm staying here, by the way."

"Staying *here*?"

"Yes, Ambrose was very peeved at my mismanagement of your fire, and was rather offensive this morning, so I packed up and came here, and here I shall stay for a little while, just in case you have another fire or anything that needs a strong man's assistance. But how are you this morning? And did you have that hot bath and a good sleep? You look 'in the pink,' as they say—quite as if you had never had a smut on your face in your life. Were you awfully tired?"

Jocelyn smiled suddenly. "Do you know, I really *enjoyed* last night. Isn't that funny? I wasn't a bit frightened. I just enjoyed it all enormously and felt it was an adventure."

"So did I," he said heartily. "I wouldn't have missed it for anything. Can't we have another—adventure, I mean?"

She coloured and looked a little confused. "Oh, I don't think—" she began.

"Oh, yes, we'll think of something else," he assured her with a laugh. "But now here's Ermyntrude. I can hear her voice upstairs, so I'll say good-bye. Don't say you've seen me. I'm still a guilty secret." He retreated through the door into his own sitting-room and closed it gently as Ermyntrude came down the stairs.

"Oh, there you are, Jocelyn," she said querulously. "Did you meet Adrian just now? He came to ask for me, but they didn't tell me he was there—so stupid of them—so he drove off before I could get down."

"How did he know you were here?" Jocelyn asked dubiously.

"Oh, of course the news of the fire was all over the village last night," Ermyntrude retorted. "I wonder he didn't go to see if he could help to put it out. It caused quite a scare when Colonel Tidmarsh called out the Fire Brigade. The poor old thing was a bundle of nerves. I've never seen any one in such a state. By the way, what did happen? I went to your worthy aunt, but the house was shut up, so I came here. I thought I'd be much better out of every one's way."

"Very sensible of you," agreed Jocelyn. "Are you ready to come home now?"

"Yes, I expect Adrian will come to see me, so I'd better get back."

The landlord's daughter had just brought down Ermyntrude's luggage, and as she stood a moment to ask if there were anything else Ermyntrude wished for, Ermyntrude said sharply: "Why didn't you tell me that Mr. Murchison-Bellaby called?"

Lucia raised her beautifully pencilled eyebrows. "I did not know that you wished to speak to him."

"He called to see me," Ermyntrude said haughtily.

"Pardon, madam," murmured Lucia with a deprecating gesture, "he did not say so."

"Probably you didn't understand."

"That is possible."

Jocelyn caught the gleam of amusement in Lucia's dark eyes as she turned away. "You are home for the holidays, Lucia?" she asked. She had known this young woman from the time she was a child, and took a friendly interest in her career.

"Yes, Mrs. Renshawe. I have a few weeks' holiday to get well. I have had influenza badly, and the doctor ordered me rest."

"Oh, I'm sorry. Are you better? I expect you find the village dull, after London."

Again Lucinda smiled and looked indolently amused. "It is dull, perhaps, but there are compensations." She went away with a smiling "Good-morning," and as the door closed Ermyntrude snorted with indignation.

"What an impudent girl! Her manners are positively outrageous, and her appearance—painted to the eyes and smothered in powder! She looks like a second-rate film actress."

"Shall we go?" Jocelyn asked. "Have you paid your bill?"

"I've no money," snapped Ermyntrude.

"I'll see to it." Jocelyn picked up a suitcase and went out to the car.

CHAPTER ELEVEN

THE dinner-party at the Murchison-Bellabys' was a rather difficult affair. The mixture of Jasmine's London friends and what she contemptuously termed "the village people" was not altogether a success. The vicar was still unable to take part in social events owing to his lumbago, but Mrs. Pomfret came determined to make the most of her opportunity to enlist the sympathy and interest of the new and wealthy parishioners in her numerous activities. Ermyntrude came resolved on creating the right impression on Adrian's people. She had never met any of them, but was convinced that she had only to be seen to conquer any prejudice that might have to be overcome. Jocelyn came rather diffidently, for she dreaded new acquaintances, especially rich and (she was sure) clever, smart people with whom she would feel shy and out of things. A few days spent in her mother's company invariably upset her usual serenity and made her feel stupid and "impossible." The surprise of meeting Gervase brought a bright glow of colour to her usually rather pale face and a deepening of the blue of her eyes, so that she was looking unusually attractive, a fact of which she was, as usual, quite unaware, for she never thought of her appearance, so she continued to feel shy and diffident in spite of Adrian's unabashed admiration and something in Gervase's greeting which suggested that he was glad to see her. Jasmine's glance told her at once that her frock was not worth noticing and that she was merely "village" and dowdy at that, but Mrs. Murchison-Bellaby shook her warmly by the hand and made her feel that she was delighted to make her closer acquaintance, whereas, her look said as plainly as possible, the sight of Ermyntrude's naked back, auburn hair and over-painted face aroused her deepest disapproval.

The round table had been arranged by Adrian, who had decided to sit as far as possible from Ermyntrude and had basely turned her over to Gervase, whom he had met playing billiards at The Roebuck and had invited to dinner on an impulse. Mr. Murchison-Bellaby naturally took in Mrs. Pomfret, and Jocelyn sat between him and Adrian, while Jasmine and Ermyntrude were separated by Gervase. There were several other guests staying in the house-party—young, noisy, and not distinguished by their good manners. The dinner was long and had innumerable courses of Christmas fare, all very rich and heavy, while the champagne flowed in such prodigious quantity as to suggest that the supply was regulated by a tap that refused to turn off.

Jocelyn found her host silent and boring, and her thoughts were occupied in wondering how Gervase came to be at the party whenever she was left free by Adrian, who was almost embarrassing in his attentions. She wished that he had not taken her in to dinner, for she was sure that Ermyntrude had expected him to take *her* in and would therefore be exceedingly bad-tempered and hurt, and would blame her for the unfortunate coupling. Across the table she could see Ermyntrude growing angrier as the time went on, and Jasmine bent on achieving the destruction of Gervase's peace of mind with all the allure of her beauty and frankness of sex appeal. Gervase, on his part, seemed to be as little attracted by Jasmine as he was by Ermyntrude, and maintained a calm imperturbability which infuriated Ermyntrude and puzzled Jasmine, who, being crude in her methods, had no understanding of subtlety as practised by one proficient in that art. Gervase fenced with a gentle irony far outside the rude repartee and badinage which seemed to be the language of Jasmine and her young friends, and his thrusts left her puzzled and uncomprehending. She consoled herself by putting him down as "a dark horse," and decided that he was too discreet to let things rip at the dinner-table. Beyond all doubt he was a "he-man" of wide experience, and worth her attention.

"Tell me," she said, cupping her thrust chin in her hands and resting her elbows on the table. "Whom do you consider the most interesting person here to-night?" Her dark eyes searched his and a confident smile played round her full red lips.

Gervase gave the matter his attention. "Do you really want my honest opinion?" he asked seriously.

"I asked you."

"Well, then, I consider myself far and away the most interesting person," he replied in a matter-of-fact manner that remained imperturbable in spite of Jasmine's wide-eyed astonishment and her sharp exclamations.

"Well, I'm damned! What conceit!"

"You asked me," he reminded her.

She half-turned in her chair and regarded him with fresh curiosity. "Why do you flatter yourself that you're so interesting?"

"I've done practically everything I ought not to have done and very little that I ought to have done. I'm lucky. I succeed. I get what I want. I *do* things."

Jasmine gave a long fluttering sigh. "That's rather *marvellous*, you know. What sort of things do you *do*?"

"Do you want the list in alphabetical order?"

Jasmine laughed. "As long as all that? What a wonderful man you must be!" she drawled with a faintly insolent lift to her eyebrows.

"I am," he replied coolly.

"And you like telling people about yourself?"

"When the alternative is listening to them telling me about themselves."

"Don't you admit that other people can be interesting, too?" she challenged.

"To themselves, no doubt."

"Like you?"

"Exactly."

"But don't you ever take any interest in other people?"

"Good heavens, yes, when they're worth it."

"A-ah!" sighed Jasmine. "*Now* we're getting at it."

"At what?"

"The real you."

He looked at her in silence for a moment. "Oh, Yasmin, Yasmin, what a dangerous woman you are!"

"Why 'Yasmin?'" she asked a little breathlessly. This was more promising!

"You remind me of a dancing girl I came across once in Quetta. She was very beautiful and very wicked."

"Aren't you flattering me?" murmured Jasmine, letting her black lashes sweep her cheeks.

"No," said Gervase decisively. "I'm not. No decent English girl ever wants to be likened to an Indian nautch girl."

Jasmine flung up her head. "Good Lord! 'A decent English girl'—what a ghastly idea! Let me tell you, that sort of slush is dead—like Queen Anne or Queen Victoria. Give me beauty and wickedness and I'll win all along the line!" She turned fiercely to him. "I *do* things, too. I don't just talk."

He considered this for a moment. "Yes, I expect you do," he said quietly. "As I remarked just now, Yasmin, you're a dangerous woman."

"Do you ever fall in love?" Jasmine was enjoying herself now.

"I? No, I'm blasé."

"I don't believe it."

"The only woman I've looked at for years is Mrs. Pomfret."

"Mrs. Pomfret! But why? How extraordinary!"

"She's so human and natural. If her nose shines, she lets it—"

"She certainly does!" agreed Jasmine.

"If her hair comes down, she lets it. She's cheerful—a regular tonic in a world of jaded artificiality. She shines like a beacon. She does good works and glories in them. She's straight all through, and she does you good just to see her smile. Now *she's* a woman who does things, not just talks about them."

He went on cracking a nut and Jasmine sat and wondered what to say next. Mrs. Pomfret? Of course he was pulling her leg!

He piled the walnuts on her plate. "And I mean every word of what I say, so you needn't look amused or superior, Yasmin. I've told you just what you are and I've told you what Mrs. Pomfret is—you can weigh it up. Your mother is trying to collect the ladies." He rose and stood aside for her to pass.

"I'd rather be dangerous than have a shiny nose, I think," she drawled, and flung him a glance over her shoulder.

In the drawing-room Mrs. Murchison-Bellaby made herself agreeable to Mrs. Pomfret. "What a charming little place Much Dithering is, Mrs. Pomfret, but coming to it fresh, as we do, we realise, possibly better than the people who have always lived here, how behind the times it is in many ways. It wants some modern ideas. It is *delightful*, of course, but so *completely* behind the times. Such a pity, but *we* can soon alter all that when we've lived here a little longer and have more influence."

Mrs. Pomfret shook her head vigorously. "No, villages will be old-fashioned still in spite of the fact that the young people go to the 'movies' and say 'Oh yeah' and 'Sez you' when they want to be up to date. You can't be really modern in the way *you* mean in Much Dithering. It's sleepy and keeps itself to itself, if you know what I mean. You'd be like a war-horse harnessed to a bath-chair, and by the end of a week the war-horse would be running loose and the bath-chair would be in the ditch or kicked to pieces, and as *I'd* be part of the crowd packed into the bath-chair, Mrs. Murchison-Bellaby, I'm not very keen on the notion. We've always been old-fashioned here in Much Dithering, and I hope we always will be. It's a dear old-fashioned place and we don't hold with 'progress,' so called."

"Prejudice," argued Mrs. Murchison-Bellaby with a tolerant smile. "It seems a pity to shut one's eyes to the march of progress. If you'd take Jasmine on to some of your committees, she would bring new ideas and waken you all up. I hope very much that Jasmine will interest herself in village affairs. We mean to live here entirely in the future. I want my son to stand for Parliament some day, you know, and he must get to know people and study rural problems. Young people should work, don't you think? They are the hope of the future—not all the local stick-in-the-muds you pin your faith to. The world is moving and you must move, too, even in Much Dithering."

Mrs. Pomfret gazed at her with horror in her round eyes. "If Mrs. Renshawe heard you she would drop stone dead with horror."

"And a very good thing, too," said Mrs. Murchison-Bellaby, shrugging her fat white shoulders. "Old women who get in other people's way are far better dead. But there, I've shocked you. I mustn't do that. I'll send my husband over to talk to you. He is interested in the British Israelites, and I'm sure you can tell him things. Leopold, come here! Mrs. Pomfret is anxious to talk to you about British Israelites." She rose from her seat beside Mrs. Pomfret. "Now I must go and talk to young Mrs. Renshawe." And she left the vicar's wife to the task of being bright with singularly little encouragement from her host, who sank into the enormous chair vacated by his wife and seemed resigned to conversation on the subject of the Ten Tribes or Plagues of Egypt—he didn't mind which.

Mrs. Pomfret, however, seized the opportunity to lay the affairs of the parish before him, feeling that the forthcoming events in Much Dithering were much more vital than the long-past wanderings of the Children of Israel. Mr. Murchison-Bellaby, stirred by her enthusiasm, actually sat up and began to take a little notice, and Mrs. Pomfret, with her usual grasp of affairs, made the most of her opportunities.

Mrs. Murchison-Bellaby found her son deep in conversation with Jocelyn. That is to say, he was telling her all about himself, his views on life, art, literature, drama, public questions—anything, in fact, in which he was pleased to take an interest. He had just got to his political ambitions when his mother bore down upon the sofa where he sprawled beside Jocelyn and inserted her bulk between them—a very efficient bulwark, Jocelyn realised with some relief, for Adrian was rather a strain on her powers of endurance.

"Now I want to know all about Much Dithering, Mrs. Renshawe," Mrs. Murchison-Bellaby said. "It takes people a little time to settle down, but now that we have really got the place to our liking and are beginning to feel at home, we must get to know our neighbours, and take our part in the social round. I don't believe in standing on the edge of things and merely looking on. We have responsibilities and we must shoulder them. You find that, I'm sure. How long have you lived here?"

"Ever since I was a child. I came home from India when I was five and lived with my aunt, Miss Pallfrey, until my marriage."

"I see." Mrs. Murchison-Bellaby studied Jocelyn with speculative interest. Not much money, she decided, not at all *smart* in the way that Jasmine and her friends were smart, or that other woman, Mrs. Lascelles, who kept looking at Adrian in such an objectionable way. Mrs. Lascelles? But Mrs. Renshawe had mentioned that her *mother* was staying with her? Surely—?

Mrs. Murchison-Bellaby glanced round the room to ascertain if there was any one whom she had overlooked, but no! she could account for every one. Only Mrs. Lascelles, now firmly attached to the man Adrian had brought in unexpectedly, was old enough to be Mrs. Renshawe's mother, and she was certainly old enough to know better than to dress herself up in tinsel brocade and paint herself. Ah! She had a wave of recollection. Jasmine had said something—So *that* was the widow woman who was making a fool of Adrian? Well! She glanced round again. At any rate, to-night Adrian had eyes for no one but young Mrs. Renshawe, so that was why that ageing female boa-constrictor was so angry with him!

She turned her attention again to Jocelyn, studying her with fresh interest, pleased with her air of quiet distinction and her old-fashioned, well-bred dignity that were so noticeable in the company of the other young people who were sprawling and smoking and shouting foolish things across the big room. Here in Mrs. Renshawe was the perfect wife for her son, with whom he could settle down and be a real country gentleman—a wife to break him of his youthful follies and guide him in the way he ought to go. Her manners and looks were "the real thing." It was essential that Adrian should marry someone local who "belonged." That would give him the standing among the right people that newcomers just beginning naturally lacked. How fortunate that Adrian seemed to admire her so much already! And she, of course, would jump at such a match—any one would!

In the meantime, while thus arranging Jocelyn's future, Mrs. Murchison-Bellaby had been busy asking questions and studying her prospective daughter-in-law with an undisguised curiosity that Jocelyn found exceedingly irritating.

"Whom did you say your husband was?" repeated Mrs. Murchison-Bellaby, whose attention was divided between her thoughts and her conversation, and had wandered a little.

"Lancelot Renshawe."

"Any relation to the Honourable Mrs. Renshawe?"

"He was her son."

"Really!" (What an asset!) "And would he have succeeded to The Priory?"

"Naturally."

"What awful luck for you! Who comes in for it now? There aren't any daughters, are there?"

"No." Jocelyn paused. She realised the drift of the question from the eagerness of Mrs. Murchison-Bellaby's manner. "The heir is somewhere abroad, I believe."

"Is he married?"

"*I* can't tell you."

"H'm!" Mrs. Murchison-Bellaby fell silent, staring at Jocelyn in such a frankly appraising manner that Jocelyn felt that she must get up and walk away. She saw Gervase Blythe watching her inquisition with a twinkle of understanding in his eyes. The young people had vanished, and only Mrs. Murchison-Bellaby, Mrs. Pomfret, and Gervase remained in the room. From the hall came the sounds of dance music.

Impulsively Jocelyn sprang up. "I'd simply love to dance, Mr. Blythe, if you were nice enough to ask me."

"I hoped you might want to," he replied, tucking her hand under his arm and leading her into the hall. "I couldn't help seeing you were making heavy weather."

"I hate people who sit and stare at you and ask questions as if they were firing a machine-gun," she said stormily. Her eyes were sparkling with anger and her cheeks were vivid. She almost stamped her foot as they paused outside the drawing-room door.

Gervase laughed. "I saw the storm brewing, so I stayed behind. I felt you would need a rescuer before long. Shall we dance?"

"I don't really dance, I'm afraid," Jocelyn said with a sigh. "I'm a folk-dance expert; but I'm afraid it's not quite the same thing."

"Can't we find somewhere in this bear-garden to hide and be quiet?" he asked as they danced.

"Oh, but I'd like to dance," she said quickly. "I feel as if I were recovering my lost youth. In fact"—she looked up at him with a pucker of surprise on her smooth forehead—"I feel as if I were young for the first time in my life. Isn't that funny?"

There was a strange thrill in the feel of his arms round her, a feeling of protectiveness, even of possessiveness, such as she had never experienced before. His eyes looking down into hers were a trifle amused, speculative—perhaps something else, too. Jocelyn felt her heart beating unevenly with a thrill of totally unaccustomed pleasure and excitement.

"If we stay here," Gervase said, "I'll have to dance with Yasmin, which I couldn't bear, and you will have to dance with Adrian; he's stalking you now."

Jocelyn was suddenly dismayed. Her inclination was to go with Gervase, but her strict upbringing asserted itself—perhaps, too, a subconscious impulse to flee from a situation that promised adventure. She felt that she could not bear to be alone with Gervase. She must not give him reason to think—oh, anything! She could not bear it if he held her cheap! If Ermyntrude noticed anything . . . Not that there was anything to notice. How could there be? But she couldn't go and sit out with him.

Gervase was extremely amused. Jocelyn's startled eyes and her delightful discomposure told him exactly what she was thinking. She was so charmingly transparent, and so very much of another world. He smiled reassuringly at her embarrassment. "I forgot you wanted to dance, Mrs. Renshawe. I was being selfish."

She gave a little sigh of relief. "Yes, I think I *ought* to."

"Come along, Mrs. Renshawe." Adrian thrust a masterful arm about her and swept her away. He held her to him with a possessiveness that made her furious, and his cheek almost touched hers. "God!" he murmured. "How I've wanted to have you in my arms. You're so beautiful and so cold. You make me want to cry."

"That's merely stupid!" said Jocelyn icily. "And I hate being hugged."

He held her closer. "You know I love you, and you're going to love me, too—oh, yes, you are!"

Jocelyn was suddenly amused and completely self-possessed. All her life she had never known what it was to arouse admiration or passion. Lancelot's decorous affection had been little different from that of her aunt. Here in one evening in this new world she had experienced two fresh emotions. One was oddly stirring, the other a novel and delightful feeling of flippancy. She felt that it would be amusing and exciting to experiment lightly with Adrian, but she was afraid to lift her eyes to Gervase's. Adrian's admiration aroused no faintest hint of the return of his ardour which he desired so much, but the silent half-understood questioning of which she was dimly aware between Gervase and herself caused a thrill she was afraid to acknowledge. With a curious perversity she sought refuge from her perplexity in dancing with Adrian while she suffered agonies of jealousy from her observation of Gervase's light-hearted flirtation with Jasmine.

CHAPTER TWELVE

THE days after the Murchison-Bellabys' party were full of interest for Mrs. Faggot at the post office. Her shop-window commanded a view of the square and the bridge, and was close enough to The Roebuck for her to lose nothing of the comings and goings of the stranger who had come there carrying his suitcase the morning after the fire at the Dower House. The reason of his arrival at such an early hour was unknown and a source of curiosity, for she did know that he had been staying with Colonel Tidmarsh and had been dining at the Dower House. *That* news had been broadcast by the Goodbuns and was of no great value. The strange gentleman had only become really interesting when he had walked across the bridge, quite unconcerned, hatless, carrying a suitcase and an overcoat. Why?

And then that Mrs. Lascelles? She had been staying at The Roebuck that night. It was possible that he had followed her there, and if so, what a sell it was when Mrs. Renshawe drove up and took away Mrs. Lascelles, who was her mother and a very grand lady indeed and lived in London and was much too dressed up and fond of gadding round to be as good as she ought to be, and every one in Much Dithering knew that the Honourable hated the sight of her, and Miss Pallfrey, who was too sweet and good to hate any one, didn't get on with her, and she had always neglected Miss Jocelyn, who was such a nice young lady, and let every one walk over her and order her about.

Mrs. Faggot's memory ran on and on as she watched those lives of Much Dithering that held so much interest for her unfold their secrets day by day. Never before had so much drama existed in Much Dithering under her very nose, and she was astute enough (for she read all the sensational fiction that her branch of a circulating library could supply) to realise that the chief ingredients for a good two-penn'orth of village scandal (the weekly fee for her library books was 2d.) existed, or were about to exist, in the hitherto blameless village outside her window.

Take that young man at The Place. Why did he want to play billiards at the village pub when he had a good billiard-room at home? Would he be sneaking in and out of The Roebuck if the Hedgecocks' daughter from London weren't home for a holiday? And if Lucia Hedgecock wasn't the attraction for young Murchison-Bellaby, did she represent the reason for Mr. Blythe's having gone there? And anyhow, had he quarrelled with Colonel Tidmarsh (that mean old skinflint who counted every ½d. of change and put threepenny bits in the collection on Sundays!)— and if so, why? Was it about Mrs. Lascelles or (unlikely) Mrs. Renshawe? Young Mrs. Renshawe wasn't the kind of woman any man would quarrel over. She was a quiet, modest, well-conducted young lady that no one would ever give a thought to, even though she was quite young and not bad-looking in her own way. Mrs. Faggot had no interest whatever in Mrs. Renshawe. There was no drama in her life, and never would be. The high spots of melodrama were Lucia Hedgecock and Mrs. Lascelles. There was Miss Murchison-Bellaby, too; but so far she had presented no particular point of interest that Mrs. Faggot was aware of.

She went back to her review of the situation. Mr. Blythe must be watched. He was a mystery—probably a dark horse—for he had something about him that suggested he was a bit out of the ordinary and had seen life (2d. coloured!). As for young Murchison-Bellaby—every one knew what it meant when a rich young man went after the innkeeper's pretty daughter (and she was half-Italian and no better than she should be—foreigners never were). Well, that left Colonel Tidmarsh to be checked up, and there was a rumour that he was a bit sweet on Mrs. Renshawe, knowing that she had a little money and a nice house (and the roof of The Brook, where he lived, was always giving trouble and the kitchen was full of black-beetles, so he'd be glad to leave it)—well, there you were!

There were a lot of little bits that wanted putting together, and it was interesting to watch what went on and what would come of it. That party last night, for instance. The milkman, Mr. Pedler, had just told her that the cook at The Place had told him the goings on of the Londoners staying at The Place were something awful—champagne flowing like milk and honey all night—beer, bacon and eggs, kippers—all sorts of odd things at two in the morning—dancing, children's games, hide-and-seek in the attics. . . . Such goings on were unheard of in the village, and did not sound at all the sort of thing the Honourable would approve of in her new tenants, and what Mrs. Renshawe must have thought of it all was beyond Mr. Pedler's powers of imagination.

It would have interested and astonished Mrs. Faggot to learn what Mrs. Renshawe did think of her evening at The Place. It astonished Mrs. Renshawe herself; in fact, she was completely unable to decide just what she did think. The only thing of which she felt certain was that the experiences of the evening at the Murchison-Bellabys had been a landmark in her career—the second landmark. The first had been the thunderstorm which had introduced her to Gervase. She had been aware that that evening in the wet darkness of the hilly road through the High Woods had divided Time into Before and After. Now she had reached another signpost, a more disturbing one. The first had been almost imperceptible and had flashed by before she had realised it existed. This one was rather startling. It seemed to point so clearly that there must be a deviation from the long, straight, narrow road down which she had passed with such a sense of security and an absence of adventure that now struck her as regrettable, for she had come upon this signpost without being in any way prepared for the momentous decision as to which direction she must take.

There were three roads from which to choose. No, not really. One, the one she had arrived by, went straight on. There were two by-roads branching off into unknown country round corners which concealed their wanderings. Again laying down her needlework and looking into the grey misty morning with a perplexed frown, she rejected another of the roads. So there was really only one! But the solution of the problem was not as easy as all that. She was faced by uncertainty instead of calm security. Her peace of mind was troubled for the first time, and she was restless and her nerves on edge. Her problem was not one she could discuss with any one or upon which she could seek advice. She must keep it hidden and make her own decision. So far she had come up against no cross-currents in her smoothly flowing existence. There had been little mingling with other streams, no rapids, no rock-strewn depths; in fact, her life had been extremely like the course of the placidly flowing Waver between its peaceful green meadows and its willow-grown banks. The metaphor made her smile a little and then look startled, for she remembered that the biggest willow had been struck by lightning when the storm had broken that afternoon. If she were superstitious she might take that as an omen. The thought was disturbing.

She folded up her embroidery and decided to put away her foolish imaginings. Anyway, Ermyntrude was coming downstairs, and there would be no peace, for she knew (and was quite unrepentant) that Ermyntrude had a full-sized grievance against her. She smiled to herself as she recalled her own unprecedented behaviour the night before, which viewed in the cold greyness of a foggy morning seemed to be quite inexplicable. The fact was that she had, so Ermyntrude declared, flirted outrageously with Adrian and behaved in the most extraordinary way altogether. Ermyntrude had solaced herself by retaining Gervase as a cavalier through what had been to her a most unsatisfactory evening, for she had never been able to come into direct contact with any of the Murchison-Bellabys and impress them with her suitability as a wife for Adrian, as she had been so certain that she would do. Indeed, it had been noticeable that Mrs. Murchison-Bellaby had avoided her except for the briefest and most perfunctory contacts forced on her by her duty as a hostess. Mr. Murchison-Bellaby had been submerged in the flood of Mrs. Pomfret's eloquence on the subject of parish affairs, and on coming at length to the surface had sought liquid refreshment in the billiard-room and remained unseen for the rest of the evening. Jasmine and her friends had other things to interest them. Adrian had been rather drunk and behaved very badly, devoting himself entirely to Jocelyn and pretending that he had fallen in love with her. There remained only Gervase Blythe, and he had nobly risen to the occasion (ignored himself by the mannerless crowd) and had joined her in her isolation and proved a charming companion up to a point. Exactly, up to a point, and that was what was so exasperating. She couldn't gauge the extent of her success. He kept her at such a respectful distance, talked with delightful inconsequence, listened to her tales of her life in India, Egypt, China, London, her conquests and successes—all her trivialities, in fact, and remained unimpressed, making no effort to declare himself her latest conquest, beyond agreeing that it would be pleasant to meet sometimes in London. He was going abroad almost immediately, and his date for returning was uncertain. He was distressingly vague when one tried to extract any real information about himself—a baffling, disappointing, perverse sort of individual, and on the whole she disliked him. The evening, in fact, had been a perfect nightmare. No wonder she had a grievance.

She came downstairs just as Jocelyn was going out, and she decided that she would go, too. There was always the chance that *someone* would be in the village. She had a suspicion that The Roebuck held a magnet in the person of the innkeeper's daughter, and a walk in that direction might prove interesting.

"I am going to get some stamps," Jocelyn explained. "I haven't enough for my Christmas letters. Can I do anything for you? It's not at all a nice day out."

"No, I shall come with you. I want a walk. I have a perfectly foul head this morning. It just shows, doesn't it? I said last night the champagne was filthy. People like the Murchison-Bellabys never know how to choose decent wine." Ermyntrude drew on her fur gloves with determination, and they set out together.

Gervase spent the morning writing letters, chiefly because the window of his sitting-room overlooked the square and, like Mrs. Faggot, he was interested in drama, and felt sure that something was about to happen. He decided that he would go and buy stamps when he looked up from his writing-table, which stood in the window of his sitting-room, and saw Jocelyn crossing the square towards the post office.

It was therefore a subject of much interest for Mrs. Faggot when she saw Mrs. Renshawe coming towards the post office with a bundle of letters in her hand, and almost immediately Mr. Blythe leaving The Roebuck and crossing the square leisurely. (Mr. Blythe, she had noticed, never hurried. He always seemed to have plenty of time for everything.) Then, just as he reached the post office and before she had to leave her observation post in the shop window to go and serve her customer unwillingly, she saw Adrian Murchison-Bellaby, hatless and in a hurry, go into The Roebuck, and at that very moment (she *had* to have one more look!) Mrs. Lascelles came out of the grocer's and, seeing Adrian go into The Roebuck, instantly set off in pursuit.

With a snort of indignation Mrs. Faggot left the window and asked Gervase what he wanted as he and Jocelyn came in together. Jocelyn was looking exceptionally well (Mrs. Faggot noticed it at once) in spite of her late night. Her colour was unusually vivid, her eyes deeply blue and more "alive" than

Gervase had ever seen them. They held a new awareness that interested him and made him speculate as to its origin. She had run out of stamps, she told Mrs. Faggot a little breathlessly as if she had hurried.

"Stamps?" Mrs. Faggot looked in the drawer and said, "I'm sorry, Mrs. Renshawe. I'm sold clean out of stamps since yesterday; but I'm expecting a fresh lot in on the next bus. I sent into Totterford this morning by my nephew, and he'll be back any moment now. It was the quickest way to could get hold of some till my next lot comes in."

Gervase laughed. "I'm surprised that Much Dithering should tolerate anything so modern as a bus. It offends my sense of values. I consider a red bus in a setting such as this village green an anachronism."

"This ain't a *green*," Mrs. Faggot informed him haughtily. "This is the *Square*, and it's' the first time any one has said the red bus was an anarchism. We ain't Red in *this* village, and we don't hold with anarchy nor socialism nor the bus company, neither." She paused and looked accusingly at him. "Perhaps you get your ideas of anarchy from The Roebuck. We don't hold with foreign madams nor bold black-eyed hussies neither in this village, and we're better without strangers, since you ask me."

"I didn't ask you," returned Gervase mildly, "but I'm sure you're right. I seem to have spoken out of my turn," he added to Jocelyn. "I think I'll wait outside—that is, if you're coming."

Jocelyn went out with him. "Ermyntrude is doing some shopping at the grocer's. I must go and look for her. She hates to be kept waiting. I must get the stamps later."

"Tell me," said Gervase sternly. "Why did you behave so badly last night? I thought you were such a nice person, and now I'm not at all sure."

Jocelyn smiled and her eyes danced. It was an exhilarating thought that her doings mattered. She had learnt, too, in her dealings with Adrian, a certain sophistication and the knowledge gave her a new self-confidence and helped her to combat the shyness which had overwhelmed her with Gervase the night before. There was a pleasurable flutter of excitement about meeting him, but the feeling of sheer panic had gone. She could meet his eyes with a confidence and security that had not been there before, a responsiveness to the hint of adventure that underlay their acquaintance from which she had recoiled the night before.

"Ermyntrude told me that my misguided efforts to dance the tango, or whatever it was, incurred your wrathful contempt."

Gervase shook his head. "I observed you getting off with Master Adrian more in sorrow than in anger. I feel sure that our friend Ambrose would have been deeply pained. May I come and see you some time?"

"I shall be delighted if you will. To-morrow, about tea-time?"

"I shall be there." He regarded her quizzically as if he sought the explanation of her new self-possession, and wondered whether he regretted the change and for how much of it Adrian was responsible. She had run away from him last night—he was perfectly aware of that—and that she should have sought refuge in dancing with Adrian worried him not at all. The fact that she had run away from *him* was what mattered.

"Are you coming to the village Social to-night? Mrs. Pomfret is very anxious that it should be well supported." Jocelyn was a little diffident. It didn't seem to be much in the line of a man who had led such an adventurous kind of life, but it was all she could think of saying at the moment.

Gervase noticed her hesitation. "No, I don't think I could bear a village Social," he said seriously. "I admire Mrs. Pomfret immensely, but I don't think I can carry my admiration to such lengths. Do you think that is churlish on my part?"

Jocelyn looked slightly relieved. "No, I think you are right. I have to go and help; I always do; but—it seems wrong of me, but I admit that I find village Socials rather dull. I am sure *you* would, and I'd hate to think you were there and being bored."

"Do you ever want to go out and enjoy life?" he asked curiously. "I don't mean fooling like last night. I mean to escape from all this and get into the outside world?"

"I've never even thought about it," she answered with a little frown of perplexity. "My life has always been here and I expect it always will be."

"And does that satisfy you?"

"I've never asked myself that question."

Gervase was aware of Mrs. Faggot peering from between the rows of sweet-jars in the window behind Jocelyn and was annoyed. "Some day when you've had a little time to consider the question I'll ask you again. Tell me—is Mrs. Lascelles staying long?"

"I don't know. She is very indefinite."

"Yes—well, it can't be helped. By the way, can I post your letters? I'm going into Totterford now. I want to catch the early post myself, and there seems no chance of it here. I shouldn't think anything was ever early here. My car is just over the road. May I drive you home? I pass your house."

"Oh, no," said Jocelyn hastily. "I must look for Ermyntrude. I can't think where she can be. But thank you. It's very kind of you."

"I shall come and see you, Ermyntrude or no Ermyntrude, but hoping against hope that I may find you alone. If I find Ambrose or Adrian, I warn you I'll go and seek consolation at the hands of Mrs. Pomfret."

"She will probably be having a practice of her glee-singers," Jocelyn said with a laugh. "She is getting up a concert, you know, and she'll rope you in if you're not careful."

"I'll come to the concert if you'll sit beside me."

"Oh, dear no, I shall be much too busy. I play all the accompaniments when I'm not singing glees myself. Oh, there's Ermyntrude coming out of The Roebuck. How odd! Oh, and Adrian, too."

"Not so odd," commented Gervase dryly. "Well, good-bye—till to-morrow."

CHAPTER THIRTEEN

ADRIAN awoke in a state of extreme depression that grey, chilly morning. Possibly, like Ermyntrude, he was feeling the after-effects of the drinks he had mixed with such careless rapture the previous night. It had been, in his opinion, a good party, and he had enjoyed himself tremendously. Aware that he was piling up trouble for himself, he had abandoned caution and gone all out to persuade Jocelyn that he had fallen in love with her. His infatuation was perfectly sincere, and his spirits were at zero this morning when he reviewed the state of affairs. His perplexities gave him a headache, and his future for the moment filled him with the deepest misgiving, for no young man can be expected to deal with a situation that embraces a Past, a Present and a Future, all inextricably mixed up, on a wet morning after a night of revelling. The Future, as he saw it, could only be achieved by eluding the Present and ignoring the Past, and just how he was to steer his difficult course was a problem that depressed him exceedingly as he sat hunched over the fire in the billiard-room and considered the situation.

He wanted to go and see Jocelyn, but he could not face an indignant Ermyntrude. He dared not go to The Roebuck. He did not know just how much Joe Hedgecock knew about his past, and he was uncertain whether it was better to go to The Roebuck and be friendly and hearty and reassuring (if that were what he meant to convey) or to stay away and never be quite certain as to how affairs stood. He wanted to go and see Gervase Blythe, to whom he had taken a curious fancy. He was a man of the world, and he looked as if he were a good sort and would be able to understand a young man's difficulties and advise him. That was why he had made friendly overtures to him and asked him to the party. He wanted to enlist his sympathy and feel he had a friend on whom to fall back. There was something *solid* about Gervase, a suggestion of worldly common sense tempered with a humour that would help him to see the human side of youthful follies. If any one could help him out of this appalling mess it would be Gervase, but it would be difficult to lay it all out before him. Where and how?

Adrian got up and went out into the raw mist that lay over the garden and hung in heavy silver drops on the iron railing that fenced off the lawn. It was not a cheerful prospect, and damped Adrian's already morbid spirits even further. The only possible thing for him to do seemed to be to return to London and have a fling and forget his troubles. Go to London? Yes, why not? He had a sudden brainwave. Why shouldn't he take Ermyntrude back to London, take her out to dinner, lead her to imagine—oh, anything she liked!—and leave her there, then rush back here and meet Jocelyn and—and then what? There was the "Social" with which she was helping in the village. He had a wild desire to dance with her and hold her in his arms again, and that would give him the chance he wanted. Could he do it? Or, alternatively, could he get Gervase to take Ermyntrude off his hands? That was an idea! He had been very decent about it the evening before. Would he see things and help him? There was just the chance he might. Adrian set off for the village without further delay.

However, his scheme did not prosper, for Ermyntrude emerged from the grocer's just as he approached The Roebuck and instantly set off in pursuit. She captured him as he stood uncertainly in the lounge, wondering where Gervase was, for the door of his sitting-room was open and the room obviously empty. At that hour so were the lounge and the bar, and the only sound in the house was the ticking of the grandfather-clock in the corner. The tempestuous opening of the door disclosed, not the return of Gervase, but the determined onslaught of a very angry Ermyntrude. Adrian stiffened.

"Adrian," began Ermyntrude urgently, "I want to talk to you. Where can we sit so that we can be alone?"

"This is the lounge. I don't know of anywhere else; but in any case I'm in a frantic hurry."

"Rubbish!" snapped Ermyntrude. "That's merely an excuse.'"

"An excuse?" echoed Adrian nastily. "You're wrong. I'm not making excuses; I'm stating a fact. I am in a hurry. I looked in to see Blythe on a matter of importance and I've got to find him."

"Why were you so rude last night?" Ermyntrude demanded. "You owe me an apology, or at least an explanation."

"I had other guests whom my mother wished me to entertain," he retorted. "You must understand that it is different here. They don't know you and they are naturally taken up with local people. I've got to pay some attention to—well, the vicar's wife and so on. Sorry, I *must* find Blythe."

He went out, banging the door, and Ermyntrude stood in the empty lounge that smelt of stale cigarette-smoke and wood-fires, and realised that if she tried to restrain Adrian he would become more restive and probably kick over the traces. Her hold had never been firm. His attentions had always been fickle—as ardent as she could wish for a week or two and then a rapid cooling off, and he would never endure explanations. If he was in the mood, he was an ardent and exacting lover, and contrariwise, if he felt fed up, he had no use for her and let her know it. Well, tact and patience would bring him to heel. She must possess her soul in patience; and, after all, she had no real rival in Jocelyn. A very little of Jocelyn's "good works" would show Adrian how dull and stupid she was, and he would seek out a more amusing companion.

"Did you wish for anything, madam?"

Ermyntrude wheeled in surprise, for she had not noticed any one come in, and saw the innkeeper's daughter in the doorway leading to the back of the house, a tall willowy girl, ivory of skin, with black burnished hair parted demurely above a broad forehead, big dark eyes that held a question she had *not* asked Ermyntrude, and a red "dangerous "mouth. Her whole appearance perturbed Ermyntrude, for she felt at once that her rival was not Jocelyn, but this unusually beautiful young woman whose presence in the bar of a country inn must be a menace to the morals of every young man (or even the not-so-young) who came under the spell of her beauty. She could cope with the danger from Jocelyn's frail charm, but she would have no chance at all if it came to a conflict with this young woman. No, she must certainly be patient and *wise*. Only infinite wisdom and the tact of a woman of experience could defeat the arrogance of superb beauty such as Lucia Hedgecock possessed.

Ermyntrude lit a cigarette with casual indifference and replied to the question: "I called to see if Mr. Blythe was in. Can you tell me?"

Lucia glanced across the lounge. "I think he must have gone out. His room is empty. Will you wait?"

"No, it isn't important." Ermyntrude went out into the greyness of the square and saw Gervase and Jocelyn standing outside the post office. Adrian had disappeared. She drew her fur coat close about her and decided that she could not bear Much Dithering another moment, especially as she saw that Colonel Tidmarsh had just opened the gate of his little place across the bridge and was coming towards her. She disliked practically every one in Much Dithering and Colonel Tidmarsh more than any one, and she was perfectly aware that he felt very much the same about her. He looked now as if something had surprised and annoyed him very much, as indeed it had, for until that moment he had not been aware that Gervase was still in the village, and it was quite a shock to find him in earnest conversation with Jocelyn outside the post office.

"I had no idea that Blythe was still here," he said peevishly to Ermyntrude as he greeted her unwillingly. "Where has he turned up from again?"

"Oh, he never left," Ermyntrude explained, pleased to be able to torment her enemy. "He's at The Roebuck. Didn't you know?"

"At The Roebuck?" echoed Ambrose. "*What* is he doing there?"

"Making love to the pretty barmaid, I should imagine," returned Ermyntrude with a shrug. "I can't think of anything else that would be likely to keep a man hanging about Much Dithering. Can you?"

"I have never been interested in barmaids," snapped Ambrose, and was struck by a devastating thought: If Blythe had been getting into any low sort of mischief, would people hold *him* responsible for Blythe's misdoings? He appealed to Ermyntrude. "Oh, I trust there is no scandal, Mrs. Lascelles. I hope that neither you nor Mrs. Renshawe think that I am responsible in any way. I introduced him to Mrs. Renshawe. I did feel at the time that there might be a risk, but I never anticipated a—a—what shall I say?"

"A low intrigue," suggested Ermyntrude, enjoying his dismay. "Just fancy, a scandal at the village pub! What will Miss Pallfrey say, Colonel Tidmarsh? She has always had such a high regard for you. This will take a lot of living down, I fear."

"But I am not concerned with what he does," Ambrose expostulated in great agitation. "Mrs. Lascelles, you *must* realise—Oh, dear me, this is most unfortunate. May I beg you to point out to Miss Pallfrey and Mrs. Renshawe that I have no connection whatever with this man. I deny—"

"Oh, Colonel Tidmarsh!" put in Ermyntrude reprovingly. "You protest and deny too much. I can only suppose that you too are drawn to The Roebuck by the lure of the pretty barmaid. Haven't I, after all, met you on the doorstep—so why should you be so bitter about Mr. Blythe, if you weren't in the same boat?"

But Ambrose could bear no more. He turned on his heel and went back to his house.

Ermyntrude felt less depressed and went to join her daughter and Gervase. "I've just been to The Roebuck, hoping that you would invite me to have a glass of sherry, Mr. Blythe. I felt that a glass of sherry would restore my somewhat depressed spirits on this wretched sort of day. Are you coming to the Social? I hope so. I believe I promised Mrs. Pomfret that I would go, and I simply dread the prospect. Do say you'll be there to hold my hand and help me to bear up."

"I'm sorry," returned Gervase. "I shall have to deny myself that pleasure. I am not going to the Social. But I'm sure that Ambrose will be delighted. He's certain to be there. And I know that Adrian is going; he told me so last night."

"Oh, yes," put in Jocelyn with a quiver of a smile, "*he's* going. In fact, he promised to call for us, Ermyntrude, in his Rolls Royce. Didn't I tell you?"

"The devil he is!" said Gervase in an offended tone.

Ermyntrude raised her eyebrows and smiled sweetly. "I shouldn't count on that, Jocelyn. The charms of the barmaid at The Roebuck will probably have a stronger claim. I fear that she exercises a spell on the hearts of all the susceptible males that come her way seeking distraction in this peculiarly depressing locality. Adrian was paying her court when I went in, and I suppose it would hardly be discreet to ask you why *you* are staying at The Roebuck, Mr. Blythe? From what Colonel Tidmarsh said just now, I fear the worst."

Gervase was annoyed. He had a glimpse of Jocelyn's swift flush and the embarrassment with which she turned away, ashamed that Ermyntrude should say such (to her) unpardonable things, even in joke. Denial was merely futile; there was really nothing to say in reply. "I hope your fears won't seriously disturb your peace of mind, Mrs. Lascelles," he said with an inflection that told Ermyntrude how angry she had made him. "I assure you I am the soul of discretion and am not likely to cause any one to blush for my misdeeds," at which he smiled to see Jocelyn flush still deeper as he said good-bye and went across to The Roebuck.

Jocelyn went home feeling more bewildered than before. Her brief meeting with Gervase had given her a kind of reassurance that had been soothing. Now Ermyntrude, with her horrible air of being so much more "understanding," so well able to realise the sort of men Adrian and Gervase probably were and their attitude where the pretty daughter of the village innkeeper was concerned, had again broken into her vexed self-questioning and made her feel unhappy and disturbed. As far as Adrian was concerned she did not care; his interest in herself or in Lucia didn't matter. He was a person of no importance whatever, although she had found him stimulating, a sort of tonic. The taste of excitement the night before had aroused a sense of impatience with her life of continual good deeds and working for the entertainment and betterment of others. For the first time she felt an overwhelming desire to live for herself. Adrian had awakened her to the realisation of all she was missing.

He was a stepping-stone (but already she had guile enough to conceal the fact). His touch as he held her close when they danced meant nothing, caused no thrill, but in some unaccountable way it helped her to realise herself as she had never done before. She achieved a self-confidence from his open admiration. She realised that she was desirable in the eyes of men, but that Adrian's admiration was not what she wanted. Her instinct taught her to assume a gay inconsequence when he tried to make love to her. She used her new experience to keep him at arm's length without realising that her attitude of being unattainable made her all the more attractive. She was not considering Adrian at all; he hardly existed. All her mind and being were centred on Gervase, but she had no sense of joy. She was prey to a thousand fears. She had fallen in love—that she knew beyond all doubt. It was terribly foolish and indiscreet. It was humiliating, agonising, to think that the merest touch, even the way he sometimes looked at her, made her thrill with a mad rapture that would have been sheer bliss if it had not been tempered with a strong conviction that it must be wrong—wrong to love a man of whom she knew nothing, who was probably playing with her just as Adrian was, or would if she let him, who probably flirted just as Adrian did with Lucia Hedgecock, and who was merely being pleasant to her as he was to Miss Pallfrey or Mrs. Pomfret, and thought it a joke that she had pretended not to have met him until Ambrose Tidmarsh had brought him to her house. She must not let any one guess her foolishness. She must stamp it out firmly, unless—oh, it was folly to think of it!—unless he really did like her, even just a little, and came to see her because he *wanted* to see her again.

CHAPTER FOURTEEN

ADRIAN, accompanied by Jasmine, called in the Rolls Royce and picked up Jocelyn and Ermyntrude. They were late, of course, which vexed Jocelyn's punctual soul, but there was still time for her to slip into the kitchen and see Mrs. Pomfret about the

Camp Coffee. She thought it might prove an admirable excuse to escape from Adrian or Ambrose, but in any case she was far too conscientious to dream of shirking any duty which she was expected to perform in the way of helping to make the Social a success. It was she who organised the games and the folk-dancing, and she who would accompany Mrs. Pomfret's musical items at the piano. On the whole it would seem that she was well protected from any possible embarrassing moment with either of her admirers.

Looking round the hall, she noticed that among the usual rustic company , from the Ditherings were the two young Hedgecocks, Lucia and her brother Victor. She was rather surprised that they should condescend to a village Social. Lucia was in a smart semi-evening frock and looked exceedingly attractive. Her dark beauty was remarkable in the gathering of stodgy country women, not one of whom was well dressed. There were, of course, Ermyntrude, massively handsome, and Jasmine, vivid and colourful, but Lucia had a perfection of carriage and a touch of southern sensuousness that lifted her above any other woman present, a fact quickly noted by Adrian, whom it embarrassed, and he felt that the evening might prove a little difficult. He had seen Lucia that afternoon and asked her not to go to the Social, explaining that things might be awkward if his mother or Jasmine came across her. It was one thing to dance with Lucia in London on adventurous evening at a Palais de danse, but here in Much Dithering, under the critical eyes of all the people with whom he wished to stand well, Lucia was quite another thing, and he wished her anywhere else in the world, lovely as she was looking.

Jasmine looked surprised. "Hallo, fancy you here! What are you doing in a hole like this? On a Christmas holiday?"

Lucia, noting Adrian's guarded recognition, smiled, "Yes, Miss Murchison-Bellaby. I was rather run-down, and Madame very kindly gave me a holiday to set me up. She expects a big season. Fancy *you* being down here, though! I was surprised when I heard it. I didn't know you had left Surbiton." She turned and spoke to the sleek dark young man behind her. "Victor, this is Miss Murchison-Bellaby, one of Madame's clients."

Victor bowed and Jasmine looked at him with interest. "Haven't I seen you somewhere?"

He bowed again. "It is possible, Mademoiselle. I am—Victor."

"Good Lord!" said Jasmine in an awed voice. *Victor!*

Victor smiled, a discreetly audacious smile, a gleam of white teeth under the thin black line of moustache, a discreetly admiring glance from his big dark eyes. "If Mademoiselle wishes, I will play a dance tune later. The music here is—well, shall I be charitable and call it amusing?—but not, I think, for long."

"Will you really play just for me?" Jasmine asked in a tone that suggested that so much honour almost stunned her. Victor to play for her! Well, she hadn't expected *that* to happen at this idiotic village Social! Thank goodness she was decently turned out. She had meant just to show the village what a fashionable young woman she was, and how condescending it was of her to turn up at all. But now to meet Victor, the leader of the dance band, whom she had worshipped from a distance for six months . . .! Victor had so many adoring young women to spoil him that one had to elbow one's way in the crowd. In the glory of her good fortune she quite overlooked the fact that he was a son of the innkeeper of The Roebuck. What did it matter, so long as Victor was here in Much Dithering and going to play for her?

"Will Mademoiselle do me the honour to dance this waltz?" inquired Victor politely.

Jasmine almost fell into his arms and he guided her languorously to the heavily thumped strains of "The Blue Danube."

"There is only one pity," murmured Victor gently, his cheek touching hers for an instant. "I cannot play this tune for you and dance with you myself. You dance very beautifully. You give me all yourself when you dance so that we dance like one person."

"Do we really? Oh, Victor, how utterly divine of you!" They danced on, giving a perfect exhibition to a row of wondering spectators.

Adrian, aware of Lucia beside him and Jocelyn across the room with Mrs. Pomfret, felt that he had better dance with Lucia and get things settled.

"Really, you know, this is a bit thick," he said in an aggrieved tone as they danced. "It's all very well, Lucia, but as I told you down here I've got to be careful."

"Oh, yes?" murmured Lucia lazily, glancing at him under her eyelashes. "And your sister, has she not got to be careful, too? It pleases her very much to be dancing with my brother before the eyes of all the village folk. Why, then, do you not wish to be seen dancing with me?"

"It's different: you know it is."

"Oh, yes, I see that the stout lady who is so fond of you is here. You must not offend her. Is that it?"

Adrian had forgotten Ermyntrude, being so preoccupied in thinking about Jocelyn; but Ermyntrude made a good excuse, and one that Lucia expected. "Well, there's *that*, but, you see, down here, Lucia—"

"Yes, down here you are the squire's son and I am the innkeeper's daughter, and I am too good-looking to be trusted. Is that it? Oh, Adrian, you make me laugh! You forget all that is past—all you say when—Oh, very well, I won't go on. I just laugh; but my father will not laugh."

"Now, listen," said Adrian angrily, "there's nothing to laugh at, and I'm just telling you I won't have you following me round in Much Dithering. I'll slip into The Roebuck whenever I get a chance. It's all right meeting you *there*."

"I understand. You need have no fear that I will give you away," laughed Lucia, preferring to remain amused at his embarrassment and perfectly aware that she could bring him to heel as soon as she wished.

"What a very striking-looking couple those Hedgecocks are," said Mrs. Pomfret. "They're half-foreign, of course, and have the allure of all Southern people. The young man dances beautifully, doesn't he? What a nice couple he and Miss Murchison-Bellaby make. Well, perhaps," she added after a pause, "*nice* is not exactly the word. They are very *modern*, not a good example for our young people, too—too—exotic; in plain words, too much hugging. I'm sure the vicar wouldn't like it. Now, Adrian and his partner are much more—more—"

"Semi-detached," suggested Jocelyn. "Yes, they are not so lost in their own society that the rest of us have ceased to exist. They are even, I should say, antagonistic and not dancing at all well; but I'm not really a judge."

Ermyntrude, as bored with Colonel Tidmarsh as he was with her, watched Adrian with jealous curiosity, and Ambrose, noting her evident preoccupation, slipped away and joined Mrs. Pomfret and Jocelyn. There was no hope of seeing Jocelyn alone in this pandemonium, but he need not remain tied to her mother.

Mrs. Pomfret, however, darted to meet him when she saw him approaching, and buttonholed him. "Now come along, Colonel Tidmarsh. I want to get the balloon race started, and you must umpire for me." She swept him off, and Jocelyn smiled as she joined Ermyntrude for a few moments.

"I'm afraid you aren't enjoying this," she said apologetically.

"I am not," retorted Ermyntrude. "I am simply *furious*. What does Adrian mean by dancing with that young woman? It's disgraceful to advertise the fact that he is carrying on a low intrigue with the daughter of the innkeeper. It won't help him to get on *here*, or so I should imagine. And the black-haired lounge lizard—who is he?"

"He is Lucia's brother. He plays in an orchestra or a dance band, I believe. His name is Victor."

"Victor?" Ermyntrude raised her eyebrows. "Why, he's not the famous Victor, is he? So that's why that odious Murchison-Bellaby girl has thrown herself at him in such a disgraceful manner! I must say I wondered at such a display of voluptuousness, but I've heard that Society women simply go down flat before him—disgusting, I call it. Oh, here's Adrian looking for me." She flushed under her makeup and grew quite pink and "girlish" at his approach. "I was just talking about you," she said playfully. "I was telling Jocelyn how well you dance. We were all watching you just now. Come and sit down. I've such a lot I want to talk about. It's so amusing, isn't it?"

"I've no doubt of that," replied Adrian in a tired voice; "but hardly here. We've all come for a jolly evening—not sitting about and talking. Isn't that so, Mrs. Renshawe? I say, come and bang that bally old balloon." He seized Jocelyn by the hand and dragged her off to take part in the revels. "Darling," he said urgently, "dance the next with me, won't you?"

Jocelyn hesitated for a moment, but decided to give him the dance and escape from a possible interlude with Colonel Tidmarsh. "Yes, I'll dance. Oh, and do let go my hand. You'll horrify the nice-minded people, and if I dance with you you simply must go and talk to Ermyntrude now, or at any rate dance with her later; she *expects* it."

"Oh, I know *that*. No, let's play with balloons and be silly, and I'll go and talk to her later."

The evening wore on. Fun was fast and furious. Jocelyn led out her folk-dancers and other sets joined in to the tuneful dances played with great spirit by Mrs. Pomfret.

"I call this drivel," yawned Jasmine.

Victor watched with interest. "No, it is excellent. The music has a lovely swing. I can use it, swing it. One day you shall hear me."

"Shall I, Victor?"

"I promise you, Jasmine. Jasmine. In the East they would call you 'Yasmini.' It sounds entrancing, so."

Jasmine looked at him with wide eyes. "'Yasmin?' Someone else said that the other night."

Victor looked at her and smiled cynically. "That is very likely. Plenty of men will think of you like that. Now the pretty country dance is over. Shall I play for you? Mrs. Pomfret has said she will be pleased for me to play."

"But who can I dance with?" wailed Jasmine, her hand on his arm detaining him. "I must have a partner or your music will be wasted."

Victor shrugged his slim shoulders. "Alas, Yasmini, I cannot do both," he sighed, and followed Mrs. Pomfret to the piano.

The vicar announced that they were to have the good fortune of hearing the famous Victor, who was so well known to every listener to the wireless programmes, but here in his own village he was more than that: he was one of their own village lads who had won his way to fame and fortune by his own efforts.

During the applause that followed Jasmine sought anxiously for Adrian. There was absolutely no one else she could dance with, and she did not want to miss a note of Victor's playing. As the opening bars of "Destiny" stole softly through the hall, now hushed in eager anticipation, she came to Adrian just, as he put his arms round Jocelyn and slid away over the empty floor. Jocelyn, not she, was to be the exhibition dancer, for Adrian was an excellent dancer, and Jocelyn, though not used to ballroom dancing of the type "featured" by Victor and Jasmine, possessed the gift of being able to follow her partner, and had danced enough with Adrian at Dithering Place to be familiar with his style. Altogether they gave a very pretty display of a more restrained type than Jasmine and Victor had treated the spectators to previously, and presently, when, Victor's seductive music having lured other dancers to the floor till it became crowded, Adrian halted by the doorway, Jocelyn thrilled with the pleasure of a perfect partner and the fascination of the lovely music woven for her enchantment by Victor's magic fingers, now turning the folk-dance tunes into a medley of waltz time, laid an impetuous hand on his arm. "Don't let's stop. Oh, let's go on. It's just heavenly." He swung her back into the maze of dancers, holding her to him so closely that she was not able to move with freedom, cramped by his close clasp.

"I can't dance," she said impatiently. "You hold me too tight."

"I don't want to *dance*," he returned, his cheek almost touching hers. "I just want to hold you in my arms."

She held herself rigidly. "Please let me go," she urged. "You've spoilt it all. I can't dance any more."

"Right!" He danced up to the door again and deftly, she was hardly aware how, pushed her through into the chilly darkness of the porch and closed the door behind them. Then he put his arms round her and kissed with a fervour that, instead of arousing any reciprocating passion, enraged her. She yielded limply until his clasp relaxed, then twisted herself swiftly out of his arms and ran into the night beyond the porch out of his sight. She slipped round to the back of the hall and into the kitchen by the back door, confronting Mrs. Pomfret with blazing cheeks and dishevelled hair.

"My dear!" gasped that lady in astonishment. "Whatever—?"

"I was so hot," explained Jocelyn quickly, pulling herself together under the inquisitive eyes of Mrs. Faggot and Mrs. Jobbing. "I couldn't dance any more. I hurt my foot. I shall stay here now, Mrs. Pomfret, and help to get the refreshments ready."

"But your poor foot, my dear?"

"Oh, it's all right as long as I don't dance."

"Shall I ask Colonel Tidmarsh to take you home?" suggested Mrs. Pomfret brightly.

"Please don't mention it to *any one*," returned Jocelyn firmly, and began to arrange piles of sausage rolls on the dishes standing ready.

Outside the hall Adrian recovered his temper, lit a cigarette and went back to the dancing. After all, he had other amusements to occupy his evening, and was not going to cry over spilt milk, and he could torment Ermyntrude by paying attention to Lucia.

When Jocelyn had finished her strenuous work in the kitchen she told Mrs. Pomfret that as soon as she had played the accompaniment for the part-songs she was going to slip away home, and in spite of protests on Mrs. Pomfret's part, she declined to be seen home by Colonel Tidmarsh, who, to his intense disgust, was left to look after Ermyntrude, who in her turn had been so cruelly abandoned by Adrian.

CHAPTER FIFTEEN

THE next day Ermyntrude departed in a rage to catch the midday train from the local junction that served the Ditherings. Her state of temper made it impossible for her to remain in the same house with her daughter, for whom she conceived a violent jealousy, blaming her for Adrian's sudden cooling off. Altogether her stay in Much Dithering had not been a success. Mrs. Murchison-Bellaby had given her very cold looks, Jasmine had been rude, and Adrian had behaved abominably in every way. She could only hope that in time, out of range of his disagreeable family, he would come round, but she felt no real certainty about it. Gervase annoyed her—he was too wily, and made her feel rather silly—and she could not stand the sight of Colonel Tidmarsh, so, as suddenly as she had decided to come, she decided to go, and shook the dust of Much Dithering off her feet.

After she had gone Jocelyn dusted the drawing-room and picked out a few faded violets from the bowl on the table by the window, dropping them out of the casement, which, although the morning was wet and blustery, stood wide open. The damp, cold air blew strongly through the room, and Jocelyn sniffed as she drew in her head.

"Yes, I think Ermyntrude's scent is fading out; but I'll leave it a little longer."

Her dusting finished, she scanned the room critically, sniffing again. "Yes, it's clear now. I can shut out the gale and light the fire."

She was still on her knees, coaxing a reluctant blaze, when Bertha came in.

"Please, 'm, a gentleman to see you."

Jocelyn, conscious of a smut on her nose and distinctly black fingers, rose from her knees to find Adrian gazing at her with an expression of fatuous admiration.

"Hallo, hallo, hallo!" he exclaimed. "So this is the secret of your busy mornings. I say, how absolutely topping you look in that flowery pinafore—it *is* a pinafore, isn't it?—and a sweet little smut on your sweet little nose. Oh, I say, you shouldn't—it isn't right."

"What isn't right?" Jocelyn asked stiffly, disliking the exuberant young man.

"That you should pretend to be angry and stand there looking completely adorable with that smut on your nose," replied Adrian, trying to laugh her out of her offended dignity; but Jocelyn was still feeling angry over his behaviour the evening before and in no way disposed to pass it over. Her dignity had never before been so injured, and she was not the sort of woman who could take a kiss as a joke. She was horrified at such a liberty, and unable to handle the situation which had arisen. To enjoy dancing with Adrian had seemed a harmless amusement, and she was too unsophisticated to realise that he had taken her obvious pleasure for encouragement and had, as he would have described the affair himself, "let things rip," unable to see her point of view. A kiss to Adrian was—well, just a kiss, and for her to be angry and offended was absurd. He tried laughing at her seriousness, but Jocelyn was not amused.

"I'm not pretending," she said stiffly.

"Oh, I say! Surely you aren't really angry with me? Dash it all, you simply asked for it."

"Asked for what?"

"*Well*, I mean, there we were dancing away and being awfully happy, and I'd got you in my arms and thought you were liking it as much as I was, and then—well, I lost my head and just felt I had to kiss you, so—well, I just did. I say, I'm awfully sorry; I should have known better. Do forgive me and let's start again."

"I'm sorry," said Jocelyn. "You see, I look at things differently. No one has ever dared to treat me in that manner before."

Her eyes were bright with anger and a pink spot of colour blazed in each cheek as she faced him, her head held very high, her scorn apparent in the tilt of her chin. She was very proud, very cold, and very desirable to the humiliated young man, who had never before come up against any one quite so unattainable, or been repulsed with such determination.

"Please go away," Jocelyn said firmly, but he declined to retreat so tamely. He felt he had to bring her round and make her realise how unreasonable she was. He simply couldn't go away and never see her again.

"No," he said equally firmly. "This is all rot, you know. I'm not going away letting you feel you've washed your hands of me and slung me out, and so on. This has got to be settled sensibly. It's not a melodrama, as you seem to think. I admit I was a damn' fool, but I've said I'm sorry. Now *you* say you're sorry for making such a silly fuss, and let's be friends. I promise I won't do it again until you ask me to."

"It isn't funny." Jocelyn was obstinate.

"No, it isn't at all funny," he agreed. "It wasn't meant to be funny. I was in dead earnest at the time and I'm in dead earnest now. I want to marry you. I wasn't insulting you. I'm just so badly in love with you that I lost my head and my heart all at the same time and went off the deep end. I didn't mean to be so crude. If you'd let me I'd have made love to you quite reasonably and sedately; but you've gone and knocked the bottom out of everything by this 'Tragedy Queen' act, so now you're hearing it all straight from the horse's mouth. Will you marry me?"

"No," replied Jocelyn with determination. "And you are wasting my time as well as your own."

"I'm not wasting my time."

"Well, you're wasting mine. I have work to do. I'm always very busy in the morning."

"Then I'll come and see you in the afternoon."

She looked taken aback, and he instantly noted the fact. "Oh, but you *can't*. I'm engaged this afternoon," she said sharply.

"So am I—to you." Adrian blew her a kiss and went out with a swagger to cover his retreat. He wasn't used to being shown the door by the ladies on whom he paid morning calls and felt very annoyed indeed, to put it mildly, but his rebuff only made him resolve to carry on and show Jocelyn that he wasn't the sort of man she could push on one side if he didn't choose to be pushed aside. Incidentally, although he was unconscious of it, he accorded her a higher value than he had previously done.

Jocelyn went to the kitchen, feeling furious and much perturbed by the likelihood of his return at tea-time. She hated him and despised herself. There had been a pleasant thrill of mischief in playing at a mild flirtation that evening at Dithering Place. She had been completely disillusioned and enraged last night when he had kissed her in spite of her genuine indignation, and now he told her she had asked for it! She was out of her depth and unable to cope with him. She had been looking forward to Gervase Blythe's visit with an eagerness that rather frightened her, and she was still finding excuses for herself. He was quite different from Adrian—she was certain of it. He would never behave as Adrian had done. It was quite an ordinary thing, surely, for him to come and call, since he had come as a guest to her house? Yes, of course it was. Perhaps he felt it would be pleasant to get to know her a little better; at any rate she hoped so. There was no danger or harm in that. Even Aunt Mellicent could hardly object or see anything wrong in what was merely politeness. And now Adrian, that senseless buffoon, was going to spoil everything! It hadn't occurred to her that any one would come in. She had declined Mrs. Pomfret's invitation to tea to discuss the final arrangements for the Children's Christmas Tree on the 6th, and she knew her aunt was going to the Priory, so she was safe from them both, and no one else was likely to drop in, especially as it looked like being a wet afternoon, but she hadn't reckoned with Adrian. In her preoccupation she let a cake get badly burnt on top, and forgot to put baking-powder in another, and had to make a third.

At four o'clock, as she sat pretending to read a *Life of Napoleon*, she heard the crunch of feet on the gravel outside the house, and her heart gave a foolish little flutter. But it was not Gervase. It was Colonel Tidmarsh—another miscalculation, she reflected dismally. There were really no words for it!

"I felt I must come and see you as soon as possible," he explained, taking a chair by the fire and, as far as she could judge, settling down comfortably for the afternoon. "You see, it was quite a shock to me yesterday when your mother told me about Blythe and the barmaid. I felt I *must* explain that I really know nothing at all about him. I cannot be held responsible in any way."

"But why must you assume the worst?" Jocelyn asked indignantly. "And why should it matter to *you*?"

"No, no, I don't mean *that*."

"Ermyntrude knows nothing about him, either, and she is fond of telling perfectly outrageous tales just to amuse herself and shock other people. You needn't believe a word of what she told you."

He looked uncomfortable. "But I gathered young Murchison-Bellaby told her—"

"*That* horrid young man!" retorted Jocelyn scornfully. "I really don't think he counts."

After a short pause he said nervously, "It is more than kind of you not to hold me responsible. I have been *very* distressed, fearing I might have incurred your displeasure. However, since I have not been so unlucky, let us choose a pleasanter subject. What a very charming house you have, Mrs. Renshawe, and what a delightful sense of colour and decoration. I suppose you are very attached to your home. You have always lived in this charming backwater unspoiled by the world, haven't you?"

Bertha opened the door to admit Adrian, whose triumphant grin of greeting faded out, and he stared in such blank dismay that Jocelyn laughed. After all, it was being funny now. That Ambrose Tidmarsh might elect to pay her a visit that afternoon had not occurred to her; but, since he had done so, it no longer mattered that Adrian had fulfilled his intention. They would both be so annoyed that they would probably leave early. But the threat to the peace of her afternoon was disturbing and her hopes of an uninterrupted tête-à-tête with Gervase, which had held such a fascinating thrill of pleasure, vanished altogether when the door opened again and Bertha announced: "General and Mrs. Wingham." And almost immediately afterwards: "Mr., Mrs. and Miss Murchison-Bellaby."

Adrian looked exceedingly annoyed and Colonel Tidmarsh even more depressed than usual, but the rest of the visitors seemed to take it for granted that it was a party, and after apologising profusely for having selected that afternoon to call, every one settled down to await the tea so ardently pressed upon them by Jocelyn, now resigned to the worst. She introduced everybody, for the Murchison-Bellabys, being newcomers, had so far been ignored by the Winghams, who now had to explain various reasons for their delay in calling. Then with an apology she slipped out of the room to hold an anxious interview with Bertha on the subject of tea for so many unexpected guests.

In the hall she came upon Gervase regarding the array of hats and coats with some dismay.

"Oh!" she gasped. "You *have* come. I hoped you wouldn't. I mean, I hoped you would; but now every one else has, and it's spoilt everything."

She was incoherent in her distress, but he smiled reassuringly. "You appear to be the centre of attraction this afternoon. Don't worry. I'll come back later. I see Ambrose's hat and coat, and I really don't want to sit and talk to him any more than he to me. Or wait a moment. There's the Hunt Ball to-night at the County Hotel in Totterford. Let's be gay and enjoy ourselves, shall we? May I call for you—say seven-thirty—and we'll dine somewhere first and go on to the bail?"

"Oh!" Jocelyn drew a long breath. It sounded so daring, so *impossible*—and yet so wonderful, so adventurous. Somehow Gervase inspired one to dare adventure. There was no time to argue or hesitate. She flung up her head on a reckless impulse and her eyes danced as they met his. "I'll come," she whispered breathlessly. "Yes, I'll come. But go away now. You mustn't—I mean—"

"Don't look so guilty," he said with a smile for her perturbation. "I'll be here at seven-thirty. Till then, be kind to Ambrose and all the others. I can wait my turn."

He let himself out and she went into the pantry to see how Bertha was coping with the emergency. She was amazed at herself for entering into such a conspiracy, but she told herself that there had been no time to consider. She would tell him when he came back that it was impossible. She couldn't go. What would Aunt Mellicent say, or her mother-in-law? Of course she couldn't go. But a sense of mischievous elation persisted. She couldn't help feeling that she had scored off her unwelcome guests. They (at least two of them) would be so furious if they guessed. (Guessed—what? If she didn't mean to go on with her adventure there was nothing to guess. What a curious feeling of blankness!) But even her hurried meeting in secret with Gervase would annoy Ambrose and also Adrian, and the thought entertained her as she went back to her guests with such a demure appearance that Colonel Tidmarsh thought of a stained-glass window and Adrian said to himself: "I wonder what the devil she's been up to. Did she arrange this blasted party on purpose? And who on earth is the crashing old bore who looks as if he'd like to murder me? He was hanging round, too, last flight."

The presence of his parents and sister was a blight, but he did not mind them so much, for he wanted them to be friends with Jocelyn. He wanted them to know he was in love with her, and he knew his mother would be pleased. The other old people didn't matter; they were just everyday sort of bores. On the whole, Adrian made the best of it, and adopted a distinctly possessive air towards Jocelyn that was not lost upon the other guests at the impromptu party, but of which Jocelyn herself was completely unaware. Her thoughts were not with Adrian or with any one else present.

It was an exhausting afternoon, and when Jocelyn was at last alone she was tired and her head ached. She wondered almost hysterically why she had said she would go and dine with a man of whom she knew nothing at all except that Colonel Tidmarsh disliked him exceedingly, a thought which was somehow reassuring. What Much Dithering would say to such a proceeding on her part she shuddered to think: her aunt, the Honourable Augusta, Mrs. Wingham—well, they couldn't be more astonished than she was herself. Why had she agreed, and what was she to say to Bertha, who was coming in to clear the tea-table?

"Bertha, I—I am going out to—to supper." (Somehow "supper" didn't sound so dashing as "dinner.")

"Oh, that will be nice for you, 'm," said Bertha cheerfully. "Shall I wait up for you?"

"Oh, no, no. I may be a little late."

"Very good, 'm." Bertha expressed no surprise and carried away the tea-tray with the remark that a little company did a person good, and wasn't it odd that every one should have come together; but, after all, better that way than to stretch it out for a week. Now every one had been, and she could put away the best china. "Funny," remarked Bertha genially, "how one thing led to another, and now here she was with someone asking her to supper. A bit of luck, that was, but then it was only manners to return a compliment."

Jocelyn suddenly realised that Bertha thought she was going to the Winghams or the Murchison-Bellabys and saw nothing odd in her going out. She must have missed seeing Gervase in the fluster of preparation for tea, or she would certainly have mentioned him!

CHAPTER SIXTEEN

ON NEW Year's Day Miss Mellicent spent the afternoon at the Priory and took the opportunity of discussing Jocelyn's future with the Honourable Augusta, a delicate matter, because that lady had a marked aversion from discussing the future years when she herself would no longer be there to hold the reins of government. So long as she lived she considered that Jocelyn's life needed no rearrangement. She was the widow of her son, and her home was the Dower House, and she was comfortably off, and lived in the village where she had always lived, and doubtless always would live, and continue the daily round and the common tasks which furnished (so far as one had ever thought about it) all she asked of life. Still, perhaps Mellicent was right. Perhaps it was wiser to ensure that Jocelyn, whose knowledge of the world was practically nil and whose capacity for looking after herself was untested by experience or opportunity, should be left in the care of someone who could be trusted to go on shielding her and cherishing her in as far as possible the state of life in which she had always lived.

"Perhaps you are right," agreed the Honourable Augusta thoughtfully. "As you point out—rather morbidly, I must say—I see no reason for such gloomy forebodings just because it happens to be New Year's Day, and I dislike good resolutions, Mellicent; they lead nowhere—but still, since you *have* pointed out the danger of Jocelyn having to face an uncared-for future—derelict and shipwrecked, I think you called it, though I see no reason for such terrifying prognostications—well, go on, Mellicent, tell me about this person to whose care you wish to consign Jocelyn's future. You tell me that *he* is attracted. But what about Jocelyn? Has he made any definite advances to make her think so?"

"Oh, no—oh, dear, no!" replied Miss Pallfrey hastily. "Not at all, Augusta. Mrs. Pomfret says she is *sure* he is falling in love—greatly attracted, at all events, by our dear Jocelyn—and has pointed out the inestimable advantages of such a possibility; and naturally, Augusta, at our age—we are no longer young and no one knows what the years may bring—"

"Keep to the point, Mellicent, and let the years go by. Who is this man, and is he the right sort of person to be Jocelyn's husband? Has he Family, Position? Why is he here in Much Dithering? Of course I remember approving his lease when my agent consulted me; but a man may be a suitable tenant without being a suitable husband for my daughter-in-law."

"I feel sure he is the right man, and that we can put the future of our dear Jocelyn in his hands without any doubts and fears," returned Miss Pallfrey earnestly. "He is worthy, in every meaning of the word. He also is bereaved and knows what it is to be severed from one's dear one. Indeed Jocelyn could find no more blessed task than to devote the rest of her life to being his comfort and stay in his old age. "

"H'm!" remarked the Honourable Augusta. "It sounds a more enticing prospect for him than for Jocelyn. I thought you were considering the affair from *her* point of view. It doesn't sound very lively for her."

"Jocelyn has never been brought up to consider liveliness an asset in a happy, well-conducted life," said Miss Pallfrey with dignity as Mellowes, the elderly parlour-maid, brought in the tray and arranged it on a table by her mistress's chair. The fire-light gleamed on the silver kettle and teapot in the dusk of the room, for there was no other light as yet though the evening was growing dark.

Mellowes lit the tall brass standard-lamp and placed it conveniently. "Will you require another lamp, madam?" she inquired.

"No, thank you."

Mellowes crossed the room and drew the heavy curtains across the three tall windows, shutting out the dimness of the terraced garden and the green vagueness of the park beyond. There was silence for a short time. The Honourable Augusta poured the tea and waited till Mellowes had handed the buttered toast and left the room. Then she resumed the subject.

"An Army man, I think you said?"

"Yes—at least, he is a colonel. He is a widower, about sixty, I fancy, very quiet and reserved. Mrs. Pomfret says he is inclined to be rather a wet blanket. But one can't altogether rely on Mrs. Pomfret's judgment; she is too impetuous to be a judge of character. *I* find Colonel Tidmarsh very pleasant and gentleman-like—cultivated and interested in music and art."

"Has he any money?"

"*Just* a little. He and Jocelyn together would be quite comfortable at the Dower House. They both have quiet tastes."

"And you really think he is attracted?"

"Mrs. Pomfret is convinced of it."

"And Jocelyn?"

"Oh, well!" Miss Pallfrey spread out her hands deprecatingly. "I haven't discussed it with her, naturally. I felt I must talk it over with you first, Augusta, but I am sure I can answer for Jocelyn's good sense. When she comes to me for my advice I shall counsel her to accept him and thus secure a companion and protector for her old age. It would be such a comfort."

"Jocelyn is twenty-five," remarked the Honourable Augusta, "so if he is sixty, he won't be much of a comfort to her in her old age. Pushing a centenarian in a bath-chair isn't much fun."

"Oh, I don't anticipate anything of *that* sort," objected Miss Pallfrey.

"Well, well, we can only hope so," returned the Honourable Augusta. "Anyhow, she is not likely to meet any one in this part of the world who would be more—shall I say vulgarly?—of a bargain, so I expect your idea is a good one. Jocelyn is a person who needs looking after. She is singularly incapable of looking after herself if anything should occur. She is a sweet girl and I am very fond of her, but I often want to shake her and wake her up. She goes through life seeing about as much as a kitten whose eyes aren't yet open; and a lot of it—most of it—is *your* fault, Mellicent. I can't imagine what would happen if she ever did wake up and took it into her head to want to see the world."

"Seeing the world in the sense you mean, Augusta, is never likely to attract Jocelyn. She would never wish to look for excitement; it has never occurred to her."

"No," agreed the Honourable Augusta dryly, "never, Mellicent; but there's always the chance."

Miss Pallfrey shook her head decisively. "No, Augusta, we can *trust* Jocelyn."

"If she's going to marry this man, I'd better ask him to come and see me. I suppose in these days one can't be *too* exclusive, but I must be sure, if possible, that he is the sort of man I can allow her to marry. There are so many odd people one cannot possibly *know*—these new people at Dithering Place, for instance. I hear they are really dreadful. Mellowes told me about a party, and Jocelyn was there, I hear. Why? She never told me she was going."

"I think Ermyntrude wanted her to be friendly with them. She knows them, I believe. Jocelyn was rather reticent and gave me the impression it was because of Ermyntrude she went."

"Ermyntrude is a bad influence. I feel convinced she will cause trouble. If she were to put the idea into Jocelyn's head, for instance, that she ought to live a life of her own choosing, and not the one we have chosen for her—" The Honourable Augusta paused a moment and went on very thoughtfully, as if she were choosing her words carefully: "There's just one thing, Mellicent—if Jocelyn is to marry this Colonel Tidmarsh, let it be as soon as possible. I would feel happier if I knew her future was safe. Someone might want to marry her for her position— her money hardly counts, and her continued residence at the Dower House will depend on the generosity of—of someone else—someone we—none of us, know anything about, and one expects nothing creditable in a man who roams about the world. He is certain to be dissolute and unmannerly, and is quite probably married to a most objectionable kind of wife or ready to pounce upon an innocent, unsuspecting woman—Jocelyn, for instance—and marry her for her social standing in a place where he himself would be quite taboo among the old family people.

"Oh!" gasped Miss Pallfrey. "That is something that never occurred to me! What a dreadful thing, Augusta! Yes, you are quite right; we must get this arranged. I'll talk to Mrs. Pomfret—she is resourceful and might drop a hint—just casually, of course, that we would accept Colonel Tidmarsh's—er—proposal—if that is the right word—I mean, that if he wished to propose, we would consider such a proposal favourably."

"If there is anything in the man," retorted the Honourable Augusta, "he is probably quite capable of proposing to Jocelyn himself without Mrs. Pomfret's interference. Please keep it out of Mrs. Pomfret's hands, and tell Jocelyn to give him any encouragement he may need herself. I must say I don't much like the sound of such a timid wooer. I like a man to *be* a man and go for what he wants without waiting to be pushed."

CHAPTER SEVENTEEN

JOCELYN was ready too early, for she dressed in a hurry, fearing to be too late, and then was in a panic, for it seemed such an impossible idea. Why had she ever agreed to go to a hunt ball with a man who was really a complete stranger (for Gervase suddenly seemed to be that)? Why had he asked her to do such an unconventional thing? Did he know what people like Aunt Mellicent and the Honourable Augusta would think of such a proceeding? Was he not risking her reputation in a very foolish way? After all, what did she know of him? Was he like Adrian? The thought made her cheeks burn and her heart beat.

She looked in the mirror, seeking an explanation of the reason why Adrian said he was in love with her and wanted to marry her, the reason why Gervase should ask her to come to this ball. She had never imagined that she was attractive. She had never heard of sex-appeal, and would have been horrified if she had been told she possessed it. Her husband had been entirely absorbed in his stamp collection and his tulips, and had never given much attention to her; certainly he had never seemed to consider her beautiful or attractive. Her life with Lancelot Renshawe had been entirely uneventful and unemotional. They had always known each other, and had grown up with the idea that one day they would marry and live happy ever after like a fairy-tale prince and princess, and in due course they grew up and it all came to pass without ever a heart-pang or sense of adventure or thrill of any kind. Lancelot had been a peculiarly cold-blooded, self-centred young man. He was not a normal human being, and normal human emotions had been left out of his composition—a fact that had escaped Jocelyn's unawakened perceptions. Her upbringing had not included any modern instruction on the subjects that Miss Pallfrey considered "indecent." She was slow in developing, had no strong passions and no knowledge to guide her. It was her destiny to marry Lancelot, and she never contemplated anything different. His lack of emotion left her indifferent; indeed, her own feelings were as tepid as his. Mrs. Pomfret had acted a mother's part (Ermyntrude being in India) and told her what she called "the facts of life," and given her a book called *Things a Young Wife Ought to Know*, and so equipped her for her life with Lancelot and the prospect of being the mother of the necessary heir, but it had been unnecessary, for the "facts of life" hadn't interested Lancelot. He had a violent aversion to anything in the nature of sex, and was relieved to find that Jocelyn was as reluctant as he to any approach to a subject that was a mutual embarrassment. The lack of an heir was a source of resentment on the part of Lancelot's parents and of speculation on that of Mrs. Pomfret, but Miss Pallfrey, clinging to the fantasy of the stork or preferring to think that the gooseberry bush was not prolific, merely murmured that she "hoped for good news one of these days." Jocelyn's emotions remained unstirred, and she developed a curious barrier of restraint in her attitude to "the facts of life." She avoided the subject and tucked it out of sight, feeling that Aunt Mellicent had been right. Some things were "not nice," and it was better to avoid them.

The matter of attraction, that a woman should arouse feelings of a nature she was unable to understand, made her feel all at sea. Why should she feel so wildly anxious to be admired by Gervase? Why did his touch, his looking at her, set her heart throbbing and make her senses swim? She must be in love, and to be in love was—just what, she could not decide. She knew nothing about men. She only knew that the thought of being loved by Gervase was a bliss on which she dared not dwell, and that "love" from Adrian repelled her and made her feel furious, while the idea of marriage with Ambrose gave her a sick, cold feeling. That she knew nothing at all about Gervase did not matter. She was far too well brought up and nice-minded to express her attitude as a mad desire to "let things rip," but nevertheless it described the situation, though she did not realise it.

Eagerly she scanned her reflection in the mirror. She had never before seriously considered her looks or set any value on the gold of her hair or the violet of her eyes, but now; she appraised them critically, for she wanted to be admired by Gervase. She thought she was too pale and serious to be attractive, but it would never have occurred to her to follow her mother's example and supplement her natural lack of colour. Her lips were naturally soft and red, and her teeth showed very white and even when her lips parted in what was really quite a nice smile. She was slim without being thin, and her black dress was becoming. Her pearls were real, quite a pretty row, and even Ermyntrude had said that pearls suited her. Anyway, she had no smart clothes, judging by Ermyntrude's or Jasmine's standards, and if Gervase did not like her as she was there was nothing to be done about it, but she hoped terribly that she looked nice enough to please him. She wanted to be beautiful for his sake so that he would feel proud of her to-night. She had no self-confidence, and her anxiety robbed her of even the little colour she usually had, and her eyes looked very big and full of apprehension. It seemed certain that it couldn't possibly happen. He wouldn't come. He would think that, after all, it wasn't quite proper; it was too daring. He had only thought of it all in a moment and hadn't had time to consider. No, he wouldn't come.

But even as she gazed at her pale reflection and resigned herself to putting away her thoughts of being beautiful for a man who wouldn't come, there was a crunch of gravel under the tyres of a car under her window and a faint squeal of brakes. She wrapped herself in her fur coat and fled down the stairs to be before Bertha in opening the door. She greeted him on the doorstep, and he understood at once that this affair was also a secret of their own. Her eyes told him so, and quite a lot more that she did not suspect.

He settled her comfortably and tucked a big rug about her knees before he got in beside her. "Now we're really off. I hardly dared to hope that your party wouldn't still be sitting round. However, if it hadn't been for the party I'd never have suggested this. I felt positively desperate this afternoon. This is going to be fun, you know."

Jocelyn gave a little low laugh of excitement. "Oh, yes, it is going to be fun. And do you know, I've never had any real fun in all my life. You probably think that very stupid and silly, but it's true. This is the most exciting thing I've ever done, and I'm just—just—oh, I don't know, but I don't care!"

"That's the true spirit of adventure," said Gervase lightly, "to seize one's opportunity without any questions or doubt and just sail off into the blue."

"Oh, but I've had terrible qualms," she confessed. "All the things that my aunt will say, that every one will say—"

"But if we keep it our secret, no one will ever know. We'll have a pleasant evening, and I'll bring you home not too late and drive away in the dark. And who will ever know? Anyhow, let's be happy, shall we?"

"I've never done such a thing before," Jocelyn said breathlessly, "and I shouldn't be here now if I'd had time to consider what I was doing. You didn't give me time to say 'no.'"

"The great thing is that you had time to say 'yes,' and now that we've left every one behind us for an hour or so, let's forget them. No, tell me how Ermyntrude got on last night. Did Ambrose rise to the occasion?"

"Not at all, I fear. I didn't see much of them. I—I was helping Mrs. Pomfret in the kitchen."

"Ambrose admires you."

"Oh, surely not?"

"Yes, he does. Don't let him be a nuisance. He's such a melancholy old bore. My chief recollection of him is that every one cleared out of a room when he came into it."

"And he remembers that you broke things up and made a noise. You don't seem really to have much in common," laughed Jocelyn.

"Well, we needn't waste time discussing poor old Ambrose. Tell me about yourself. "

"No, I don't want to talk about myself. I am such a very dull person. What about you?"

"No, I want to satisfy my curiosity. What do you do with yourself in a place like Much Dithering?"

Jocelyn sat up very straight with a sudden defiance. "I? What do I do? I'll tell you: I exist, I moulder. I've never been allowed to be myself. I've always been guided and shielded and steam-rolled, according to the pattern designed for me by other people—all with the best intentions in the world, no doubt. I keep my house nice and I weed my garden—and oh, how I hate tulips!" she ended inconsequently.

Gervase laughed. "Yes, you hate tulips. Anything else? I'd like to know what subjects to avoid."

"Postage stamps," Jocelyn said with a sudden bitterness that surprised Gervase.

"Well, that's easy," he returned. "Suppose you tell me what you would like to do if you hadn't got to live in this mental gabbery and do good works."

"I've never imagined such a possibility. My life is fated to be spent here, and I shall never escape."

"But is there any real need for you to live in Much Dithering?" he persisted. "You are a free agent, aren't you? An independent woman who can please herself, surely? You aren't really tied to Much Dithering."

"Oh, but—but I am," she said rather helplessly. "I've never even thought of going away."

"But that's merely stupid."

"Yes, I—I expect so."

"Why not consider the subject seriously—stretch your wings and fly out into the world?"

She laughed suddenly. "Why, yes, I believe I could. My aunt is so anxious for me to marry Colonel Tidmarsh and have someone to take care of me."

"That's impossible!" he said heatedly. "It isn't even funny. You mustn't talk like that."

Jocelyn was silent.

"Do you *want* someone to take care of you?" he asked after a pause.

"I—oh, I don't know. I think I've always been so much taken care of that I'm almost a nonentity. I have no experience—of anything. I feel like a cabbage!" She broke off, a little startled by her outburst and wondering if he thought her a fool. She felt one. Only a complete fool would have been content to lead her life without ever striving to attain any freedom. He was right. Of course she ought to be independent, but she was too cowardly to break loose. She was a despicable idiot.

"Here we are," said Gervase in a matter-of-fact tone. "This is The Angel, quite a good pub, and one gets an excellent dinner. We'll go on later to the Hunt Ball. I rang up about tickets when you said you'd come."

"Dare I?" Jocelyn wrinkled her smooth forehead and looked at him in sudden panic as they went into the hotel.

He laughed. "Why, of course you dare. I'll just park the car and meet you in the lounge. I ordered dinner on the phone."

There were several parties gathered in the lounge when she went there to await Gervase. The women were very smart and she thought ruefully of her unenterprising black lace and hoped that he would not be ashamed of her. It was obvious that the other people were also dining before going on to the Hunt Ball, and the pink evening coats gave Jocelyn a queer little thrill of pleasure. She sat in a corner unobserved and looked about her, feeling rather like a stray cat.

A party of four came in and sat down a little way off and ordered cocktails: Adrian Murchison-Bellaby, Jasmine, and two others that Jocelyn recognised with surprise as the Hedgecocks. Lucia looked amazingly lovely and was beautifully dressed, while Victor was sleek and had something intangible about his well-groomed appearance that was just not right. Adrian was wearing a pink coat and was very well pleased with himself. He ordered the cocktails, and as he stood with his back to the corner where Jocelyn was sitting, Gervase came in and looked round. Recognition was mutual, and neither seemed to exhibit any pleasure at the encounter, but Gervase was less visibly put out of his stride and took the fence with more ease. He took in the situation at once, saw Jocelyn in the corner looking rather stricken, and realised that there was no way to avoid the unfortunate discovery of their being together. He smiled as he caught Adrian's no less stricken glance and nodded cheerfully as he passed the group.

"Good hunting!" he said with an intonation that made Adrian redden and then grin rather sheepishly.

"Same to you, old chap," he returned and glanced after Gervase with a casual curiosity that faded out and was replaced with a stare of amazement as he saw him sitting down beside Jocelyn. "Well, I'm damned!" he stuttered and stood staring in silent dismay. His own pleasure in the evening suddenly smashed. Why had he ever agreed to this party? It had been Jasmine's bright idea, for she wanted to dance with Victor, and this was the only way to achieve her ambition. But who could possibly have dreamed that Jocelyn would be here with Gervase Blythe? What were they doing? Were they, too, going to the Hunt Ball? Lord, what a frightful bit of luck! Gervase Blythe? What had she to do with him? It was extraordinary—not a bit what he had expected of her. And what would she think of his being here with Lucia, for of course there was no other explanation. Lucia was so decorative and self-assured, and so damnably, patently possessive that there was no mistaking that she considered him her property. But who could have thought—?

He sat down feeling like a pricked bubble, and Jasmine, who had been too deeply engrossed in Victor to notice his sudden moodiness, became aware that Lucia's dark eyes were fixed with an amused, satirical expression on someone across the room.

"Ah!" Lucia raised her pencilled eyebrows. "So the visitor at The Roebuck, too, entertains this evening? And why not? Mrs. Renshawe, no doubt, has moments when she is not so devastatingly dull as would appear. It is well known that still waters run deep, and she has lovely eyes—such long lashes and so much earnestness." Her glance flickered over Adrian's sullen face and she laughed. "You hadn't thought of Mrs. Renshawe being deep? And now you feel that Mr. Blythe is 'offside,' as you are so fond of saying? Adrian, you make me laugh."

"I don't see what the hell there is to be funny about," he growled. "I didn't think there was the slightest possibility of any one from Much Dithering being here to-night. What filthy luck!"

"Yes, isn't it?" scoffed Lucia.

Jasmine shrugged her shoulders. "I don't care a damn. There's no one in Much Dithering that matters."

"Only one," observed Lucia sweetly and laughed at Adrian's scowl.

In the corner of the lounge Gervase sat beside Jocelyn and made light of the encounter. "I assure you there is no harm in dining with me and dancing afterwards. Lots of people do it."

"But *I* never have," objected Jocelyn unhappily.

"Then it's quite time you did," he retorted. "Where's your spirit of adventure now?"

"We can't go to the Ball," Jocelyn said miserably. She felt like a naughty child caught stealing jam.

"We most certainly are going to the Ball," he returned firmly. "We are not going to run away from a third-rate party and admit we knew we were doing something wrong. There's nothing *wrong* in what we're doing. I wouldn't have asked you if there were. I think you might give me credit for so much. Or are you placing me at Ambrose Tidmarsh's valuation, or even on a level with the gay Adrian?"

Jocelyn looked perplexed. "I don't really know what to think."

"Then let me think for you." He gave her a glass of sherry and looked at her gravely. "Now please don't worry. I've set out to give you a perfectly harmless evening's amusement and you mustn't crumple up in despair because someone has seen us. Why worry about people who don't matter to any one? *I'm* not worrying, and I don't want you to feel that your adventure's spoilt. It isn't, and I'm sure you have enough spirit to forget your fears. Enjoy yourself, Jocelyn—that's all I ask. Please!" He leaned a little closer and touched her hand for a moment. "Please!"

His tone awoke a new courage in her. After all, what did anything in the world matter but that she was here with him and he wanted her to be happy? He was looking at her with a deep tenderness that made her heart leap and flutter. "If it pleases you—yes. Nothing else matters." She looked back at him with all her transparent soul in her eyes and forgot her qualms.

"Let's go in to dinner." He stood up and helped her out of her low chair, walking beside her to the dining-room and admiring her calm poise and dignity as she crossed the lounge, passing Adrian's party with a smiling greeting that held no suggestion that she had so recently been petrified by their entry. It seemed to be the most natural thing in the world that she should be dining at The Angel and going to the Hunt Ball. She had recovered from her panic and felt completely happy. Gervase had taken charge and she was content to follow where he led.

CHAPTER EIGHTEEN

IT WAS worth it, Jocelyn decided, once she had succeeded in putting aside her qualms as to what her mother-in-law and Aunt Mellicent would say. It was a wonderful evening, such as she had never believed possible. Gervase was a perfect host, with his grave courtesy and care for her. She saw the admiration in his eyes when he looked at her, and had a glimpse of herself in a mirror across the room, looking transfigured and radiant. His eyes told her she was beautiful, but he said no word of his admiration and made her completely at ease.

The ball was like every other Hunt Ball. It was very crowded and almost impossible to dance; the supper accommodation was inadequate and the corridors were full of draughts. Nevertheless Jocelyn enjoyed the discomforts with a zest of which she had not thought herself capable. Dancing was merely marking time in a crowd with the firm protection of Gervase's arm about her as he warded off the inevitable collisions in the traffic jams.

He looked at her once with a smile and remarked; "What a lovely hugging tune this is. I feel dangerously sentimental, so I'm going to take you home."

"Oh, not yet," she pleaded. "I'm so happy. I don't want to go home just yet. To-morrow you'll be gone and there will only be— Much Dithering. I want to put it out of mind."

"Sentiment is dangerous."

"Is it?" She glanced up at him, but he wasn't looking at her, and they danced on with the crowd.

Then he looked down at her and said gravely: "You are very sweet, Jocelyn—very sweet and very lovely."

"I like you to think so, even if it isn't true," she said breathlessly.

"But it is true."

"It doesn't matter—so long as you think so."

"My dear!" He guided her out of the crowd and stood a moment looking at her. "It's time I took you home, Jocelyn. Get your coat and meet me at the top of the steps."

"Gervase—"

"Please, Jocelyn." He left her and walked quickly down the long corridor, and she turned with a little sigh and went to fetch her coat.

There was light snow falling as they drove through the darkness of the silent country roads. It was bitterly cold and the joy of the evening faded in the suggestion of anti-climax that is inevitable at two o'clock of a winter's morning when the music and lights and gaiety have been left behind and a sense of weariness creeps over the spirit. Gervase found the roads slippery, and driving became difficult as they went on. He was also preoccupied and silent because he feared that words were dangerous, and he was at a loss for the first time in his adventurous career, hesitating, unable to decide on his course without proper consideration. He was frightened of Jocelyn's unbelievable innocence and unsophistication, and filled with doubts as to his own worthiness. After all, his past, though it could easily have been blacker, was lurid enough to startle, even horrify, a woman of Jocelyn's almost terrifying purity. Gervase, in short, was scared stiff at the situation, and was at a deadlock as to his future procedure.

Jocelyn, chilled by his silence and constraint, grew colder and more depressed with each mile. She was at a complete loss as to the reason for his withdrawal. All her happiness faded and her mind was full of doubt and despair. It seemed to be only too evident that Ermyntrude was right: she would always prove so hopelessly dull that no one would think her worth bothering about. Gervase had taken her out hoping to find her amusing, and she had failed. She had made the fatal mistake of taking his casual admiration seriously and had let him see it. No wonder he was cold and embarrassed and had to put her back where she belonged—into the company of the dull, stupid people of Much Dithering. Yes, that was where she definitely belonged. Her foolish dream was shattered.

Both were glad when the long, cold drive ended.

Jocelyn paused doubtfully on the doorstep at the Dower House. "It seems so inadequate to say 'Thank you.'"

"I don't want you to say 'Thank you,'" he told her quickly. "And I'm not coming in for last words at this hour. You are very tired, and I have a lot I want to say, but not at a time like this. I'll come back, Jocelyn, in a week or two. I have to think out a big problem, and I dare not make a mess of it. Good-night. It's been rather priceless, hasn't it?"

Jocelyn smiled at him a little wistfully. "Oh, far above price," she said with a little catch at her breath. "Don't—don't be away too long." She said that without meaning to.

He stood a moment looking at her. "You know, I ought to warn you that I'm not—I mean—well, the truth is, Jocelyn, I'm a bad hat. You shouldn't—oh, it's terribly difficult to explain."

She shook her head. "Then don't bother to explain. The truth is that I—well, I *like* a bad hat."

She slipped into the hall and closed the door behind her, standing to listen to the sound of his departing car before she crossed to the stairs. The ticking of the grandfather clock echoed in the silent dimness, and she seemed to hear a cold disapproval of her return in the measured chime as it struck three o'clock. She sighed with a gesture of despair as she went slowly up the stairs, pausing to turn out the lamp in the bracket at the stair-head before going to her room.

She lay awake, her feelings too disturbed to allow her to rest. She acknowledged that she had fallen in love with Gervase and was at a loss whether to be glad or sorry. To be glad seemed to be an indication that she had definitely put all her past life behind her and was reaching out to grasp something she hardly understood, something that Would cause a revolution in her carefully supervised existence, something that demanded her complete obedience to a new influence and attitude to life, an opening of a door into the Unknown. Dare she open that door? To be sorry—well, to think of being sorry or to have regrets—merely seemed to mean that she was bolting that door firmly instead of opening it.

Of Gervase she tried not to think too much. It made her feel weak. If Gervase loved her—oh, but how could he love her? She dared not dwell on the possibility. If Gervase loved her—no, she couldn't get beyond that, and to let herself imagine it would be folly. And if he didn't love her, and it only meant that he had been just kind and friendly—but that was such agony that she dared not let herself dwell on that aspect, either. In fact, Jocelyn was just very badly in love and experiencing all the doubts and fears and agonies and ecstasies of that state of mind, augmented by her previous lack of experience in anything of the nature of love, and complicated by placing herself at her mother's valuation. And yet—why had Gervase looked at her just as he did when he told her he was a bad hat? And what did it matter if he were?

CHAPTER NINETEEN

"JUST imagine," said the Honourable Augusta in a tone of indignation. "He had the impertinence to call to see me after you had gone yesterday—quite late, about six o'clock. He said he wished to see me alone, but I told Mellowes to say that I never interview strangers on business, and referred him to my agent. He said his business was with me, and I replied that I had no business with *him*, and that defeated him."

"Quite right, too," agreed Miss Pallfrey. "But what *was* his business?"

"How do I know? I didn't inquire."

"Quite right," agreed Miss Pallfrey again, but rather doubtfully, and added: "I believe in knowing people's business, even if it has nothing to do with me. If you know people's business, it gives you an advantage and you can deal with them more easily."

"I have no wish to deal with this Mr. Blythe," said the Honourable Augusta loftily. "I understand he is staying at The Roebuck with that odious Joe Hedgecock, who wants to have a petrol pump and a garage—a common commercial traveller, I expect."

"*Who* did you say?" asked Miss Pallfrey suddenly, looking perturbed.

"A Mr. Blythe," repeated the Honourable Augusta.

"Dear me!" ejaculated Miss Pallfrey. "How odd! How almost *unpleasant*! You were quite right not to see *him*. I don't understand it at all."

"What are you talking about?" demanded the Honourable Augusta sharply. "You don't know him, do you? Or"—she paused—"was that the man Colonel Tidmarsh brought with him the night of Jocelyn's dinner-party? The one who helped to put out the fire?"

"Yes," replied Miss Pallfrey. "But Colonel Tidmarsh told me he was highly undesirable, and begged me to understand that *he* had no connection whatever with him. He merely knew him years ago in the Army, and was most annoyed when he came here, self-invited, to stay for Christmas."

"Self-invited? How peculiar!"

"Well, practically self-invited. Colonel Tidmarsh had, I believe, vaguely said, 'You must look me up some time; I'll be delighted.' But no one expects that sort of invitation to be taken seriously."

"Of course not," agreed the Honourable Augusta. "He certainly sounds a person to be avoided."

Just then Mellowes opened the door and ushered in Jocelyn, who had come to spend the afternoon with her mother-in-law.

Jocelyn had recovered her spirits and had an unaccountable suggestion of happiness about her this afternoon. She was looking particularly well, the Honourable Augusta thought, younger, and with a sparkle and colour about her.

"You are looking very well, my dear," she said, "quite five years younger than last week. What have you been doing?"

Jocelyn was taken aback. "Doing, Aunt Augusta? Why should I have been doing anything?"

Miss Pallfrey patted her shoulder. "Perhaps," she said archly, "the attentions of a certain gentleman may have something to do with your pretty colour, dear. Love is a most wonderful rejuvenator."

Jocelyn's cheeks flamed scarlet and she sat down and stared at her aunt in consternation. So they knew already! But how?—

"Ah, my dear," crowed Miss Pallfrey jubilantly, "I see I am right! Don't say a word, Jocelyn—all in good time."

"But really," gasped Jocelyn, "there's nothing, Aunt Mellicent. He never said a word to lead me to suppose—"

"No, my dear, of course not," said her mother-in-law soothingly. "Very naturally, being more or less a stranger, he feels that he must proceed with circumspection, but I am glad that you appear to be taking kindly to the idea. We have been much concerned, your aunt and I, over your future, and we are greatly relieved at this solution of the difficulty."

"Oh, but—"began Jocelyn faintly.

"There, there!" said Miss Pallfrey kindly. "We'll say no more about it at present, but Augusta is right—it is a great happiness for us to know that you have a happy future before you. We are getting old—at least, getting on, and life

"Oh? Mrs. Pomfret only seems to have noticed Colonel Tidmarsh going in your gate, and she thought . . . She scented romance, in fact."

"Oh, did she?" Jocelyn began to laugh. Surely people couldn't imagine that she was falling in love with Colonel Tidmarsh? Why, she had forgotten his existence. How utterly absurd! But her secret adventure was safe. She collected her scattered wits and sat prepared to be on her guard.

"Has Colonel Tidmarsh ever mentioned Mr. Blythe to you?" Miss Pallfrey asked suddenly.

Jocelyn looked surprised. "I don't see that we need discuss him at all," objected the Honourable Augusta. "Tell us who came to your tea-party, Jocelyn."

"How is it that we never heard about it?" asked Miss Pallfrey in a hurt tone.

"It just happened," explained Jocelyn with a laugh. "Every one arrived out of the blue, and no one was more surprised than I was."

"Well, who were they?"

"The Murchison-Bellabys came, and the Winghams, and Colonel Tidmarsh."

"Oh, those new people? I suppose one day they'll go every-where, but whoever calls, *I* shan't," remarked the Honourable Augusta. "I stand for the 'Old Order,' and I resent the coming of the new."

"I suppose I shall have to call," sighed Miss Pallfrey, "but I feel as you do, Augusta."

Jocelyn walked over to the window and stood looking out over the sloping park. Down there, hidden by the beeches, ran the road to Totterford. The happenings of last night were

dream-like. She almost doubted now, in the familiar surroundings of the Priory, that last night had ever been. To-day Gervase
had gone away, but he had said he would come back, and that
thought was responsible for her feeling of new hope. It also
made her feel impatient with all the futile indignation on the
part of her mother-in-law and aunt over the coming of new
people and new ideas to their age-old village. To her Gervase
belonged to the new order, repudiated just now by her mother-
in-law. (The Murchison-Bellabys didn't count.) He had spoken
of progress and the impossibility of standing still and letting
the world go by. Improvements and innovations were bound
to come—so he had said—and she found she was agreeing with
him and becoming impatient of the stagnation in the village life
she had endured so unthinkingly all her life. Because things had
always been so there was no reason why they should continue
to be so while other places followed on the progress of the years
and left them here in Much Dithering still living in the traditions
of the past.

She was aware of the usual tea-time arguments and discus-
sions on parish and village happenings; but she was not thinking
about them. She was wondering how it was that she had been
content to waste her life as she had been doing, how it would
be possible to break the chains of tradition which bound her,
how to venture to assert a new viewpoint, how—oh, but it was
all a dream! She was paying her usual weekly visit to Lancelot's
mother. She was going on presently to discuss the approaching Social and children's Christmas tree with Mrs. Pomfret, and
choose the glees and part songs for a concert, and arrange prac-
tices and so on. She would be taking out the *Parish Magazine* in
a few days to the people in Little Dithering, and magazines and
papers to her old ladies in the Almshouses, and she would pass
the pile of wood by the roadside where the big willow was being
sawn up for removal.

She got up, unable to bear the Priory and the Honourable Augusta and Aunt Mellicent another moment. She must
get away and walk through the cold darkness and collect her
self-control before she went to Mrs. Pomfret.

"I must go," she said. "I have to see Mrs. Pomfret—the concert and—and other things."

"Surely there is no hurry," expostulated her aunt. "Wait a few minutes, Jocelyn, and I'll be ready to go with you; but I haven't finished my tea yet."

"I'm sorry," replied Jocelyn hastily. "I *have* to go. I've just remembered, Aunt Mellicent, that I must go home and fetch some music before I go to the Vicarage."

She made her adieux and escaped. She walked briskly down the long avenue through the park, rejoicing in the crisp cold air. The stars were bright and there was frost in the air. The snow that lay thinly crunched under her feet and gave her a sense of exhilaration. Oh, surely, surely Gervase would come back? Surely she had justification for her strange happiness?

"H'm!" remarked the Honourable Augusta as the door closed behind Jocelyn's abrupt departure. "In love, I suppose; the symptoms point to it. She's been odd ever since you mentioned Colonel Tidmarsh."

"Dear Jocelyn!" murmured Miss Pallfrey fondly. After a pause she remarked: "Purely as a matter of curiosity, I'd like to know why that man called."

"What man?"

"Mr. Blythe."

"What does it matter? If his business is important he can take it to my solicitor or the agent. I never interview any one until I know his business. I'm too busy to waste my time over people who come begging for donations or trying to sell me something. I've had advertisements of all sorts of electric rubbish by post lately, and I expect this man was selling them."

"Oh, I can't believe that Colonel Tidmarsh could be connected with a commercial traveller," objected Miss Pallfrey in a shocked tone.

The Honourable Augusta was silent for a moment. "I have a mistrust of any one who comes and asks to see me on business. I have the feeling that one day someone will come and say he is Rupert's nephew, and there will be trouble."

"Oh, but why—? I mean, you know he is in Australia or something like that."

"I know nothing of the sort. He was in Australia, I believe, when Rupert died; but he may be anywhere now."

"What a dreadful thought!" sighed Miss Pallfrey. "What would happen if he turned up?"

"Naturally if he wanted to live here, I should have to go elsewhere. He wrote at the time and said he was travelling abroad and would not be in England for a long time, and in the meantime, if I wished to go on living here, I could do so. He had no ambition to come and settle down here then, and it was arranged that everything should be carried on as before. Of course the money all has to be accounted for. We spend what is necessary on keeping up the estate and the rest is paid into this person's account in a London bank. Naturally I spend my own money on my personal expenses. So far I have merely been placed in charge of everything and am allowed to go on living here free of rent, which is, I consider, quite fair; but the thought that is always lurking in the background is that one day he is bound to come, and my reign at the Priory will be over—not at all pleasant, Mellicent, I assure you, so I always refuse to see strange men."

"I understand," Miss Pallfrey sighed, shaking her head. "And then, of course, it would affect Jocelyn at the Dower House. She is very fortunate to have another home open to her. Colonel Tidmarsh has a very pleasant little place—small, of course, but quite charming, and it is a great happiness that we shall not be losing our dear child. She will still be with us and able to carry on all her village interests without interruption. That is a very happy thought. Dear Jocelyn would never transplant into another sphere. She suits her surroundings and would be quite lost if she had to make strange contacts in another part of the world. She is essentially of her own little circle. She asks nothing else."

"No," answered the Honourable Augusta rather sharply. "But she is a bit of a fool in some ways."

CHAPTER TWENTY

ADRIAN was an exceedingly perplexed young man. Lucia's attitude was infuriating when he tried to persuade her that their love affair had never been serious. There had never been anything more in *his* love-making than in *her* casual acceptance of a few brooches and earrings, all *pour passer le temps*, or so he had assured himself, not bothering to think very much about her side. Now Lucia seemed to think she could corner him, and was threatening to create a local scandal if he refused to marry her. She realised that down here in Much Dithering it would be easy to get what she wanted. The family would pay up to keep Adrian's name clear. She had heard all about their ambitions, and knew just how to make herself unpleasant.

Adrian had met Lucia in London, where she worked as a mannequin at the shop where Jasmine bought her frocks, but posed as a girl of good family who chose to earn her living and live in London rather than remain buried in the country place where her old-fashioned and not very well-off parents lived (so said Lucia). She went about quite a lot in the gay set of young people in which Jasmine and Adrian spent their London life, and their acquaintance had blossomed into a hectic love affair, as much a relaxation from the somewhat wearisome entanglement into which he had got himself with Ermyntrude as for any more serious reason, for he was a fickle youth. Ermyntrude bored him. Lucia was lovely, and her southern sensuousness was alluring. Well, that was all as far as *he* was concerned! And now here was Lucia, the daughter of the village innkeeper in Much Dithering, his parents' new country residence! Could any one have believed in such a ghastly coincidence! And as if *that* wasn't bad enough, she must needs have as a brother the dance band leader for whose sleek, oily charm Jasmine had fallen, insisting on a party to go to the Hunt Ball so that she could dance all night with him and carry on an ill-timed flirtation. And the crowning disaster of all the wretched affair was meeting Jocelyn Renshawe with Blythe at the ball. What was he to do? He knew quite well that

Jocelyn would never understand the affair or make allowances for a young man philandering with a pretty girl. Besides, there was Ermyntrude to account for!

There seemed nothing to be done but to do as he had always done in a tight corner when his affairs had reached a critical turn that was beyond his somewhat limited intelligence. He therefore confessed his misdoings to his indulgent mother, confident of her forgiveness and ready resource in dealing with difficulties. He also confided in her his desire to marry Jocelyn, and implored her assistance in his endeavour to persuade Jocelyn to listen to him.

Mrs. Murchison-Bellaby was most upset at the tale of his entanglement with Lucia. It was so common—an innkeeper's daughter, and at their very gates! A scandal would be a terrible business and must be avoided at all costs. How could he ever stand for Parliament in the district with a local scandal hanging over him? Where would all his hopes vanish to? What chance was there to get on in the county? Think of Jasmine—

"Oh, as for Jasmine!" Adrian laughed and shrugged. "It doesn't rest with me to mess up things for her; she can do that for herself quite well. As a matter of fact—oh, well, it's no affair of mine."

"What do you mean?" demanded his mother suspiciously. "What is it *this* time? You'd better tell me."

"Yes, perhaps I ought to. You know Jasmine, though; she'll do as she pleases in her own way."

"Adrian, tell me at once!"

"She's running after the leader of some dance band—I forget what it's called. As a matter of fact, he—well, he is the son of—I mean, he's Lucia's brother. Funny, isn't it?"

"Funny?" stormed Mrs. Murchison-Bellaby furiously. "Funny! What have I done to deserve that both my children should disgrace me?"

"Call it 'reversion to type,'" suggested Adrian nastily. "After all, Old Man Bellaby was a grocer, wasn't he? And on the other side we don't owe much to the worthy Ezekiel Hobbs, do we?"

Mrs. Murchison-Bellaby was a rich purple, almost speechless with mortification. "Whatever your grandparents were, they were *decent*. They raised themselves to a good position and were respected. You and Jasmine will never be *that* if you go on in this way. Your grandfather's money bought us *our* position and gave you all the money you want; but you've got to make your own position, my lad, you and Jasmine. We can't help you there. Your father and I are fixed here, and it's your look out to go farther and build up a family that will be a credit to the decent old folks who spent their lives putting by the money that's going to be the ruin of you, from the look of things."

"Oh, for heaven's sake don't nag," Adrian implored. "I've told you that Lucia pretended to be someone quite decent—said her people were in the country, not well off or something. I never really worried, for I only meant to fool round a bit. It was the shock of my life when I found her at The Roebuck."

"Well, you'll have to get clear of her. Pay her anything you like so long as she understands it's for good and all. Oh, Adrian, if you could only marry that sweet woman it would be the making of you—the making of us all. I'll go and see her and do all I can. I'll go to-day. She mustn't hear about this girl."

"She was at the Hunt Ball and saw us all together, but she doesn't understand that a fellow can rag and not be serious." He stopped pacing the room and faced his mother. "Now she herself was with a funny bloke that night. I was as surprised to see her with him as she could have been to see us, if you know what I mean."

"Oh?" Mrs. Murchison-Bellaby looked shrewdly at her son. "She was, was she? Well, you *do* surprise me. Who was he?"

"That fellow I brought in to dinner here. He was staying at The Roebuck till yesterday. No one knows a thing about him. He just blew in and blew out again, I hear."

Jasmine flung herself into the room in a state of distraught excitement. "My pearls—my earrings—my diamond bracelet—they're gone! Everything!"

"Gone?" echoed her mother. "Gone? Stolen, do you mean?"

"Yes, I suppose so. I pushed them into my dressing-table drawer yesterday morning, and I never looked again till just now."

"Damn' fool!" growled Adrian unsympathetically. "What do you expect if you leave valuable stuff lying about? You're simply asking for trouble."

"But here, in this house, who—?" began Mrs. Murchison-Bellaby, and stopped. "I wonder—my emeralds—"

She left the room hurriedly and Adrian looked at his sister. "Are you sure?"

"Of course I'm sure! I took them off when I got back from the Hunt Ball and just pushed them into the drawer as I always do."

"Worth a couple of thousand, those pearls, aren't they?"

"Yes, and my bracelet was £150 and the earrings another £50, and there was a diamond pendant on a platinum chain and a couple of brooches."

"A nice little haul!"

Mrs. Murchison-Bellaby burst into the room, wailing. "My emeralds—all my rings—and brooches—gone! Oh, what shall I do? All gone! This is awful!" She sat down and began to cry. "All this to happen—I don't deserve it—I don't deserve it."

"Oh, shut up!" snapped Jasmine rudely. "It's just as bad for me, but I'm not howling about it. Let's get on to the police and *do* something. Adrian, you ring up the police."

Adrian went away, leaving Jasmine and his mother alone. Mrs. Murchison-Bellaby stopped crying as soon as the door closed behind him.

"What's this I hear about the people at The Roebuck?"

Jasmine flushed. "I don't know and I don't care."

"I dare say you don't; but *I* do, and I'm not going to have any low-down behaviour ruining our prospects here just as we are starting to make our way. You needn't look so black. I've heard all about you."

"Oh, so Adrian's been trying to cover up his mistakes by getting me into a mess, has he?" scoffed Jasmine. "Well, I'm quite able to carve my own career, and I'm not going to stand any interference from any one. The opinion of a lot of old frumps doesn't worry me. My life's my own, not theirs, and what I choose to do is my own affair. See?"

She left the room, banging the door behind her, and joined Adrian, who was in the library ringing up the County Police.

CHAPTER TWENTY-ONE

MRS. Murchison-Bellaby called on Jocelyn that afternoon in spite of the unpleasant weather, for it had been snowing all night and the roads were in a very slippery condition. However, as Mrs. Murchison-Bellaby said comfortably: "What are motor cars for, and servants who eat their heads off, if not for the convenience of the people who pay for them?" So she paid an unexpected call and found Jocelyn alone, to her great relief, for she had come on a delicate mission. She believed in the good old-fashioned principles and proverbs such as not beating about the bush, and striking while the iron was hot, and a bird in the hand being worth two in the bush (which latter had an ironic significance at the moment).

Jocelyn was surprised at receiving the visit and wondered what was at the back of it, for Mrs. Murchison-Bellaby was obviously flustered and ill at ease.

"I'm thankful to say," remarked Mrs. Murchison-Bellaby presently, after a somewhat disjointed prelude about nothing in particular, "that our decision to live here has had an excellent effect on Adrian. You know the sort of life a young man leads in the Army when he has all the money he wants and nothing to occupy his spare time. But it was all to the good, really. He has sown his wild oats and is steadying down very sensibly and cultivating country tastes. I want him to stand for Parliament, you know, when he leaves the Army."

"For the Ditherings, do you mean?" asked Jocelyn doubtfully.

"Yes, for this part of the world where we have a stake in the country, as the saying is."

"Is he a Conservative?"

"I think so," replied Mrs. Murchison-Bellaby comfortably. "We haven't really discussed it yet, but I'm sure he'll decide on that. I'd sooner he was a Conservative. All the *best* people are. Of course one meets all sorts of people in politics, but far the nicest are Conservatives, I always think—more *chic*, if you know what I mean, and Adrian is rather particular who he knows. He's been about with really smart people such a lot; and the Labour, or even Liberal, women always seem so dowdy." She paused and looked at Jocelyn in sudden alarm. "You are a Conservative, of course?"

"I call myself a Conservative," said Jocelyn. "But I'm not really keen on politics. I'm not clever enough to understand them."

Mrs. Murchison-Bellaby looked relieved. "No? Well, that's like me."

"I hope I'm not exactly dowdy, but on the other hand I don't claim to be at all smart. I have always lived such a quiet sort of life," apologised Jocelyn.

Mrs. Murchison-Bellaby was obviously delighted at finding Jocelyn so reasonable in her views. "As I was saying about Adrian," she went on after a slight pause, "I hope he will marry soon. The woman who marries him will be very lucky. He will be able to give her everything she can possibly want—a villa in the South of France, a service flat in town, and of course he will have a separate suite of rooms at The Place. We are prepared to build on a new wing, if necessary. Or he might find a nice suitable house somewhere near. That might be better, don't you think? For instance, have you ever thought of letting this house? Adrian has taken such a fancy to it. He's very artistic and seems to like old places. If he spent some money here he could make it quite charming."

"I have never considered letting it," Jocelyn said firmly, "so he needn't waste time deciding now to improve it. Besides, it isn't mine: it goes with the Priory."

"Oh, I see! The Priory? When that old lady dies I suppose the Priory will be on the market?"

"I should be sorry if it were. There have been five or six generations of Kenshawes there, and it is heart-breaking when old families die out and their homes are sold to outsiders." Jocelyn spoke stiffly.

"Yes, but on the other hand," rejoined Mrs. Murchison-Bellaby with some heat, "it's the new families who are going to count in another generation or two. You, for instance, are a childless widow. You are going to die and leave no one behind you. Your old aunt will die an old maid and leave no descendants. The Winghams have no children, I understand. Half a dozen other old families round about here are in the same way. And who will carry on in their places if a new and vigorous growth of new people don't take their place? When all you old families in Dithering are buried, *we* shall be going strong. Adrian's children and Jasmine's will take *your* places in due course. But who else will there be anywhere round about here?" She patted Jocelyn's knee. "I dare say this seems brutal, but it's perfectly true. Now, if you married Adrian, what a sensible arrangement it would be—a blending of the old and new. Think about it, my dear."

"I'm afraid not," replied Jocelyn gravely. "I—I've never considered marrying again. The idea doesn't appeal to me at all."

"It is my dearest wish," Mrs. Murchison-Bellaby said earnestly. "With you to guide Adrian, he will soon be the right man in the right place. I shall have no further doubts for his future happiness or success in his career. This is confidential, I needn't tell you, Mrs. Renshawe, but I must add that I would never have mentioned it unless I had noticed that Adrian is very much attracted by you, and I know he is ambitious and very anxious to marry the right woman."

"Thank you," said Jocelyn feebly, unable to cope with the embarrassing situation or to stem the eloquence of her visitor, "but I'm afraid—"

"No, no," broke in Mrs. Murchison-Bellaby. "Just now you think I'm an interfering, common person trying to push my way in among you people here. Well, perhaps I am, my dear, but I have my ambitions. We are very rich people, and I'd like to think that our money could be spent on some worthier object than giving Adrian and Jasmine what they call 'a good time.'

I'd like to make our home worthy of the respect that your villagers here give to the people who employ them and live in the big places. I'd like to come among them and help in any way I could. I'd like my Jasmine to be loved like you are, and marry a country gentleman and settle down, and above all I'd like to think that Adrian would marry you and realise all the things I've ever wanted for him. He's a good boy at heart, and I can assure you of all my love and welcome. Think it over, my dear. I'll say goodbye now. I've said more than I meant to; but I just *had* to." She began to cry suddenly. "Oh, my dear Mrs. Renshawe, forgive me for coming like this and saying things perhaps I shouldn't say, but I'm a very unhappy woman and I seem to have no real friends I can confide in or ask advice from, and there comes a time sometimes when a person is in sore need of advice and no one to appeal to. You are so sweet and gentle, I—I felt you might be sorry and perhaps see what I meant and be able to help me."

"I don't think I can possibly help you in the way you suggest," Jocelyn said unhappily. She felt very sorry for the poor lady, but really did not think she was called upon to sacrifice herself to the extent of marrying Adrian in order to comfort his sorrowing mother. It was all terribly embarrassing, but she could not see what she could do in the circumstances. She was too kind-hearted to speak sharply or to refuse to grant the absurd request in words that might cause her afflicted visitor more pain, but at the same time she had to make it quite clear that she could not possibly consider marrying Adrian.

"I'm very, very sorry indeed that you are so unhappy," she said sympathetically; "but really, Mrs. Murchison-Bellaby, your suggestion is out of the question. I hardly know your son and—and in any case—why, such an idea never occurred to me."

"No, of course not," agreed Mrs. Murchison-Bellaby hastily. "I'm sure of that, Mrs. Renshawe. You are far too much of a real lady to think about being fond of a man or wanting to marry him before he gave you any reason to think he was fond of you. That is the way nice people brought up their girls, I know; and you are a nice-minded, modest young woman and to be respected. Adrian realises all that, I assure you. That is why—I mean, he confided his hopes to me and I said I'd help him, and so—so I just rushed off in a regular state. I didn't think—I was too upset—"

She wept again.

"I'm very sorry," repeated Jocelyn. "I can do nothing to comfort you—unless, perhaps, a cup of tea—"

"Oh, thank you—but no, I think I'd better not stay any longer. I'd quite forgotten—there has been a burglary. Adrian was telephoning to the police. I'd better go home. All my jewellery, and Jasmine's, too—it's dreadful, dreadful, and being so vexed and upset about—other things as well,—Oh, dear, what a day I'm having!"

"A burglary?" repeated Jocelyn. "Good gracious! such a thing has never happened in Much Dithering before. How dreadful!"

"Yes, indeed." Mrs. Murchison-Bellaby dried her eyes and sat up, looking at Jocelyn with quite a different expression. "Yes, it is funny the way things happen. *You've* had nothing stolen, have you?"

"No."

"No? Well, perhaps you've nothing much to tempt thieves here."

"Possibly not, but Much Dithering people are honest. No one has ever even thought of being burgled. As long as I can remember, it has always been the same here."

"Very likely, Mrs. Renshawe; but you know strangers have been about lately—staying in the village, they say. And who knows anything about strangers these days? Why, they might be any kind of criminal!"

Jocelyn found her hard, sharp eyes searching hers as if she had a clue concealed about her. She felt a moment's vague alarm. "Burglars? How—?" she began.

"That man Adrian brought in to dinner with us," said Mrs. Murchison-Bellaby sharply, "what was *he* doing here? He'd never been here before. He'd been all over the world, he told me. He was quite a gentleman to look at and talk to, and he had nice manners and a nice way with him. But what do we know about him, I ask you?"

"Do you mean that—that *he* is a burglar?" Jocelyn asked in a startled tone, and her cheeks were suddenly white and her eyes dark and horror-stricken. "Oh, no, no, I can't believe it. It's not possible!"

"Not possible?" echoed Mrs. Murchison-Bellaby derisively, following up her advantage. She had hurt Jocelyn; she saw that clearly and rejoiced. Yes, she'd make her eat a little mud in return for her refusal to be nice about Adrian. Adrian wasn't good enough for her; but anyhow he was honest. And who could say whether this other man over whom she had given herself away was honest? "It's quite possible, Mrs. Renshawe. Anyhow, the jewels are gone, and *he* has gone—make what you like of that!"

"I don't believe it!"

"Why does it matter to you so much?"

"I—I only think it isn't right to assume that he is a burglar without any proof whatever."

"I've no doubt the police will find the proof," retorted Mrs. Murchison-Bellaby, rising. There were no further symptoms of tears or distress visible, and Jocelyn felt that for some reason she had become an enemy. She obviously was hinting that she imagined that there was a reason why Jocelyn was interested in Gervase Blythe, and was hurting her deliberately. "It's funny," said Mrs. Murchison-Bellaby, "yes, it's funny the way the sky seems to fall. Oh, I tell you, I've had a day. I feel as if I'd been under a steamroller. Do you ever feel like that? Well, I expect every one does, sooner or later. Good-bye, Mrs. Renshawe, and if you've any sense you'll think about all I've been telling you." She conveyed a threat in the hostile glance she cast at Jocelyn as she drew on her gloves and took her leave.

Jocelyn went back to the drawing-room when her visitor had driven away. "'Funny how the sky seems to fall,'" she quoted and laughed. "Oh, what a horrible woman! What a horrible thing to say—or even think." She clenched her hands till the knuckles showed hard and white. "I won't believe it. It isn't true. It couldn't be true. I'll never believe it!"

CHAPTER TWENTY-TWO

ADRIAN went himself to pay a visit to Jocelyn, deciding that a straightforward discussion was the best move. Obviously his mother had not been as successful as she might have been. It was all so very difficult. In the first place there had been Ermyntrude following him down here, and the strange coincidence of her being Jocelyn's mother, and then his own violent head-over-heels infatuation for Jocelyn at first sight, and his realisation of the fact that here was the woman he must marry, the woman who could bring him all that he sought in his future career, the woman his mother desired for him—and that was a consideration to be respected, for his mother was a very rich woman and was prepared to finance his future, provided he married into the "landed gentry" circle she so ardently admired. And then there was Lucia—Lucia, who had discovered that he was spending Christmas at the new country place his parents had rented with the intention of becoming landed gentry in a small way before spreading themselves in a wider sphere. "A quiet place to begin with," had been his mother's idea, and when they had learnt the ropes and found their feet they could move on and buy a bigger place. But now, even if they moved on, the damage was done. Here was Lucia threatening him with breach of promise and exposure, saying she would tell Jocelyn all about their engagement and create a sordid scandal that would finish any hope of his ever getting anywhere in county circles. It was infuriating—damnable!

The party for the Hunt Ball had been Jasmine's idea, not his. She had wanted to dance with Victor, for whom she had conceived a crazy infatuation: Victor, the popular dance band leader who was the idol of half the female hearts in Mayfair, but who had never been within her reach till now, for he moved in very high circles indeed. It was the chance in her lifetime to come across him in the country and find that she could attract him and make him notice her. Jasmine, thought Adrian furiously, was a bloody fool, had no pride, was ready to fling her cap over the windmill for any dirty dago that she fell in love with, and now here she was running after Victor—and Victor, by the hideous irony of fate, was Lucia's brother, and their Italian mother was married to the innkeeper at The Roebuck in Much Dithering of all places in the world!

There was no doubt that if Lucia meant to be nasty she held the best cards and could wreck his career; but if he could explain things to Jocelyn and put them in as favourable a light as possible, she might be reasonable, or if she wasn't—and he recalled her cool, uninterested acceptance of the fact that the Murchison-Bellabys and the Hedgecocks should be together at the Ball and felt that she had "placed" him and Jasmine to their disadvantage—well, what was *she* doing out with a man of whom no one knew anything at all? A young man in the Army was permitted indiscretions in search of amusement, but a young widow of high social position was not supposed to cause comment—not in Much Dithering, anyway—and he had a very shrewd suspicion that she had been "out on the tiles," as it were, without the knowledge of her well-bred relations. He'd soon find out for himself, so he went to pay a morning call on Jocelyn.

Jocelyn was busy in the kitchen, making cakes, and was annoyed when Bertha told her that Mr. Murchison-Bellaby was in the drawing-room and wanted to see her.

"Didn't you tell him I was very busy?"

"Oh, yes, 'm, and he said to tell you it was important and that he had lots of time and would wait till you were disengaged, please, 'm."

Jocelyn took off her overall of flowered linen and then put it on again. She wouldn't let him interrupt her morning work. She would let him see that she was really busy and not to be hindered, so with a firm resolve to cut short his visit, she washed her hands and went in. There was a faint suggestion of defiance about her, and a smudge of flour on her cheek that Adrian found enchanting, and again he noticed the distracting way her hair had of curling round her ears in gossamer golden tendrils. His first glance told him that she was going to be stern and serious. But how could she expect him to take her seriously when she had a smudge of flour on her face and was wearing such a decorative pinafore?

Jocelyn was disconcerted by his enjoyment of the situation, for he grinned cheerfully and said, "Yes, I know without being told so that I'm a nuisance, and that you are frightfully busy and never see any one in the morning, and that you simply hate me for coming, and quite a lot more of stuff like that; but you've got flour on your face and your hair isn't tidy and your pinafore is marvellous and you look simply adorable, and I'm *not* sorry for coming, and I mean to stay." He sat down on the fender-stool and laughed at her quick flash of anger.

She stood by the door and made no movement to join him. "I am very busy, Mr. Murchison-Bellaby, and I have no time to stay and talk to you."

"Just come and sit down over here one moment, Mrs. Renshawe." He indicated the low fender-stool beside him.

"I only want to explain a small matter. I particularly don't want you to misunderstand me, and I simply must stand all square over it."

Jocelyn still stood by the door. "You probably know your mother came to see me yesterday."

"Yes, I know. She simply would butt in. I'm awfully sorry. She's quite incurable, and we can't do anything about it; but let's wash her out and start again—it's the only way."

"I'm afraid I cannot start at all," returned Jocelyn stiffly. "I told your mother all that, and I have nothing to add. And I really am very busy indeed this morning. Good-bye, Mr. Murchison-Bellaby."

"It's just about the Ball the other night. I don't want you to get that wrong. It was all a rag, and Jasmine's party, by the way, not mine. She wanted to dance with Victor—he's the fashion in town, you know. I don't know what girls see in dagoes, myself. Lucia works at the place where Jasmine gets her frocks and I've danced with her in town; one *does*, you know—I mean, one knows people in town one doesn't meet on—well, on equal terms in the country."

Jocelyn was silent, realising that this was an attempt at justification, which amused her. Her silence seemed to embarrass Adrian.

"I expect you thought it odd—I mean, to see our party. It's a bit hard to explain to a person who is completely out of—I mean, you don't understand a rag. How could you? You've led a very quiet life. That's why I was completely staggered at seeing *you* at The Angel."

"Oh, I'm sorry if I give people the impression that I never go out," remarked Jocelyn in a distant tone. "And as for thinking it odd about *your* party—why, I never even thought about you. I think Lucia Hedgecock is a very charming girl, and I've always understood that young men had friends they don't take home to their parents. Ermyntrude puts me wise to quite a number of things that don't happen in our village."

The mention of Ermyntrude jarred him. He had forgotten all about her in his anxiety to "explain" Lucia. "Oh—er—yes," he said rather lamely. "Look here, Mrs. Renshawe, let's get things straight between us. I know, and I know *you* know, for I expect Ermyntrude's been talking, that I've been a fool. Well, most men are fools now and then; but—"

"I know nothing at all about you," interrupted Jocelyn, "and I'm not at all interested, so please don't tell me about your follies; there's no need."

"Oh, look here, Mrs. Renshawe, please don't be so—so *icebound*. I'm in dead earnest. I want you to understand about that Ball and about Ermyntrude and—and everything."

"There is no need that I should understand."

He got up, suddenly angry at her continued coldness. She shouldn't get away with things so easily. "Mrs. Renshawe, it was just as big a surprise for me to see you at The Angel, I assure you; but, as a matter of fact, I found it rather reassuring, for it seemed to suggest that the ice-cold goddess has a human side if one's only lucky enough to find a method of thawing her a bit. To find the highly respected Mrs. Renshawe enjoying a night out with a perfect stranger of whom no one knows the smallest thing except that he—"

"I have no intention of discussing my reasons for going to the Hunt Ball. They do not concern any one."

"Oh, yes, they do. Quite a lot of people are very interested in what you do. You have a reputation to consider in Much Dithering, Mrs. Renshawe."

Jocelyn's eyes flashed angrily, but he went on blandly:

"'Boys will be boys,' as mother says, and I don't deny that the siren at The Roebuck is very seductive, but that's by the way and quite harmless. But to catch the more than charming Mrs. Renshawe, the pattern of all the virtues, on the hop really *is* a different matter. Mother *would* be surprised. D'you know, I sat all through dinner one night and listened to an inexhaustible catalogue of your perfections, and I don't mind admitting that it left me cold; but when I discover a flaw in the crystal—then I sit up and take notice! It's all very well to cling to what mamma calls 'your charming Victorian dignity'—it's an excellent camouflage, incidentally, but it's really time to realise yourself as an ordinary human being and acknowledge that you are just like the rest of us."

"Where does all this lead to, and what is your object in being insulting, Mr. Murchison-Bellaby?"

"Oh, I say, now you're upset."

"I'm not upset. I'm merely telling you that all this is of no interest to me."

He stood in front of her. "Oh! Then am I to understand that you are interested in that bounder from the pub? What's the attraction? Do you know they say *he* is the burglar? What do you think?"

Jocelyn's colour flowed and ebbed, but she looked at him steadily. "That it's a lie," she said sharply.

"It's quite probably true. No one knows who or what he is, and there were tracks half-covered by the snow leading to the pub from The Place, *and* he left in a hurry the next morning. Where did he go? He left no address. He came here out of the blue and went away into the blue."

"I really can't waste any more time, Mr. Murchison-Bellaby." Jocelyn turned to the door and opened it. "Good-morning."

Adrian shrugged. "Since you *will* have it, Mrs. Renshawe, good-morning."

He went out, looking very angry, and as the hall door banged behind him Jocelyn sat down on the fender-stool and wondered why her knees suddenly felt weak.

However, she determined not to give way to her alarm and set herself to write some of her Christmas letters which had been neglected. But she was not destined to get far, for glancing up from her writing-table she saw to her intense disgust the approach of Colonel Tidmarsh, and was instantly filled with a suspicion that she was about to receive a second proposal. She resolved to settle that matter definitely, so she called Bertha and told her to say she was at home to Colonel Tidmarsh and to bring in some tea and biscuits.

"My goodness!" said Bertha brightly. "Ain't we having a day! The next thing will be that there burglar gent blowing along. Shall I let *him* in, too, 'm?"

Jocelyn was annoyed at the damsel's naive familiarity. Bertha always was "difficult," being spontaneous in her human interest in domestic and social happenings. "Bertha, you must not talk like that," she said severely. "Show Colonel Tidmarsh in, and make *no* remarks to him."

"No fear!" retorted Bertha. "He ain't the kind that calls for remarks. He gives you a stony stare and freezes you up. One sight of his blue nose gives me the shivers, 'm."

Colonel Tidmarsh had played with the idea of presenting Jocelyn with a pot of bulbs that had come on nice and early in his greenhouse, but as he was far from sure of the result of his effort to come to a satisfactory understanding, he had decided that he would postpone the presentation until he was certain that he would have a share in the pleasure of the future unfolding of their scented loveliness. For the moment, therefore, he was merely presenting his more or less unadorned self, and as Adrian's earlier call had been accompanied by a presentation of expensive hot-house blooms, which now decorated the drawing-room overmantel, Ambrose's unadorned self made a remarkably unimpressive entry.

Jocelyn shook hands with resignation. "It's such an unpleasant day that you really shouldn't have come out at all, Colonel Tidmarsh."

"I came," he exclaimed, warming his cold hands at the fire and rubbing them to restore the circulation, "because, Mrs. Renshawe, I thought I could count on not being interrupted by other visitors. I really don't think any one will venture out on such an inclement morning. Anyhow," he added with an awkward laugh, "I hope not, most sincerely. I have something important to say to you."

Jocelyn stiffened and realised that escape was impossible. She would, it seemed, have to endure another proposal of marriage. It was really very annoying.

"You must have a cup of tea," she said, without concealing any of the resignation she felt.

"I have had a long talk with Miss Pallfrey," Ambrose explained, settling down in a comfortable chair. "I won't disguise from you that I have a very high opinion of Miss Pallfrey. She has the rare gift of sympathetic understanding that so few people seem to possess. She is indeed a woman in a thousand. She has made me very happy, Mrs. Renshawe. She has given me reason to *hope*. There is a poem I expect you know—'Hope springs eternal,' and so on."

Jocelyn did not quite know what he meant. It was not the beginning she had expected. She looked at him in perplexity. "You are telling me about Aunt Mellicent? Did she—? I mean, are you—?"

"She and I understand each other. I have faith in her judgment. I can only assure you, Jocelyn—I may call you 'Jocelyn,' may I not—?"

Jocelyn felt dazed. This was most mystifying. "Oh, yes, in the circumstances, why not?" she returned. "This is quite unexpected. I had no idea—But I'm very glad indeed. I think it's a splendid idea. Dear Aunt Mellicent, she thinks such a lot of you. She never ceases to sing your praises."

"Jocelyn!" He got up and stood beside her, holding out his hand. "My dear Jocelyn, you make me very happy. I can scarcely believe my good fortune. This moment has been worth waiting for."

His fervour startled her, and she had the alarming thought that she had, after all, misunderstood him. Had he been talking of her and not of Aunt Mellicent? Did he think that she had accepted him? He had taken her hand and bent to kiss it.

"You have made me the happiest of men," he said solemnly.

Jocelyn was appalled and took the only course that occurred to her shattered senses. "I think," she said hastily, "that Aunt Mellicent is a lucky woman. I mean, you are a lucky man. She will make you an ideal wife. She and you—I mean, you and—she—"

She stopped in unhappy confusion and he released her hand, staring at her uncomprehendingly.

"I've always thought," she went on in desperation, "that you and she would be an ideal couple. I hoped you would realise it for yourself, and now you—you have. It will make her so very happy. She is so sweet, so full of sympathy, so—oh!" She had to stop, breathless, incoherent, incapable of talking any more to stave off the horrid explanation that she knew was inevitable.

He looked at her in chilly displeasure. "What do you imagine I meant?" he inquired coldly.

"Why, that you are going to marry Aunt Mellicent, of course." She recovered herself and was able to smile. "I think it's a splendid idea!"

"If you think so, Mrs. Renshawe, I have no more to say. I am deeply hurt. I will trouble you no longer." At the door he turned. "Is this your last word?"

"I still think," replied Jocelyn firmly, "that you and Aunt Mellicent will be an ideal couple. I wish you every happiness, Colonel Tidmarsh. She will make you far happier than I could ever have done. After all, you are sixty, she is fifty-eight, and I am twenty-five. Doesn't it really sound more suitable as it is?"

He stood looking at her for a moment in stern displeasure. "I am deeply disappointed, Mrs. Renshawe. I had hoped for a kinder hearing. You have displayed a spirit of mockery I had not imagined you to possess. You have shattered my ideal." He bowed very stiffly and left her.

Jocelyn watched his departure with relief. "Poor Aunt Mellicent! I wish she would step in and soothe his injured feelings. I hope I haven't implied too much."

CHAPTER TWENTY-THREE

THE news of the burglary naturally came as a shock to the residents of Much Dithering, which had maintained an aura of respectability for so long that crime was practically unknown in the locality. The snow was lying rather deep and a hard frost had made getting about somewhat difficult and unpleasant, but Miss Pallfrey sent her maid Eunice (locally pronounced "Euniss") round with some invitations and gathered a few friends to discuss the latest details.

Mrs. Pomfret came in on her way to a practice of the glee-singers, and Colonel Tidmarsh was glad to drop in and air his views and theories. The Honourable Augusta looked in for a short time; but as she was walking she left early so as to get home before dark.

Jocelyn came unwillingly, feeling that it might look odd if she failed to put in an appearance. Two days had passed since Adrian's visit, and she was unnerved and shrank from hearing the subject discussed. Still, she dared not give any one the idea that it was of particular interest to her, and she maintained an attitude of unruffled calm and was even a little more noticeably cheerful than usual, for she was fighting against allowing herself to harbour any suspicion and kept her flag flying in a sort of gay defiance of the dark suggestions that she knew were being made regarding Gervase.

The news came that the Priory also had been broken into, but that the burglar had been foiled of what he no doubt hoped would be a good haul. The Renshawe sapphires and diamonds were celebrated, but they were safe in the bank, and only a few old gold bracelets and a brooch or two had been taken, and the silver was still intact. On the whole there was plenty to talk about at the tea-party, and it promised to be enjoyable.

The shock to Much Dithering was shattering and created as much stir as a volcanic upheaval. Much Dithering was in the news. Public attention was suddenly focused on its hitherto almost unguessed-at existence.

"Our names," wailed Miss Pallfrey, "are being bandied about by vulgar newspaper reporters. One tried to interview *me*— goodness knows why, except that someone might have told him of my dear mother's gold locket with papa's hair, and the diamond ring that was my grandmother's—vulgar curiosity, no doubt—and I refused to see him."

"Quite right," said the Honourable Augusta, who was a little shaken by the knowledge that her house had been actually entered and prowled about in by an intruder while she had been sitting in her drawing-room talking to Miss Pallfrey, for it was at that time that her dressing-table had been ransacked and her old-fashioned jewel-case taken, which contained some gold bracelets and brooches and a pair of gold-crested cuff-links. No doubt the thief had explored the whole house and learned his way about in that quiet house while the servants were safe in the servants' hall at tea and she was occupied with her guests.

"It's evidently a jewel thief," she said, "for the silver was in the dining-room and in the pantry as usual, and he never touched it. He is evidently the sort of man who slips things into pockets and doesn't want to be burdened with bulk. It is very disturbing."

"Dreadful! He may return and remove anything that he observed while he had leisure to notice."

"No." The Honourable Augusta shook her head. "No, I don't think so. He will know that the police will simply swarm in the place now, and that any attempt to return and take the silver would be found out at once. No, he won't come back. It was the sapphires and diamonds he came here for; he knew about their value."

"Colonel Tidmarsh," said Miss Pallfrey, "has grave suspicions of that Mr. Blythe. He is greatly distressed because he feels responsible for having introduced him to people here. He knows nothing—absolutely nothing—about his character, or what he does for a living since he left the Army. He poses as a rich man, it seems—and of course he would be if he lived on the proceeds of valuable hauls of jewellery. It looks highly suspicious to me; and, what is more, he has left the village—a most suspicious coincidence, to my mind."

"And the coming of the snow just then has been so hampering," put in Mrs. Pomfret. "Somehow one has felt one could do nothing—not that one could, I suppose, in any case."

"The police have the matter in hand," said Colonel Tidmarsh in an important tone. "Of course, as far as Blythe is concerned, I have no real reason to think that—but one never knows, one never knows."

"Yes," agreed Miss Pallfrey. "And it is odd—isn't it?—that he was out somewhere that very night and left early next morning."

"Rubbish!" broke in Mrs. Pomfret. "The evidence is so clearly against him that it is quite obvious that he didn't do it. No one would be such a fool as to stay in the village and commit a burglary under every one's nose—on a snowy night, too—and then skip."

"Ah!" cried Miss Pallfrey. "But Eunice says there were tracks that led back to The Roebuck, where we know he was staying, from The Place by a side gate."

Colonel Tidmarsh shook his head. "It is very remarkable," he said gloomily. "I feel terribly guilty about all this."

At this point Jocelyn arrived. She overheard the last remark. "Guilty?" she echoed. "What are *you* guilty of, Colonel Tidmarsh?"

"Oh, but of course you've heard!" cried Miss Pallfrey. "The burglary the other night—"

"But why should *you* feel guilty?" Jocelyn asked, sitting on the sofa beside Colonel Tidmarsh. "Surely no one could connect *you* with a burglary?"

"Ah!" sighed her aunt, shaking her head. "Burglary nowadays seems to be almost a gentleman's profession. In the old days when people like Bill Sykes were the burgling class one knew where one was; but nowadays any one might be a burglar. Still, we really needn't conclude that this Mr. Blythe is really guilty."

"Mr. Blythe?" cried Jocelyn indignantly. "How utterly absurd!"

"Circumstantial evidence certainly points to him," maintained Colonel Tidmarsh. "And I shouldn't be at all surprised. After all, what do we know about him?"

Jocelyn sat very still. She glanced at Ambrose and noted the mulish obstinacy in his narrow face and the gleam of satisfaction in his eyes. He was evidently determined to believe the worst because he disliked Gervase. For a moment she thought of telling them that Gervase had an excellent alibi for the evening in question, but as she was about to speak she changed her mind and said quietly:

"What is the evidence?"

"Footsteps in the snow leading from The Place through the shrubbery to the short-cut to the village and The Roebuck, and the fact that Blythe was not in for dinner and came in very late," explained Ambrose. "It didn't snow till after midnight, I know, and *some one* left The Place after it began to snow."

"I don't believe a word of it!" said Mrs. Pomfret. "Not about Mr. Blythe, I mean. He told me the other night that he knew every note of the tenor line in 'The Messiah.' *Burglars* don't sing 'The Messiah.' And he is devoted to opera."

"'Music hath charms to soothe the savage breast,'" murmured Miss Pallfrey irrelevantly.

"Orpheus with his lute worked all sorts of miracles," said Mrs. Pomfret, and sang a few bars, "but there's not a word of *his* being a burglar."

"We're getting away from the point," put in Colonel Tidmarsh. "The point is, who is the burglar? We all have our suspicions, and if I'm asked I shall naturally tell the police all I know about Blythe."

Miss Pallfrey suddenly gave a little cry. "Jocelyn! That man— Mr. Blythe—went to see Augusta that afternoon. No doubt he was spying out the land then and went back later. No one would suspect anything, and it would be so easy to steal anything he fancied. Oh, dear! Evidently he stayed at The Roebuck in order to become acquainted with the neighbourhood."

"I can't really feel responsible for him," said Colonel Tidmarsh, "because he actually stayed at The Roebuck before he knew I lived here. Or—wait! No, I see it all now. No doubt he found out—all crooks have means of finding things out—yes, no doubt whatever, he tracked me to Much Dithering and stayed at the inn in order to pretend he was here by accident. From the window of the inn he could see me leave my gate, and he had nothing to do but walk out and meet me casually on the bridge. Mark you, he knew *me* at once, but I hadn't the slightest idea who he was. He was always the sort of man I disliked—a good-for-nothing bounder who thought practical jokes were funny and got drunk and went round smashing things up. He was always in debt and finally cleared out of India in most reprehensible circumstances in order to evade arrest—something to do with a native moneylender, I believe. Anyway, he vanished, and no one heard any more about him, and I had forgotten he ever existed till that day when he came up to me and told me a cock-and-bull story of his successful career in Australia and what a rich man he was, and promised to give me a tip to make a little money on the Stock Exchange—said that he stood to make fifty thousand himself—completely fooled me. I can't think why I ever believed in him; but he was always a plausible scoundrel. No, I don't feel that I am responsible for this at all. My only regret is that I was the means of introducing him to Mrs. Renshawe and actually took him to her house. I've no doubt her house is the next on his list if he ever dares to come back. We must take precautions at once. Mrs. Renshawe may I offer you my assistance in any way that may be necessary? A man can sometimes be helpful in many ways. He has resource in dealing with emergencies that a woman lacks. Let me—"

"Thank you, Colonel Tidmarsh," returned Jocelyn calmly; "but I think your assistance had better be offered to Aunt Millicent, who has no resources to fall back on either. As you see, she is far more nervous and perturbed than I, and I'm sure she will be very grateful for your protection. Mrs. Pomfret, isn't it time we were going along to the Parish Hall? The glees and folk-songs demand our attention." She rose and began to button up her suède jacket. "Good-night, Aunt Mellicent."

"Mrs. Renshawe," said Colonel Tidmarsh in an agitated tone, "let me see you home after this practice. I am seriously alarmed. You might come to harm. You might—Why, anything might happen! You are wearing your pearls—I've noticed that you always wear them—so might someone else. Mrs. Renshawe, you have no one to take care of you—I must insist—"

"Oh, Jocelyn!" wailed her aunt, wringing her hands. "Colonel Tidmarsh is right. You need a protector, my love. If you must go to the practice, let him go home with you afterwards. And another thing, Jocelyn; while you have been here, anything may have been happening at your house. He may have watched you go out and taken the opportunity to burgle the Dower House. The miniature of grandmother—he may have noticed it when he was dining with you, or the silver candlesticks, or Aunt Alice's silver soup-tureen. Oh, my dear, don't worry about the glees to-night. Go straight home with Colonel Tidmarsh and see if all is well."

"Come, Mrs. Renshawe," commanded Colonel Tidmarsh, holding open the door, "I will see you home and deal with anything that may be necessary."

"I've already told you that I require no assistance," returned Jocelyn with spirit. "I have no fears for my very few treasures; no burglar would be bothered to steal them. I shall certainly go to the practice with Mrs. Pomfret. She and I are not in the least nervous. Are we, Mrs. Pomfret?"

"I'm certainly not," laughed Mrs. Pomfret. "And I'll see you home, if you, like—or Percival will. Good-night, Miss Pallfrey. Good-night, Colonel Tidmarsh. No, no, we'll be quite safe. My dear man, it's only a few yards to the Parish Hall. We are in no danger, I assure you. Stay and protect Miss Pallfrey."

Jocelyn and Mrs. Pomfret succeeded in making their escape and stood for a moment outside in the clear starlight to breathe in the crisp cold air that was such a relief after the over-heated, stuffy little room they had left.

"Oh, dear!" laughed Jocelyn. "What a commotion!"

"Jocelyn," said Mrs. Pomfret sternly. "What has come over you? And what's this I hear about Adrian Murchison-Bellaby visiting you?"

"Oh, him!" Jocelyn closed the garden gate and they went along the road to the Parish Hall. "Do you know, he has actually proposed, and so has his mother?"

"Oh, but you can't!" protested Mrs. Pomfret, aghast. "I—oh, no, Jocelyn, be guided by me and by your aunt. These new people—Oh, I know, my dear. I told you we had to be friendly and help them to get on in the parish and all that; but to *marry* them—I mean, him—oh, no, it would be a great mistake."

"Do you think I ought to marry Colonel Tidmarsh?" demanded Jocelyn.

"Well, I think it would be a good thing in many ways. Not exactly romantic, dearie; but, after all—" she sighed—"what is romance? Common sense lasts, romance doesn't. Colonel Tidmarsh would be kind and take care of you, and he's very fond of you, I'm sure. Why, he was so fierce just now, so strong and manly, that it gave me quite a thrill. Didn't it you? He showed so plainly that he wanted to take care of you and protect you. The love of a good man, my dear—it's not to be despised. Yes, since you ask me, duckie, I think you ought to marry him."

They arrived at the hall, and Jocelyn was saved the necessity of a reply as the vicar greeted them in the porch and they all went in together.

CHAPTER TWENTY-FOUR

THERE was no news of Gervase and no new development in the search for clues regarding the burglaries. Local opinion was firmly convinced that the stranger who had so suddenly come to stay at The Roebuck, and as suddenly left, must have a connection with the affair, and no one was louder and more emphatic in his denunciations than Ambrose Tidmarsh. He could not let the matter rest. The fact that Jocelyn refused to listen to his courtship and had been flippant enough to suggest that he and her aunt would be an ideal couple rankled badly. He did not actually connect her peculiar conduct with a preference for Gervase—that would have been unthinkable; but he felt that she was upholding the belief that the story was false in order to annoy him—feminine perversity, of course, and he consoled himself with the reflection that sometimes women behaved in a foolish, irresponsible way to conceal their real feelings and goad their despairing suitors. Mrs. Renshawe was a very shy and modest lady who possibly shrank from a display of natural feeling. He would proceed with caution and play a waiting game, a determination that was strengthened when it came to his ears (via Mrs. Goodbun, who had got the story from Bertha, who had been greatly interested in Adrian's morning call and could not help overhearing quite a lot when she was dusting the hall) that Mrs. Renshawe hadn't half given young Murchison-Bellaby what for and fair wigged him till he left the house looking as angry and red in the face as Mrs. Faggot's old turkey-cock, from which remarkable statement he gathered that Jocelyn had dismissed Adrian as unkindly as she had himself, and from which he took fresh courage. With a woman one never knew where one was, but he found consolation in the sweet reliability and tenderness of Miss Mellicent, who seemed to understand his feelings so well and reassured him as to Jocelyn's one day relenting and coming to realise what happiness and devotion a good man would bring her.

"Only those women," said Miss Mellicent with a wistfulness that touched him deeply, "who have never had the inestimable happiness of knowing the love of a man for the woman he desires for his wife can realise what the lack of it must mean. Our dear Jocelyn married so young, and was widowed before she had time to estimate the blessings of a good husband, so we must make allowance for her reluctance to face the problem of matrimony again. Give her time, Colonel Tidmarsh."

"Time?" Ambrose looked gloomy. "But time goes on. Miss Pallfrey; it passes so quickly when one is no longer young. I want to be married and settled. I haven't any time to waste.

I'm not young, I need the care and attention of a wife. I'm tired of Mrs. Goodbun and her filthy cooking. I want to be properly taken care of and—well, for want of a better word, 'cherished.'"

"There is no better word," said Miss Mellicent with a gentle sigh. *"Cherish!"* She repeated it with a lingering tenderness that gave it a significance he had not realized before. "Ah, Colonel Tidmarsh, 'to love and cherish!' What a beautiful phrase! Like a poem!"

"'Pon my soul," said Ambrose, deeply touched by her understanding, "'pon my soul, Miss Pallfrey, you are a—a true friend. I have the deepest regard—I—well, really, I can hardly tell you what your sympathy means to me. You give me courage. You restore my self-respect. Bless you, dear lady!" He laid his hand on her shoulder for a moment and pressed it gently. "It is at a time like this—of doubt and uncertainty—that a man learns who are his true friends. He learns, too, his own mistakes and how it might be possible to—ah—er—start afresh with—ah—er—fresh hopes. But I will say no more. I must think. This is serious. I have had new light—but no, I will say no more." He seemed very agitated, and Miss Mellicent was quite upset when he took his departure, still talking, she considered, rather incoherently.

Jocelyn was really behaving in a very silly way, her aunt thought, feeling vexed at her unkind refusal to consider Colonel Tidmarsh's formal proposal. She had hurt him deeply, and he had brought his lacerated feelings to *her* for comfort and sympathy. Poor man, he was quite angry, and justly so, for he had never anticipated such a rebuff. Possibly, thought Miss Mellicent a little guiltily, it had been her fault, for it had been because of her encouragement and her belief that Jocelyn felt for him what she hoped Jocelyn *was* feeling—

"Dear me, I'm getting rather mixed," she murmured aloud.

The truth was. Miss Mellicent was so romantic that she had invented a moving love tale about Colonel Tidmarsh and Jocelyn, true enough about Ambrose, if a trifle over-idealized, but entirely imaginary as far as Jocelyn was concerned, and now the pretty castle in the air had crashed in ruins. Poor Colonel Tidmarsh was sadly disillusioned and his faith in women shattered, and Jocelyn had retired behind a cold barrier of reserve and refused to discuss the affair with her aunt or her mother-in-law. Everything had gone wrong, and Miss Mellicent was quite upset and unhappy.

Meantime the burglaries continued to be the chief topic of interest in the Ditherings. Joe Hedgecock admitted that the evidence against Gervase was distinctly nasty, but maintained that he was a nice sort of gentleman and had a way with him—told a good story, too, and had knocked about all over the world and knew his way about.

"No doubt about that," agreed Adrian with a laugh. "All these gentlemen burglars are up to that sort of thing. Confidence tricks always go well—nice hearty blokes who can talk well and get you off your guard—all part of the trade. No one has ever seen this chap before, and it is rather odd that he went off into the blue directly he'd got what he was evidently after. He'd been able to get a good look at my sister's jewellery that very evening, for he was at the Hunt Ball we all went over to Totterford for."

"You don't say so?"

"Yes, I was rather surprised to see him; but I dare say he poses as a hunting man if he thinks it's a good line to take. He was in good company, I will say." Adrian laughed again.

Joe Hedgecock gave him a sidelong glance as he refilled his glass with brandy. Adrian had dropped in at The Roebuck in a friendly fashion to hear the local gossip. Lucia and Victor had gone back to London, but he felt it politic to keep in with Joe. He had an uncomfortable feeling that Joe guessed something, or possibly Lucia had laid her story before him; and he was pretty sure he could be unpleasant if provoked. He went to The Roebuck against his will, but unable to stay away. He wanted to keep an eye on Joe and judge whether it was safe to let Much Dithering gossip couple his name with Jocelyn's or whether he would be wiser to exchange into the other battalion of his regiment and go abroad for a few years. Lucia might chuck up the business if someone else took her fancy. It was all a very tricky problem, and Joe Hedgecock was a dark horse who needed watching.

"Old Muleface is all for throwing mud at Mr. Blythe," remarked Joe presently. "He don't like him; but all I can say is, give me Mr. Blythe rather than *him*—nasty old tom cat! He's prowling round after Mrs. Renshawe, that's easy to see, but she's got too much sense—at least I hope so."

"What! That melancholy old bore? Good Lord, she wouldn't think of *that*, would she?"

"Well, the old woman is trying to persuade her to marry him. The girl what works for Mrs. Renshawe is a rare little gossip and brings out some funny tales at times." Again Adrian didn't quite like the look the landlord gave him. Something seemed to amuse him, and there was a gleam in his genial blue eyes, but his mouth set wryly.

Adrian had not gathered whether Joe knew about Jocelyn's having gone to the Hunt Ball. Any approach to the subject was a blank draw where Joe was concerned.

"Oh, so her maid is a gossip, is she?" Adrian asked lazily. "A smooth little piece, I should think; but I shouldn't imagine she had much to talk about. Mrs. Renshawe isn't the sort of woman who would be likely to cause the faintest whisper of scandal, surely? All the women here are so virtuous and well-bred that scandal must be dead and buried."

Joe's cheerful blandness did not vary. "You've said it, sir," he agreed briskly. "The Honourable and the old aunt keep her all wrapped in cotton-wool. They don't stand for scandal, and they're right. Scandal's a nasty thing, and don't do a place any good. Look at this here burglary—the cheap papers have got hold of it and worked it up in blinking great headlines, and the next thing is press photographers coming along and putting you in their dirty rags, and busloads of nasty-minded people crowding along and gaping."

"All good business, though," laughed Adrian. "Teas and gallons of beer."

"I don't stand for notoriety," returned Joe. "Business is business, I know, but I can't stand vulgar curiosity into a man's private affairs. The old ladies are right there. It's only the cheap kind of people that go out for publicity. Good breeding is out of date these days, but we could do with more of it—good blood and good manners—yes, sir!"

On the whole, Adrian thought he had better be getting along. The brandy at The Roebuck was excellent, but the landlord's manner was a trifle brusque now and then, and his occasional sarcasm had the peculiar effect of causing Adrian's mouth to feel dry and sawdusty.

On his return to The Place, Adrian found his mother in hysterics. A telegram from Jasmine, who had gone up to London that morning, had just been telephoned up by Mrs. Faggot from the post office to the effect that she and Victor had been married that afternoon and were leaving for a honeymoon on the Riviera, where Victor had an engagement with his band—a piece of news, incidentally, which had caused Mrs. Faggot so much excitement that she was extremely incoherent when she telephoned, and it was a matter of so much difficulty to understand her peculiar squawkings that Mrs. Murchison-Bellaby had had to call the butler to take down the message, which no doubt had been broadcast in the servants' hall as well as in the post office, where it had been given all the publicity that might have been expected. Mrs. Pomfret had been buying stamps at the moment the message had come. Mrs. Faggot had said, "Excuse me one minute, Mrs. Pomfret," and gone to answer the ringing of the telephone bell. "Yes! . . . What? 'Married . . . Victor . . . Going . . . Monte Carlo . . . Aeroplane . . . Casino . . . Band . . . Engagement. . . Jasmine.' Lor! Oh, my! Well, I never! But what else can you expect? Sows' ears don't make silk purses. Didn't I say that lot aren't no good? Oh, Mrs. Pomfret, did you ever! There, I've come over all funny-like. Gladys! Gladys, bring me a glass of cold water—I'm queer. Oh, dear! Oh, dear!"

Mrs. Faggot staggered from behind the post office counter and collapsed on the chair in the corner, opening and shutting her mouth and emitting little squeals that alarmed Mrs. Pomfret as she hastened to her side and began to fan her with a copy of the *Parish Magazine*, which she happened to have in her hand. Gladys hurried in from the kitchen with a glass of water, which unfortunately provoked an attack of hiccoughs that alternated with Mrs. Faggot's squeals, which became more excited as she endeavoured to impart the startling information she had just received and which it was her unpleasant duty to telephone on to The Place.

"Such a thing—hic—Mrs. Pomfret—hic—never in all my life—hic—and me a mother myself—hic—to tell that poor lady. Oh, dear—hic—dear! What have I always said—hic—Mrs. Pomfret? Them there people calling themselves landed—hic—gentry—disgraceful, that's what it is—hic."

"But what is it, Mrs. Faggot?" demanded Mrs. Pomfret, twittering with curiosity and impatience.

"It's that girl—hic—at The Place—gone off with the chap at The Roebuck—hic—*married*. Oh, dear—hic—drat it!"

"Oh, dear!" echoed Mrs. Pomfret, and, realising that Mrs. Faggot was in such a demented state of mind that she would almost certainly be indiscreet and convey the news to the whole of Much Dithering should any one else come in, she took her arm and said firmly, "Now, Mrs. Faggot, pull yourself together. This is serious, and you ought to remember that you received that message *confidentially* and must not shout it aloud like this. Private messages must not be spread over the village. Come into the other room till you are better and let Gladys stay in the shop—and mind, Gladys, don't tell any one about this."

A little later Mrs. Faggot recovered sufficiently to telephone the devastating message to Mrs. Murchison-Bellaby, and Mrs. Pomfret, cramming on her hat firmly against the strong wind, hurried on to the Parish Hall, where the preparations for the Mothers' Union Social were in full blast. Jocelyn was cutting a ham in wafer-like slices for the meat tea—"real genteel," as Mrs. Goodbun remarked approvingly, laying a clean tablecloth over the dish. Mrs. Pallfrey was cutting "slab" cake at another table, and there was a pleasant atmosphere of bustle and gossip flavoured with a strong odour of coffee.

"Jocelyn," said Mrs. Pomfret, who felt that she must tell someone or burst, "a message has just come for Mrs. Murchison-Bellaby that Jasmine has married that strange man at The Roebuck and gone to Monte Carlo."

"I don't believe it," returned Jocelyn, looking up from carving the ham. "I simply don't believe it; but I—I think I'm going to faint." And she did.

Mrs. Pomfret declared it was the heat, but the coincidence startled her.

CHAPTER TWENTY-FIVE

ANTIBES seemed to Gervase to have a climate preferable to that of England at present, to judge from the reports of the weather which he read in a copy of a Continental issue of a London newspaper as he sat in the sunshine under the tall pines and looked out over the deeply blue sea breaking in little dazzling wavelets on the rocks below where he sat. Snow, frost, thaw, and fog—how dreary it sounded, and how it must hamper the round of social activities in Much Dithering and other villages buried in charming but mud-soaked surroundings all over England! The Ditherings lay low in the valley of the Waver, and would therefore be fogbound and even more depressing than during the fortnight he had spent there. Jocelyn would be busy always, and no doubt taking the fog and other vileness as part of the scheme of nature and therefore a seasonable happening to be endured as cheerfully as possible. In places like Much Dithering, he imagined, one always endured unpleasant circumstances without question or effort to elude them.

What would Jocelyn think of the colour and sunshine out here, he wondered—the Alpes Maritimes rearing their glittering white crests against the blue of the sky behind Antibes, and here by the rocky shore the sun beating down warmly and bringing out the scent of the tall pines that grew everywhere. Across the Bay, just behind the Hotel du Cap, Cannes stretched gleaming whitely against the long range of the blue Esterels, and the hills all along the coast were dotted with villas among the grey-green of the olive groves and the blue shadows of the pines.

Gervase had been here for some days on a matter of business that, after the manner of all business matters, moved slowly, and the days went by, and still he waited for its conclusion. He had a great deal to think about, and in a way was not sorry for the delay. He thought about Jocelyn. Would she break loose from her moorings and brave the wrath of her mother-in-law and aunt to marry an adventurer? Would her sense of duty tie her for ever to the trivial round of village life, or would she have the courage to put her hands into his and come away with him— out here, for instance? There was a villa for sale that he would like to buy for her. He could picture her in the garden under the pine trees. She would probably be faintly sunburnt, her pale skin smoothly golden-tinted, her hair full of sunshine, and her lovely eyes bluer and not so serious. He wanted Jocelyn not to take life quite so seriously, to smile a little more often, for her smile was so enchanting. She needed rousing from her placid lethargy, to come alive. A life spent entirely in the Ditherings lacked experience of practically everything he considered made life worth living. The seasons went round inevitably, and Jocelyn followed their course serenely and indifferently. She probably picked her first violet or primrose with the same annual ecstasy, worried over the weather for the Parish Fête with precisely the same annual anxiety (and with the same justification!), grieved over the annual difficulty in saving the harvest, sighed when the evenings began to grow shorter and the leaves to turn yellow, and applied herself with the same earnestness to sing glees and practise country dances in the winter season. She was like a plant that had been brought up in twilight and was under-developed. She needed the tonic of sunshine in her life.

He wondered if she was missing him. He had stirred her senses, made her realise that her life lacked something she had not previously known to exist. He knew that she was falling in love with him, that if he had kissed her and asked her to marry him the night he had brought her back from the Hunt Ball she would have consented. She had been so transparently happy, so transported from her usual placid existence. But he wanted her to have a little time to realize things, to decide whether she wanted him when she had time to consider. He had not played quite fair, and he had to climb out of a difficulty which he had not foreseen and go back presently and put the matter clearly before her. Then, perhaps, he would bring her out here, and she would learn a little about colour and sunshine and being alive.

He lit a pipe and picked up the English newspaper again without any particular interest, for his attention was not on the pages he turned over. But strangely enough his eyes caught the name "Much Dithering "in the headline of a small paragraph and he read, at first with interest and then again in perturbed astonishment, that there had been a sensational jewel robbery at the country residence of Mr. Leopold Murchison-Bellaby at Much Dithering, and that there was good reason to suspect that a stranger to the neighbourhood passing by the name of Blythe, who had disappeared the day after the theft had occurred but before its discovery, was connected with the affair and was believed to be in league with a large gang of jewel thieves on the Continent. Colonel Ambrose Tidmarsh, it was stated, had had a slight previous acquaintance with Mr. Blythe, and had declared him to be a man of dubious character of whom he could only say that in the days when he had known him in India he had borne a bad reputation. (Good old Ambrose!) Also there had been a robbery of some important jewellery at the Priory, the home of the Honourable Mrs. Renshawe, whose family jewels, which were of great value, were fortunately in safe keeping at the bank, and so escaped the fate of Mrs. Murchison-Bellaby's emeralds and diamonds. Mr. Adrian Murchison-Bellaby had called in the local police, and the case was now being fully investigated. The movements of Mr. Blythe were being traced, and it was known that he had taken a car abroad, and Colonel Tidmarsh was able to supply the important information that he was going to Monte Carlo. (Again, good old Ambrose; quite a mine of useful—even if inaccurate—information!)

What about Jocelyn? What was she thinking? And what had started the suggestion that he was concerned in the matter? It was extremely disconcerting to think that the police were on his trail and that Monte Carlo was so uncomfortably close to Antibes. On the whole, he thought, with a sudden resolve, he would give them a run for their money. The adventure of the idea appealed to him, and he felt quite a pleasant exhilaration as he folded the paper and went into the lounge of the hotel to order an apéritif.

It was certainly a day of surprises, for as he sat and waited for his Martini, looking round the tables in the lounge, he saw Jasmine and Victor staring at him with as much surprise as he felt at seeing them. He decided at once that he would behave as if he had no knowledge of the news he had just read, and lead them to suppose that he had no idea that he was a suspected person. He rose and crossed to their table.

"This is a pleasant surprise. May I join you?"

Jasmine smiled at him and Victor jumped up and placed a chair for him. "Yes, it is a surprise, Mr. Blythe—and, may I, too, say a pleasant one? We are on our honeymoon. Perhaps that is also a surprise?"

"It most certainly is." Gervase looked exceedingly astonished, then laughed and sat down. "You young people don't waste much time, do you? May I congratulate you and wish you good fortune and so on?"

"That's awfully nice of you," drawled Jasmine. "Yes, I expect it's a bit of a shock to Much Dithering; but it's a place that deserves a shock. It needs a good shaking up. I expect it's simply aghast at our bolting like this."

"I shouldn't be surprised," agreed Gervase, and raised his glass. "Your health, Yasmin!"

Victor looked at him quick as if he would say something, but stopped and, with a sharp glance at Jasmine, sat down and took up his glass. "Thank you, Mr. Blythe, for my wife and myself. And now tell me what *you* are doing here."

"I'm cruising along the coast to Monte Carlo, as a matter of fact. I'm going to meet a friend of mine from South Africa, and then we're thinking of going on to Austria for a week or two— winter sports and so on. I'm staying here for a day or two. I like it. There are nice people staying here, and it's quiet—well, when I say 'quiet,' it's not as crazy as some of the places along the coast—ideal for a honeymoon, in fact. I must remember that. Are you staying long?"

"No, we, too, are going on to Monte Carlo. Victor has an engagement to play at the Hotel Superbe for six weeks. It will be marvellous. Shall we see you there?"

"I shall make a point of meeting you," Gervase assured her as he got up. "Perhaps I shall see you to-night at dinner—or afterwards? The Casino is quite a good spot about ten o'clock."

"We will look out for you. Come on, Victor. I'm starving."

Gervase watched them go into the dining-room and stood for a moment considering the situation. Then he had a leisurely meal and sat over his coffee till he saw the Hedgecocks leave the dining-room and go towards the lift. "And now," he said to himself, "I think I'll do what I can towards shaking up Much Dithering. As Yasmini says, it deserves a shock—or two."

As a matter of fact, he received a considerable shock himself that evening when, meeting the Hedgecock couple in the cocktail bar at the Casino, he joined them as they went to the tables for a game of roulette. Jasmine sat at the table and Victor and Gervase stood behind her. Jasmine lost once or twice, and then Victor won on the Number 9 and stretched forward to pick up his winnings and stake again. As he did so, his sleeve slipped back over his shirt-cuff and Gervase remarked that he wore gold cuff-links with a distinctive crest. Leaning forward, he watched with close interest while Victor placed his stake. The cuff-links took his fancy, and he wanted to be sure of the crest; he believed he had seen it before.

A little later he was on his way back to England.

CHAPTER TWENTY-SIX

JOCELYN's shock on hearing Mrs. Pomfret's sensational news came as a climax to her strained emotions and left her feeling limp and spiritless. She felt unable to cope with the rush of Mrs. Pomfret's "Festive Season," but was fortunately spared the necessity of inventing excuses for a sudden attack of influenza laid the Honourable Augusta low, and Jocelyn's constant attendance was demanded, since Mellowes was an indifferent nurse, and the patient refused to have a trained nurse. As usual Jocelyn slipped into the breach and retired to spend a few days at the Priory, out of reach of the sensations and excitements of the village. At the Priory she was safe from Adrian and Ambrose, and, although her peace of mind was shaken, she was free to be quiet and collect and rearrange her chaotic thoughts.

She had heard, of course, that Victor Hedgecock and not Gervase was the hero of Jasmine's elopement; but there was still no news of Gervase, and she was completely in the dark as to the solution of the mystery that undoubtedly existed. Her mother-in-law declared that the visit she had had from him was a ruse to get into the house, and that it was he who had stolen her jewel-case, hoping it contained the family sapphires. She, too, was troubled and full of suspicions she refused to discuss with any one, and made her influenza an excuse to be snappy and unbearable to Jocelyn and Mellowes. In fact, she went so far as to blame Mellowes for the robbery, since it seemed that Mellowes had asked Mr. Blythe to wait in the hall while she took his message to the drawing-room, thus allowing him to look about him and find out the probable direction of stairs and landings and so on. Jocelyn pointed out that he couldn't possibly have left the hall and found her bedroom, taken the jewel-case and returned to the hall in the time, but her mother-in-law retorted that he had probably—in fact, must certainly have—slipped in later when Mellowes had gone to her tea, and he had learnt just enough of the house to enable him to go quickly upstairs, take the case, and make his escape. Gervase had called on *her*, Jocelyn remembered, on the afternoon on which the Honourable Augusta accused him of the robbery, but there had been, she realised, the interval between the time he left her owing to her throng of visitors and the time at which he returned to take her out to dinner, and there certainly had been time to call at the Priory, but she could not think that he had time or opportunity to carry out the burglary at The Place, seeing that Jasmine had actually been wearing at the Hunt Ball some of the jewellery said to have been stolen, and, according to

Adrian, his party had got home a great deal later than the hour at which Gervase had left her at her door.

What had Gervase meant, she wondered, when he told her that he was a *"bad hat"*? It was as if he had withdrawn himself—been ashamed of something. If he hadn't been so obviously embarrassed during the drive home from the ball, she would have felt less perturbed; but there had been something she was unable then, and now, to account for satisfactorily. Yet she acknowledged to herself that if he ever came back . . . But she hardly got beyond that. If he did come back—what then? She couldn't take it for granted that he thought of her as she was foolish enough to think of him—for she admitted to herself despairingly that she *did* think of him, recalled his every look, treasured the memory of the feel of his arms round her as they danced, regretted (this was *wrong*—still, she couldn't help it) that he hadn't been bold enough to take her in his arms and kiss her when he said good-bye. The fact that he evidently held her in respect was comforting in a way, but comfort of that sort was cold when she wanted to thrill and glow and rejoice that she was loved by the man she loved. If he came back and was proved a burglar, would she still love him? It was dreadfully perplexing.

She had to spend a lot of time sitting with her mother-in-law and listening to theories about the burglaries with which she did not agree, and was so inattentive and absent-minded that neither Miss Pallfrey nor the Honourable Augusta, could understand her lack of interest in the gossip they discussed with such animation when the Honourable Augusta was well enough to come downstairs and have Miss Pallfrey to tea.

"I don't understand Jocelyn at all," the Honourable Augusta complained to Miss Pallfrey the afternoon that Jocelyn left the Priory to return to her own house and occupations. "She has been mooning in the clouds all the time she has been here and taking no interest in anything—a very poor companion, I can tell you. What Jocelyn needs is someone to shake her."

"She is certainly not her usual self," agreed Miss Pallfrey; "but I think the reason, my dear Augusta, is quite clear. She is in love and a little unbalanced. She is such a nice-minded girl that—"

"Nice-minded fiddlesticks!" snapped the Honourable Augusta. "If she wants to marry that old stick, why doesn't she say so and have done with creeping about like a nice-minded broody hen?"

"He came to see me the other day," said Miss Pallfrey. "He asked my advice. He was so *touching*, so diffident. I told him I was sure everything would be settled satisfactorily, and to be brave and go forward and not be faint-hearted." She giggled a little and her hostess stifled an impulse to throw a cushion at her. "'Faint heart never won fair lady,'" went on Miss Pallfrey. "I've told him women liked a bold wooer and—"

The Honourable Augusta exploded. "Mellicent, you make me sick! You are a sentimental old fool. Why don't you marry the man yourself and leave Jocelyn in peace? I can't believe she's in love with a man old enough to be her father—any way, I sincerely hope not. I dislike the little I know of him. Hand me another piece of toast and put a log on the fire."

Mrs. Murchison-Bellaby, meantime, was in a terrible state of despondency. A seven-years' lease of a country house in a village in which her family had disgraced itself was a millstone round her neck. There was no covering up any of the reprehensible behaviour, either of Jasmine or, she feared, Adrian. The head-lines in all the cheap newspapers spread the unpleasant gossip abroad. Every day brought fresh humiliation. She could never lift her head in social circles in the county.

She was dreadfully alone in her trouble, for her husband, not having any particular ambitions beyond a rock-garden and the cultivation of mushrooms, and never having the smallest admiration for his offspring and their goings-on, was unper-turbed and unable to sympathise in a disaster on which he had always looked as more or less inevitable. Mrs. Pomfret was Mrs. Murchison-Bellaby's only comfort. She rallied round and sustained her by assurances that in striving to do her share in the work of the parish and sitting on committees she would find new interests and gradually establish her own reputation as a woman of sterling worth. No one would hold the disaster against *her*, Mrs. Pomfret declared. She personally would vouch for her and help to "establish" her, and in a short time all would be forgotten, and Much Dithering would have learnt to know Mrs. Murchison-Bellaby as an excellent friend.

The afflicted lady confided in Mrs. Pomfret her frustrated hopes of Adrian's alliance with Jocelyn.

"Ah!" remarked Mrs. Pomfret doubtfully. "No, somehow I don't think Jocelyn would ever really have considered *that*. She is a serious sort of girl and her upbringing has been so excessively—well, to put it plainly—priggish—that she is rather inclined to be, shall I say, *exclusive* in her ideas. Mind you, I don't altogether approve. I think she'd be a far nicer young woman if she had a few human faults and did not live in the clouds. Virtues are all very well, but carried to excess they can be tiresome. I am very, very fond of Jocelyn, but I admit that her excessive *goodness* is apt to pall."

"Excessive fiddlesticks!" scoffed Mrs. Murchison-Bellaby bitterly. "That's all *you* know! Her excessive virtue is merely a blind; you ask Adrian. That's what makes him so mad. She pretends to be what you and the stuck-up old women round here think her, and she's no better than she ought to be. I know what I'm talking about; you needn't look so unbelieving. Didn't she tell you that she'd been out on the binge at the Hunt Ball at Totterford with the chap that stayed at The Roebuck and stole our jewels and cleared out, leaving no address? No, I dare say not. Well, she *did*. You ask her, and see what she says. And after *that*, she doesn't think my boy is good enough for her! Well, I don't know that I think she's good enough for *him*. I'd like him to marry a respectable woman, but I'd say nothing about this and overlook it if she'd come off her high horse and be reasonable. Her position would help Adrian, I don't deny, and *we* can't afford to chuck our weight about just now. I wonder if you'd put it up to her, as you are a friend of hers, and she might see sense."

Mrs. Pomfret sat speechless, hardly able to realise what Mrs. Murchison-Bellaby was implying.

"Jocelyn? I—I—Would you mind saying all that again?"

Mrs. Murchison-Bellaby, encouraged by the fact that Mrs. Pomfret had not walked out of her house, was only too glad to repeat her story, with embellishments here and there.

"You surprise me," was all Mrs. Pomfret found to say. "Jocelyn—I couldn't have believed it."

But it didn't occur to her to doubt it. After all, Jocelyn had been "peculiar" just lately; she had noticed it on several occasions and had remarked on it to her husband and to Miss Pallfrey, who naturally attributed it to Jocelyn's being in love and not wishing to disclose the fact. Mrs. Pomfret was quite staggered at Mrs. Murchison-Bellaby's tale and, being a candid as well as an affectionate friend, went straight to Jocelyn, feeling she had to know the truth one way or the other.

Jocelyn was busy cutting out and pinning up materials for the costumes for the forthcoming Shakespeare play in preparation for the sewing party which would presently assemble and stitch the garments under her expert guidance.

"Jocelyn," panted Mrs. Pomfret, breathless from her haste to know the worst. "*What* is Mrs. Murchison-Bellaby talking about?"

Jocelyn's mouth was full of pins and she took a little time to be sure she had safely removed them all before she replied: "Why not ask Mrs. Murchison-Bellaby?" But her colour had risen perceptibly, Mrs. Pomfret noted.

"Well, I did, and she said to ask *you*."

"What Mrs. Murchison-Bellaby says is of no interest whatever to me."

"It concerns you, so it *ought* to interest you!" retorted Mrs. Pomfret indignantly. "And if it isn't true, it must be contradicted at once. Jocelyn, it—it can't be true!"

"Then no one need worry, surely." Jocelyn replaced several pins between her lips and turned to snip away a loose bit of material from a cut-out pattern.

Mrs. Pomfret walked round the table and faced her with determination. "She says you went to a ball with the man that every one says stole your mother-in-law's jewel-case and all that stuff from the Murchison-Bellabys."

"I quite thought you liked him," Jocelyn said rather indistinctly and began to pin the sleeve together.

"Jocelyn—"

"As it happens, I did!" flashed Jocelyn, removing the pins again and looking very angry. "And it is *my* business and concerns absolutely no one but me. I'm not going to explain and apologise. I went—that's all."

"But, Jocelyn—"

"I'm making Hero's petticoat out of that old cream satin. It's a bit weak in places, but I've darned it lightly and it holds together quite safely, I think. I'll put a band of gold tinsel round the hem and use this turquoise stuff for the overdress."

Mrs. Pomfret flung her hat on the sofa and sighed in exasperation. "I see." She picked up the sleeve-pattern and examined it critically. "I'll tack it up as I'm here."

"Thank you." Jocelyn handed her a reel of silk and a needle. "Beyond telling you very firmly that I am not discussing the matter in which Mrs. Murchison-Bellaby is so interested with you or any one else, I shall not refer to it again—not if you sit here and tack up stuff for a week."

"Then I must form my own opinion and—"

"And draw your own conclusions," Jocelyn finished for her. "Yes, that is your only course, I'm afraid."

"I don't like your tone," snapped Mrs. Pomfret.

"And I don't like silly curiosity. Nor do I like this magenta silk that Aunt Mellicent gave me. It's perfectly hideous and kills all the other colours it goes near. I don't think I'll use it at all. We can keep it till next time!"

"Miss Pallfrey won't like that," sighed Mrs. Pomfret. "She thinks it will do nicely for Beatrice."

"Not with Benedict wearing royal blue and old gold, and that's all we have for him."

"It would be a contrast and be nice and bright."

"The very idea gives me a pain!" snapped Jocelyn, and flung the bundle of offending magenta silk into a corner so fiercely that Mrs. Pomfret dared say no more, and threaded her needle in puzzled silence.

CHAPTER TWENTY-SEVEN

ERMYNTRUDE arrived unexpectedly that evening in a state of intense anxiety. The news of the Murchison-Bellabys which Jocelyn had written (not without a touch of malice) had alarmed her and made her decide to return to Much Dithering without delay. This, it seemed, was the psychological moment to swoop upon Adrian and earn his distracted mother's eternal gratitude by picking up the fragments, as it were, and piecing them together. She, and she alone, could help Adrian to climb to the position to which he aspired. A year or so abroad with his regiment and all would be forgotten, and then he would be able to retire and stand for a nice constituency where she would shed lustre as the Member's wife.

Jocelyn, as a matter of fact, was relieved at her arrival, for it occurred to her that she would prove an effective barrier against Adrian, who still called daily with a dogged determination to break down her refusal to admit him.

"Now tell me everything just as it stands. I must get to the bottom of this affair." Ermyntrude sat on the fender-stool and lit a cigarette after her late supper, for she had caught an evening train and reached Much Dithering in a taxi from the junction.

"Oh, well"—Jocelyn hesitated for a moment—"I really only know the local gossip—that Jasmine fell in love with the boy who played the piano that night at the social. You may remember; you were there. He's dark and good-looking. He's got an Italian mother. I expect you've seen her. The girl Lucia is very attractive, too."

"She's back in London," Ermyntrude interrupted hastily. "I saw her. I went to the place she works at. Adrian's here, I suppose? He hasn't gone away?"

"Oh, no, he's still here."

"She's a dangerous creature, that girl. I took a great dislike to her when I saw her at The Roebuck—the sort of common harpy always chasing young men and trying to ruin them. I warned Adrian not to be foolish enough to go about with her; and yet you tell me he actually took her to a Hunt Ball. But are you sure? How do you know?"

"I was there," returned Jocelyn calmly. She decided that to Ermyntrude the fact that she went to the ball would probably seem an entirely immaterial affair and cause no great surprise. She was right, for at the moment Ermyntrude was concerned only with the Murchison-Bellaby story, and she brushed aside anything that was outside her particular line of inquiry.

"Oh, were you? Well, and did you think there was anything between them?" she asked anxiously.

"Between Jasmine and Victor?"

"No, stupid! I don't care a hoot for Jasmine. Did Adrian seem—?"

"He seemed rather upset at being caught out," laughed Jocelyn. "It didn't seem to occur to him that any one would know. He tried very hard to explain, but I told him it was not of any interest to me."

"He was afraid you'd tell me." Ermyntrude laughed indulgently. "Yes, I expect he was a bit annoyed. Silly boy! I'll teach him that one simply doesn't do these things in the country. To take out a pretty shop-girl in town is nothing, but down here it's another matter; and when he is just beginning to make his way, so to speak—Still, perhaps no great harm's done, and he's had a fright." She stopped and looked suddenly at her daughter. "But fancy *you* going to a ball with your elderly admirer! I suppose he's trying to pose as a gay young spark—or have you restored his lost youth? Jocelyn, what a perfect scream! How is your romance progressing? And what are you waiting for? Haven't you actually fixed anything? Why this delay? Is he bashful?"

"Bashful?" Jocelyn looked thoughtful and smiled. No, she really saw no reason to explain. Ermyntrude could think what she pleased. "Yes, perhaps he is a little bashful."

"Has he *said* anything?"

"He doesn't seem to be in a hurry."

Well, he *ought* to. It's just silly to play about. I'd like to have you settled comfortably."

"Oh, don't worry about me," Jocelyn begged. "Aunt Mellicent is doing all that."

Ermyntrude's brain seemed to be unusually active this evening. "Where is the man I met here? Is he still at The Roebuck?"

"Oh, no," returned Jocelyn carelessly. "He went away some time ago. They say he's the jewel thief, by the way; but I don't believe it."

"Oh, my dear, how frightfully thrilling!" exclaimed Ermyntrude. "Why, of course he is—he simply must be! He was a complete mystery, and I put him down at once as something he shouldn't be. That fascinating type always is. He appealed enormously to me. There was something terribly attractive about him. He was so very much 'all there.' Of course, you probably wouldn't realise that. You just put him down, I suppose, as not a very nice sort of person—not exactly a Sunday School type. You wouldn't see his charm, since Colonel Tidmarsh is your type, and I don't imagine *he* even realised you existed."

"Then you're wrong," said Jocelyn, suddenly realising that she could go on talking quite easily, and that it was an enormous relief to treat the matter with the casual ease she caught from her mother. It had been a mistake to bury it, to behave as if it were a guilty secret. "As a matter of fact, it was *he* who took me to the Hunt Ball. It was a nice change to go out and enjoy an evening away from here. Remembering that you always say I'm so dull, I just determined I would go and have a little amusement once in a way. Needless to say, I did *not* tell Aunt Mellicent or mother-in-law. They would have had a fit; but I thought, since you had advised me to be less of a bore, it was a good idea."

"Jocelyn! How priceless! Did you have a good time?"

"I enjoyed it very much, and it really seems quite a good thing I went, because people are saying that Mr. Blythe stole the Murchison-Bellaby jewellery that night, but I can prove that he was at the ball with me and that Jasmine was wearing those jewels that night. I noticed them."

"Yes, and so did he, I expect," said Ermyntrude dryly. "My dear, there's absolutely nothing to prove that he didn't go and steal them afterwards. If I were you I wouldn't step in and interfere. I'm *sure* he's a bad hat. Still, he's an amusing person, and I quite fell for him. Don't tell me *you* did—that would be too funny!"

Under her mother's rallying eyes Jocelyn's reserve suddenly broke down. "I did," she confessed, "and—and—Oh, Ermyntrude, I don't find it at all funny. I don't believe he's a thief; but there is a mystery somewhere, and I don't understand it. May I tell you all about it? You'll know—I don't. You're quite right. I'm a perfect fool, but I can't be quite as dull as you think; for if I were, surely three men wouldn't be in love with me?"

"Three men?" Ermyntrude looked incredulous. "But who . . . ?"

"Adrian and Colonel Tidmarsh and—and Mr. Blythe!"

Ermyntrude stared. "*Adrian?* Oh, but that's absurd!"

"Quite, but he wants to marry me, and his mother came and begged me to marry him, and it's all very troublesome and impossible."

"Oh, his mother is quite impossible," agreed Ermyntrude. "You needn't worry about Adrian. I'll deal with him if you like."

"Thank you," said Jocelyn gratefully. "That will be a help. I'm leaving Colonel Tidmarsh to Aunt Mellicent; but I have no one to talk to about—the other, and he's the only one that counts."

"Rubbish, my dear! You can't possibly be in love with him," said Ermyntrude practically.

"I am. I don't care if he *is* a burglar, but I don't believe he is, and I don't believe it was so dreadfully wrong to go to a ball with him; but Mrs. Pomfret got a fearful tale from Adrian's mother. You see, he was jealous and—"

"My dear, you are being quite absurd." Ermyntrude lit a cigarette and looked scornful. "It just shows that you've had your head turned because this Blythe man took you out, just for amusement, naturally, and you've been silly enough to imagine the rest. Did he make love to you?"

"No-no."

"Well, there you are!" Ermyntrude shrugged and laughed. "Really, Jocelyn, you are a simpleton. It's quite ordinary to go to a dance with one's partner nowadays, but it doesn't follow that the man is in love with you because he asks you to dance. Only an idiot would imagine such a thing. You really must learn sense and worldly wisdom. If you've been silly enough to fall in love with a man you know nothing whatever about, you'll just have to fall out again and forget all about it. I do wish you'd be sensible and marry your old colonel. It's quite obvious that you can't look after yourself and need someone to do it for you."

"I couldn't possibly marry a man I didn't love," objected Jocelyn.

"Love!" scoffed Ermyntrude. "What do *you* know about love? You make me tired, Jocelyn. You had much better stick to good works."

When Adrian paid his morning call next day, he was agreeably surprised and elated at being admitted at once by Bertha; but his elation faded when he entered the drawing-room and found Ermyntrude obviously ready to tackle any sort of situation that might arise.

"My *dear!*" she said gushingly. "How *very* nice of you to come round so early, and what *lovely* tulips! *Thank you*, darling! Come and sit down and tell me *all* about it and we'll straighten out the mess. I expect you feel rather under the weather, poor boy, and no wonder. Still, 'nuff said! I'm not going to tease you."

Adrian sat gloomily. "Everything is in the hell of a mess."

"Why, of course it is!" agreed Ermyntrude. "That's what comes of sowing wild oats too near home. But, then, she should have told you where she lived. It's been an absolute ramp. Is the old man very troublesome?"

"Which old man?"

"Heavens! Is there more than one?" Ermyntrude looked alarmed.

"Well, my father's a bit peeved."

"He would be, quite naturally. But does he count? I thought mamma was the family snag?"

"Oh, *she's* unbearable, of course."

"And that's not to be wondered at. After all—"

"Oh, don't nag! It's all a bloody mess."

"No, darling, I won't nag; but you must see that as it *is* such a mess we've got to clear it up. Now, listen, and for goodness' sake don't argue—just listen. I've thought it all out, and my plan is absolutely watertight and unbreakable. We'll get married in London. Adrian, don't interrupt! We'll get married in London immediately, and you can exchange into the other battalion in Hong Kong and we'll go abroad till all this blows over. Your lady friend won't know anything at all about it, and she'll forget it in a very short time and get hold of someone else—they always do, darling; I'm well versed in the unfortunate love affairs of the British Army."

"But look here, Ermyntrude—"

"I shall go and see your mother and put it to her perfectly candidly, darling, that I am absolutely the only person who can restore you to the position she wants for you. Oh, yes, I know, Adrian, you think you're in love with Jocelyn. She told me all about everything, so you've got no surprises to spring on me. Well, it's no good; she won't look at you. You're the sort of man she's been brought up to absolutely *abhor*. She's terribly narrow in her outlook and would cramp your style badly, dear boy. You'd lead a dog's life. You'd simply have to break loose. No man could stand undiluted Jocelyn for more than a week."

"But look here, Ermyntrude—"

"Is your car outside? Yes? Well, just wait a minute and I'll put my hat on and we'll go straight back to your mother."

Ermyntrude, relentless in her attack, overbore all obstacles and eventually found herself in Mrs. Murchison-Bellaby's lounge, facing her enemy and all prepared to do battle for the possession of Adrian. Dressed for the occasion in a becoming hat and an exceedingly handsome fur coat, her hair and complexion a real credit to those responsible, her air of well-bred assurance quite unmatchable, Ermyntrude was a winner from the start. Mrs. Murchison-Bellaby, taken completely by surprise at half-past eleven in the morning, was untidy, and felt and looked inferior. She hated Ermyntrude, but she was awed by her complete mastery of the situation. She realised that Ermyntrude's assurance that she could lift Adrian out of the mess and give him the position he wished to attain was no mere boast. It was quite clear that a woman of Ermyntrude's personality could do just what she liked and achieve success in whatever she set out to accomplish—or so it seemed to Mrs. Murchison-Bellaby, who had never before encountered any one quite in Ermyntrude's class. Adrian's future seemed to be secured without any further effort on her part. Ermyntrude would sweep him with her on a path of glory (paved with Murchison-Bellaby gold), and the Murchison-Bellabys themselves could settle down quietly and lead useful lives in the village and save money in order to promote the fortunes of Adrian. But—here was the snag—Adrian might achieve position, and even a certain sort of happiness, with his brilliant wife, but there would be no founding of a new county family. If he had married Jocelyn, how different it would have been! Fate was very bitter! Even Lucia Hedgecock could have been the mother of Adrian's children; but the alliance with such common people would have been a set-back from which there would have been no recovering. No, if Adrian wanted social position and success in political circles, he could achieve it with Ermyntrude, but he must forgo his ambitions to found a family. Adrian's mother accepted defeat and accepted Ermyntrude as her future daughter-in-law in stony resignation, noting the fact that Ermyntrude's eyes were already busy appraising and valuing the arrangement and furnishings of the room in which they were sitting.

"I think that's all," said Ermyntrude, smoothing a white glove absently as her gaze wandered round the room. "We shall be abroad for a few years—possibly more if Adrian gets promotion and shows promise of being a good officer. I have influence, of course—that will help his career in the Army if he's really keen on it—and I've lived such a lot abroad and know Hong Kong very well indeed, so we ought to get on famously. I'll do *my* bit, Mamma (if I may call you so?), and the rest is up to Adrian, bless him!" She blew a kiss to the completely disgruntled young man whose future she had arranged so competently.

CHAPTER TWENTY-EIGHT

WHEN Ermyntrude had taken her departure with Adrian, Jocelyn tried to concentrate on her needlework and put aside the disturbing thoughts aroused again by her conversation with her mother and also by the things implied by Mrs. Pomfret. What had Mrs. Murchison-Bellaby been saying? And to whom would she say—whatever she was saying? Was it about Adrian or Gervase? Oh, well, Ermyntrude knew the whole story now. She was glad she had had the courage to tell her all that there was to tell. If Mrs. Murchison-Bellaby had tried to tell her anything, Ermyntrude would have been wise as to the real truth. But it was all very disturbing and made her unhappy and too restless to sit and sew at the gay costumes that were all ready for her finishing touches. She stood fingering the cream satin underdress of Hero's wedding-dress, a little doubtful of its standing the strain of the gold fringe with which she wanted to trim it. It was very old and she had had to darn it carefully. Should she tack a piece of muslin behind it?

The door behind her was flung open violently and Bertha stood in the doorway, distraught with excitement. "Oh, 'm, what did I tell you?" she gasped. "Look who's here; and, my word, hasn't he brought you some lovely flowers! Better'n Mr. Murchison-Bellaby's—and they wasn't to be sneezed at, neither."

She stood aside hurriedly to let Gervase enter, and remained a moment in speechless excitement before she went out of the room.

Gervase came in carrying a gigantic sheaf of crimson roses, from which Bertha had already stripped its wrappings so that his arrival should lose none of its effect. His eyes held a question that was answered by the radiance in Jocelyn's and the smile, half shy, wholly enchanting, with which she held out her hands and took the roses.

"You've come!" was all she said; but it told him all he wanted to know.

"You knew I'd come."

"I wondered. I—I hoped." She clasped her roses and looked at him shyly as she bent over their fragrance.

"There have been some odd stories since I've been away," he began, but she looked gravely at him and said: "Yes, but they are so fantastic that no one could possibly believe . . . And, even if they had been true, it would have made no difference—to me."

He smiled, but he was serious. "I'm glad of that, but as it happens, I'm quite honest, really. I don't want you to put me on a pedestal and manufacture a halo for me, for I've never qualified for either, but I'm not as bad as some of the things I hear old Tidmarsh has been saying about me. You've taken me on trust from the beginning, haven't you? And even now you don't know anything at all about me. I warned you that I was a bad hat, and then I went away to argue things out with myself. I didn't want to—to—well, I thought you—I mean, I wanted you to have a little time to find out if I was really worth bothering about. I didn't want to rush you. I haven't done that, have I? You've had ten days—"

"No, no," she protested, "not ten days—ten years! Oh, it's been so long!"

"And you've found out?"

"Yes, oh, yes, I found out at once—when you—you didn't kiss me." She still held her roses. She found them an effective barrier, a fact which also occurred to Gervase. He took them from her and laid them aside.

"When did you want me to kiss you?"

"That night, when you drove away and left me alone, not knowing whether I was just being a fool, whether you—I couldn't be sure—it was just a blank."

He took her hands and drew her to him. "I didn't think it would be fair, Jocelyn, *then*. I had to be sure, too. Now—well?"

"Crumbs!" murmured Bertha, and withdrew from the cautiously opened chink through which she had been an enraptured audience. She retired to the pantry, where she wept in sheer ecstasy. It was just like the Pictures!

"Let me take some of this rubbish off the chairs and you can sit down," Jocelyn said, becoming more or less sane and coherent again.

"What on earth is it all?" Gervase asked, looking about him in surprise. "What are all these garments?"

"This is a wedding dress," Jocelyn explained. "How odd, isn't it? I mean, just now. It's Hero's—Shakespeare, you know."

"A wedding dress?" Gervase touched the frail stuff gently. "A good omen, isn't it. I like it. Wear it at your wedding."

"Oh, I couldn't," objected Jocelyn. "It would fall to pieces, it's so old. It's only for a Shakespeare Festival with which I'm helping Mrs. Pomfret."

"When—" he began; but Jocelyn turned firmly:

"I can't be married until that is over. Mrs. Pomfret would never forgive me."

"When?" he said again.

"In February—the 16th."

"We'll be married the day after. I want to take you away from Much Dithering and show you what southern sunshine is like. I've bought a villa at Antibes. The mimosa will be out."

"Oh, Gervase!" She clapped her hands softly. "How lovely. How *lovely*! But"—she looked a little doubtful—"I must see what Mrs. Renshawe says—and of course Aunt Mellicent, too."

"You must please yourself for a change," he retorted. "All that is over, Jocelyn. You have only your own wishes to consider—and mine, of course," he added with a laugh.

She paused. "Yes, how—how odd! I've always had to ask permission from someone. I've never dared please myself. I'm going up to the Priory for tea. I—oh, Gervase, it's going to be very difficult. She thinks you are the burglar, and even if you aren't the burglar, she has an idea that you are a—a commercial traveller." She stopped, confused. "Are you, Gervase?"

He took her in his arms again and looked down at her with a smile. "Would you mind, Jocelyn?"

"Oh, no, *I* shouldn't mind," she said vehemently. "Nothing matters—nothing!"

"That's a good thing," he returned, laughing at her serious face, "for I've been all sorts of queer things in my time. That's why I went away—to think it out. I felt you wouldn't—couldn't possibly care for a fellow who had been such a crazy sort of—well, I told you I was a bad hat, didn't I?"

She looked up at him with wade serious eyes. "I don't think anything matters, Gervase, if you'll only go on loving me."

He drew her down with him to the settee and put his arms round her. "I'll do that, never you fear. I can promise you that I am a reformed character. All my wild oats are harvested, and I've learnt all that a man needs to know to make him a nice, steady, reliable, stay-at-home husband. Does that sound very dull, Jocelyn?"

She put up her hand and touched his cheek. "I think it sounds lovely. I was afraid you might find me—not very exciting; but perhaps you won't mind that."

"I'll put up with it."

She sighed happily, content to feel his arms round her and his lips on her hair. Nothing else could possibly matter now. Whatever queer things he had done or had been, he was here now, holding her in his arms.

After a pause, however, her conscience began to stir. After all, there was her mother-in-law—she would be astonished, to say the least of it. To have to explain that she was actually engaged to Gervase was going to be difficult. Aunt Mellicent would sweep and wring her hands, of course. She no longer counted.

"Gervase!" She sat up and looked at him. "We've got to go and see my mother-in-law."

"All right, don't worry. I'll go and see her and explain that I am neither a burglar nor a commercial traveller, and when I've soothed her down you can come along in complete safety."

"And you'll tell her—I mean, about *us*?"

"Would you rather I did?"

"Yes, *please*, Gervase."

"What a coward!" he said, laughing at her alarm. "Yes, I'll tell her all about everything. Now I have to go and see to some other matters. I've been in communication with the police, as I prefer not to run the risk of being arrested. I'll see you later at the Priory."

"What will you tell her?" Jocelyn asked a little nervously.

"The truth, the whole truth, and nothing but the truth," he replied. "Nothing to cause you a moment's anxiety. Just go on taking me on trust till tea-time. Don't be late. It will be rather fun."

"Fun?" echoed Jocelyn doubtfully. "You don't know Mrs. Renshawe?"

Gervase looked at her reflectively. "Possibly you have been taking her rather too seriously. "You are a serious young woman, and I rather fancy you may have got a wrong line of Mrs. Renshawe. You're quite frightened of her. Well, I'm not. I'm going to beard the lioness in her den and get away with it."

"Am I really serious?" Jocelyn asked in a puzzled tone. "Aunt Mellicent has always told me to learn to take my responsibilities seriously, and I have tried."

He laughed. "You have certainly tried. But now I'll take the responsibilities and *you* must learn to laugh and not care a damn for any one or anything—just for a change. Will you—to please me, Jocelyn?"

She put her hand out shyly and touched his arm. "Gervase, what an odd idea—not caring a damn. But it sounds as if it might be a—a pleasant change."

She stood by the window, watching him go away before she turned to pick up her roses. "Fancy not caring a damn!" she said aloud, and laughed happily as she bent to smell their fragrance.

CHAPTER TWENTY-NINE

THE Honourable Augusta and Miss Pallfrey were sitting by the fire in the gloomy drawing-room at the Priory when Mellowes opened the door and announced in a very subdued voice: "A gentleman to see you, madam. He says his business is most important and won't wait. It isn't my fault, madam."

Before the Honourable Augusta could rise in indignation and protest, Gervase was in the room.

"I'm very sorry to intrude in this way, but I really must see you, Mrs. Renshawe. My business can't be put off indefinitely, and I would prefer to settle it personally as far as possible instead of writing a vast number of letters, or rather paying my solicitor to do so. My name will explain what my business is and why I must settle it. I am Gervase Blythe Renshawe."

The Honourable Augusta stared at him in dismay. "You are— my husband's nephew?"

"Yes. I'm sorry, but there it is."

"Gervase Blythe?" cried Miss Pallfrey. "Good gracious, Augusta, it is the *burglar*! Ring the bell! Send for the police!"

"I don't think that would really help," Gervase said soothingly. "I've already seen the local policeman and told him where I am staying and given him all sorts of references and assured him that I shall stay and see everything through. He has seen my passport and rung up the family solicitor and Scotland Yard and been very busy indeed all day. So have I, and now I'm here to tell you that I am going to many your daughter-in-law, Mrs. Lancelot Renshawe. We shall live a wandering life, as I have various interests in different places, and she is rather anxious to travel and see a little of the world outside the Ditherings. I expect it's something of a shock for you, but I am breaking it to you, at Jocelyn's request, as gently as possible."

Both ladies sat and stared at him in blank consternation, scarcely able to understand what they were hearing.

"Jocelyn marrying you?" quavered Miss Pallfrey. "I don't believe it. She has never *mentioned* you."

"Gervase Blythe Renshawe?" repeated the Honourable Augusta. "It was the name 'Blythe' that made me uneasy from the first. I knew nothing to your credit and I expected the worst."

"Yes, that was so obvious that I came to Much Dithering unofficially, just to see for myself. You refused to see me, so I never got a chance of reassuring you as to my respectability personally. I fell in love with Jocelyn—unofficially. I expect you think it's rather—I mean—"

"I don't understand," interrupted the Honourable Augusta. "This story about your being a burglar, for instance—or the other idea. You didn't come here to sell me anything?"

"Sell you anything?" Gervase looked surprised. "What sort of things?"

"There seemed to be an idea," explained the Honourable Augusta, "that you were a commercial traveller. I don't know where it started; but, being a stranger, it caused a certain amount of conjecture in the village, so Mellowes told me. And I have been given to understand that a person who alleges he knew you some years ago says some *very* queer things."

"Dear old Ambrose!" murmured Gervase. "You mustn't mind what he says. He is rather warped on the subject of my lurid past. Yes, I'll admit it *was* a lurid past. I did some appallingly silly things, but I have never been really dishonest. I had sufficient sense of what was due to my family and my old school tie, and so on, to steer clear of some of the pitfalls and gins that beset the path of the young officer in India with a taste for good horses and sport and all that goes with it. No, Aunt Augusta, I may have been a black sheep, but I've never disgraced myself or the name of Renshawe, however much I may have annoyed my old friend Ambrose Tidmarsh. I once painted a blaze and two white stockings on a bay polo pony he was rather pleased with, and rode it in a polo match when I was short of a mount. I knew it was no good asking him to lend it to me. Unfortunately I lamed the beast, and he found me out because the syce lost his nerve and gave the show away. He never forgave me for that—and other things."

"But why did you paint the animal?" asked Miss Pallfrey, looking puzzled.

"So that he wouldn't recognise the pony when I rode it, and rush out and tell me I mustn't!"

"You are certainly a person of resource," remarked the Honourable Augusta with a grim amusement.

"Colonel Tidmarsh declares you are the man who stole the jewels from The Place and the jewel-case from here. He worked it all out," declared Miss Pallfrey obstinately.

"Yes, I know he did, but he was always like that—working things out, I mean. It amuses him and does no one any harm. Let's leave him out of this."

The Honourable Augusta suddenly laughed and got up and held out her hand. "I believe I like you. You're a sportsman. I've been foolish and tried to avoid you. I—well, to be frank, I was afraid to meet you. I hated the idea of having to leave the Priory. You're an unexpected sort of person, but you're worth a dozen old women like the Tidmarsh creature, and I'm sure you'll be good for Jocelyn. She's been too well brought up; but she's all right when you get over her being rather too well meaning."

"Really, Augusta, what an extraordinary thing to say about dear Jocelyn!" protested Miss Pallfrey indignantly. "Surely it is nothing to her discredit that she has been well brought up and is a very sweet and gentle woman—a very rare thing these days, Mr. Blythe, or I suppose I should say Renshawe. I hope you are the sort of man who can appreciate her true worth and will cherish her—"

"Don't blither, Mellicent!" snapped the Honourable Augusta. "What Jocelyn needs is a good shaping up, and I'm sure she will get it. But, dear me, I'm very much surprised. Our dear Jocelyn has been very dark and secret in the affair. Does she know all about you?"

"Not yet. I wanted to see you first and talk things over."

"That was kind of you. Please sit down and stay to tea. I expect Jocelyn. Did you know that?"

"I think," said Miss Pallfrey with some asperity, "that an explanation is due. I mean, Augusta, that you have always led me to understand that Mr.—er—Renshawe was distinctly undesirable, and I cannot willingly consent to Jocelyn agreeing to place her future in the keeping of a man for whom I must confess I have the deepest distrust." The Honourable Augusta looked at Gervase. "Well, I dare say Mellicent is justified. I admit I expected the worst myself. You were always regarded as a black sheep."

"Say a dark horse," suggested Gervase. "It is less blighting."

Miss Pallfrey refused to yield. "I would like to hear something definite as to your past life, Mr. Renshawe."

"You mean that you have heard such a damning account of the little of my past known to Ambrose Tidmarsh that you feel I ought not to aspire to marry Jocelyn? Well, I'll tell you the story of my life, omitting the more lurid details, which I feel sure would only distress you and which, after all, belong to the past. As you know, Aunt Augusta, I was turned out as a 'Prodigal Son' by my stern parent when I got sent down from Cambridge for climbing the roof of King's College Chapel one moonlight night. Then I enlisted, but managed to make good and eventually got a commission. When in India I exchanged into a native cavalry regiment and had the time of my life until I got into debt and into the hands of a native money-lender. In fact, things were so bad that I had to be smuggled out of Karachi disguised as a bearer to a pal of mine who was helping me to get off. I went to Australia from Bombay, and was lucky enough to win quite a big sum on the Tote at Melbourne races the day after I landed. Very reprehensible, you'll say, of course, but my ill-gotten gains multiplied. Stocks and shares prospered. I went to South America and bred polo ponies—did well at it, sold my ranch and went to Texas, where I became involved in oil, and finally floated out of oil pretty well a millionaire. Since then I've travelled a good deal and enjoyed myself, and finally I came here just to look at things. Then I met Jocelyn and saved her from drowning, or at any rate from getting exceedingly wet. She did her best to snub me. I saw at once that she had been very well brought up and that she considered strange men who spoke to ladies on lonely roads when thunderstorms were raging all around were not to be encouraged, and I determined to become better acquainted, so I stayed the night at The Roebuck, and by sheer chance I ran into my old friend Ambrose in the village and thought it was an excellent idea to improve my acquaintance with him. A hint that I was now rich and of some importance in the world brought forth an invitation to stay with him, so I promptly accepted and came to spend Christmas with him. The rest you know."

"But if *you* weren't the burglar," persisted Miss Pallfrey, "who was? It's all very odd."

"Don't tell me it was Colonel Tidmarsh!" exclaimed the Honourable Augusta. "You know, he worked it all out very cleverly, down to the last detail. Could he possibly have been the actual thief?"

"Augusta!" wailed Miss Pallfrey. "No, oh, no! It couldn't be. It would break my heart, were such a thing possible."

"Rubbish!" retorted the Honourable Augusta. "Any one would think you were spoony over him yourself."

"Have you ever seen these?" Gervase asked, leaning forward and dropping a pair of gold sleeve-links into the Honourable Augusta's lap.

"Yes, of course I have. They were my husband's. They were in the jewel-case that was stolen. Good heavens, what a strange thing! How did *you* get them?"

"I didn't. These are mine; they belonged to my father. But I saw the others quite recently. I know where they are."

"Does any one else?"

"I don't think so. I haven't straightened things out yet. I wanted to be sure about the links first."

"And here's Jocelyn." The Honourable Augusta gave him back the links as Jocelyn came in and stopped in surprise on seeing the group by the fire. "Jocelyn, you haven't met Mr. Renshawe. Let me introduce you."

"Mr. Renshawe?" Jocelyn looked blankly at her mother-in-law and then at Gervase. "You—is—is this what you didn't tell me? Oh, Gervase!"

"Gervase?" echoed her mother-in-law. "This is very remarkable, Jocelyn. You never told me—"

"But I didn't know he was Mr.—Mr. Renshawe," stammered Jocelyn with crimson cheeks and startled eyes; "and it was only to-day—I mean, that there was anything to tell you, and now—has he told you that, too?"

"He mentioned that he had seriously interfered with our plans and hopes of a happy future for you."

"Oh, Jocelyn!" said Miss Pallfrey reproachfully. "How could you be so unkind? I am terribly upset about all this. I feel responsible—"

"Responsible?" cried Jocelyn. "You, Aunt Mellicent? Why, you only knew Gervase as a burglar."

"I mean, that I raised false hopes in poor dear Colonel Tidmarsh's heart. It was only yesterday I told him I was sure you would reconsider your first unkind decision. He asked my advice."

"And I," returned Jocelyn blandly, "told him that I thought you and he would be an ideal couple, and wished him joy."

"Oh!" murmured Miss Pallfrey faintly. "Oh! And—and what did he say, Jocelyn, dear?"

"He was quite overcome by his feelings," replied Jocelyn truthfully.

"I don't care twopence about Colonel Tidmarsh's feelings," snapped the Honourable Augusta; "but I would like to know just what has been happening about this—to me—complete stranger who appears to have become engaged to you, Jocelyn, and seems to be a person with whom you have been acquainted for some time. Where did you first meet him?"

"Delivering *Parish Magazines* in a thunderstorm," Jocelyn said demurely.

"It seems to be an occupation with many possibilities," remarked the Honourable Augusta dryly.

"It is, if one knows how to make the most of them," agreed Gervase. "Well, as to the future, Jocelyn and I intend to go to the South of France. I've just bought her a villa there. We shall be more than grateful if you will continue to live here and look after things in the extremely efficient way you have always done. We'll leave it to you to do just as you please, and we'll come back now and then just to see you and so on—if that suits every one," he added politely.

"Mrs. Pomfret, madam," Mellowes announced, and Mrs. Pomfret entered in a state of intense excitement, obviously bursting with news of the most startling description.

"My dear Mrs. Renshawe," she exclaimed, "and you, Miss Pallfrey—oh, my dears, I've just met Colonel Tidmarsh—and what do you think he told me? Only it isn't—it can't be true. I told him I couldn't believe it."

"What isn't and can't be true?" asked the Honourable Augusta impatiently. "Mellowes, bring tea at once."

Mrs. Pomfret turned and became aware of Jocelyn and Gervase, who were standing a little apart. "Jocelyn and Mr. Blythe—why—then you *are* back? Colonel Tidmarsh *said* . . ."

"You have been misinformed in one matter," corrected the Honourable Augusta grimly. "This is my nephew, Gervase Blythe Renshawe, and he assures me he is *not* the burglar. Now what is *your* news?"

"Jocelyn!" cried Mrs. Pomfret. "It's not true? You can't be going to marry *him*?"

"Oh, but I am," Jocelyn assured her calmly; "but not till after the Shakespeare Competition. I was quite firm about that."

Mrs. Pomfret sat down looking dazed but relieved. "Oh, well, I must be thankful for small mercies," she said philosophically. "No wonder Colonel Tidmarsh looked as if he had been eating worms."

"But he's going to marry Mellicent," said the Honourable Augusta with a touch of malicious enjoyment.

Mrs. Pomfret was past further thrills. "After to-day I can believe anything," she said in an exhausted voice; but after a moment she sat up and looked at Gervase inquisitively. "If you are *not* the burglar, what are you? They said in the village that you travelled in petrol pumps and were trying to sell one to Joe Hedgecock at The Roebuck."

"I'm afraid I gave Mr. Hedgecock the impression myself. I had to account for my interest in the village, and it seemed to fit in with his own ideas, so I just let him think so, and I dare say I probably gave Ambrose a false impression by allowing him to assume I was something I ought not to be. I must clear it all up, I suppose."

"I think I'd like to assist at the clearing up," said the Honourable Augusta. "I'll have a dinner-party to-night to present the new owner to my friends. You and the vicar must come, Mrs. Pomfret, and you, of course, Mellicent, and I'll send a message to our friend Colonel Tidmarsh. I'm sure he'd be interested. And I'd like to do the introducing myself." Mrs. Pomfret gave a delighted chuckle; but Miss Pallfrey looked reproachful.

"Yes, I know," broke in the Honourable Augusta before she could speak. "What's one man's meat is another man's poison. All the same, I'm going to have that party. But not a word about all this to any one till we're all collected here to-night. Mrs. Pomfret, can I rely on you?"

CHAPTER THIRTY

WHEN Gervase went back to The Roebuck, to dress for dinner he found Joe Hedgecock in the private bar, clearing away some glasses in an extremely bad temper. Joe nodded curtly in reply to his cheerful "Good-evening, Mr. Hedgecock. May I have a word with you, if you aren't busy?"

"If it's important, Mr. Blythe; but, to tell the truth, I ain't feeling fit to throw a word to a dog this evening."

"Under the weather?"

"Not so much weather!" retorted Joe bitterly. "Feels more like a blooming earthquake—that's what!"

"You've been through a bit of a—well, call it a mess, haven't you?"

"Been hearing the news, I dare say," said Joe sarcastically. "Heard the latest, perhaps?"

"This village provides so much excitement just now," returned Gervase, "that at present it's hard to say what is the latest. I'm in the headlines myself, as a matter of fact."

"You were that before," grinned Joe, with an indication of returning geniality. "Quite shook us up, you did; but I always said you were a gent, even if it looked a bit queer."

"Thank you, Mr. Hedgecock. I'm glad to know I have your goodwill. I like dealing with friends."

"Dealing? That's a funny word, Anything behind it?"

"Yes, quite a lot. Shall we sit down and have a heart-to-heart discussion on a rather important matter?"

"You're not here to talk to me about that damned young rooster at The Place, are you?" demanded Joe truculently, flaring up again. "Waste of time, Mr. Blythe. He won't get away with this. I'll have him up for breach of promise, and get my girl whacking good damages. It's no good discussing the business—I've made up my mind. I'm not going to have a man of his class playing with my girl and then leaving her for someone else. I'll have all I can get."

"Good Lord!" Gervase felt almost as tired of "late news" as Mrs. Pomfret. "This is a new one on me, Mr. Hedgecock. No, no, I'm not here to discuss that. I knew, of course, that he was—er—attracted by your daughter; but I didn't know there was anything behind it, and I was informed to-day that he and Mrs. Lascelles were going to be married; but that's as far as I'd got. No, Mr. Hedgecock, I don't want to discuss that matter at all; but, as a matter of fact, I think your daughter is to be congratulated. He's not a nice young man at all, from all I can hear, and he's getting all he deserves, if that's any comfort to you."

"Oh, I don't want *him*—nor does Lucy, neither," retorted Joe; "but I'm going to lift a tidy bit of damages out of him. He'll have to pay for his fun."

"Oh, yes, quite," agreed Gervase. "What about a 'spot' with me, Mr. Hedgecock? Scotch and soda's mine. You've got rather deeply involved with that family, haven't you?"

Joe placed some glasses, a bottle of whisky and a siphon on the table and took a cigarette from the case that Gervase held out. "Yes, that's a fact, more's the pity."

"Rather more deeply than you know, I fancy." Gervase lit a match and held it to Joe's cigarette before he lit his own. "It has nothing to do with what I wanted to talk to you about just now; but that lad of yours will land himself in a much queerer mess than Adrian Murchison-Bellaby if he's not pulled up *very* sharply. I don't quite know how the matter stands as regards the burglary at The Place. If this is a case of 'first offence' I'll take no steps beyond asking him to return my uncle's sleeve-links and other things which have a sentimental value for my aunt."

"What do you mean?"

"I mean that he was wearing the facsimile of these"—Gervase stretched out his wrist and showed his sleeve-links—"when I saw him at a casino in Antibes a few nights ago, and I happen to know that they were in the old jewel-case that was stolen from my aunt."

"Your aunt? Who are *you*, then?"

"Blythe Renshawe is my name. Lord, this is all getting terribly mixed up! One thing's led to another."

"Renshawe? Renshawe? And you think Victor's stole them jewels, do you?" Joe asked in a dazed voice. "My God, what a thing to happen to a decent, honest man! It's the mixed blood— it's no good. Not but what Louisa's a good enough sort of woman in her own way. I've no grouse against Louisa except the mixed blood in the kids, and her temper when she's upset. She's taken a knife to me before now. This'll be terrible!"

"I'm awfully sorry about it," said Gervase; "but I think there is really no doubt that she—I mean Mrs. Victor—was wearing a pair of earrings when I last saw her that were supposed to be stolen by *me*, which is really more than I can stand for. Up to a point it is a joke, but I'm not going to let it become a nuisance. Who first said that I was the thief?"

"Victor, I believe. He said the footsteps in the snow that led here were yours, and started the story just to keep things going till he and the girl went off, I suppose."

"But why the Priory?" asked Gervase. "Who put him on to the jewel-case there?"

Joe thought for a bit. "His mother talked a lot about the Honourable Augusta's jewellery—said it was worth a fortune, and that she kept it knocking round and didn't lock it up; at least, she didn't use to. That's all I can think."

"And a nice quiet little village to play in where no one suspected that anything would happen," laughed Gervase. "Any one with a talent for it could have gone round and cleared every-thing up in one evening. He scooped some brooches from my aunt, I believe, worth a couple of hundred, but she keeps the good stuff at the bank these days. Well, Mr. Hedgecock, I must be getting along. We got too deeply involved in family affairs to allow me to discuss the business of my having become your landlord and so on. I expect you'll want to make a few alterations here. We'll talk about a petrol pump and lock-up garages to-morrow. I simply hate that kind of hen-house into which I have to push my new car here—no good at all. We must be a little up to date in the village. Oh, by the way, I'm going to be married. We must drink the lady's health. I give you—Mrs. Renshawe!" Gervase stood up and raised his glass. Joe got to his feet. "Mrs. Renshawe? Who is the lady?"

"Oh, you know her quite well, as a matter of fact. Dear me, do you mean to say that bit of news hasn't got round yet?"

Joe shook his head.

"It's Mrs. Renshawe, my cousin's widow."

"I haven't got it all clear yet," said Joe rather helplessly.

"No, it's all a bit sudden, isn't it? Well, I'm dining at the Priory, so I must be getting along."

"I'd just like to tell Louisa," Joe said. He was feeling the need of support, and his wife was quick off the mark and able to see farther than he was. He went to the door and called her in. "This gentleman is our landlord, Louisa. He's the new owner, Mr. Renshawe. Queer, isn't it?"

Mrs. Hedgecock looked in surprise at Gervase. "Good-evening, sir. I—I hope you find things to your satisfaction?"

"Oh, quite, Mrs. Hedgecock, thank you."

"Louisa, he's been telling me some queer things about our Victor. You'd better hear them from Mr. Bl—Renshawe, for I'm not good at telling things, and I'd sooner he told you than me."

Mrs. Hedgecock looked steadily and warily at Gervase. "Yes, Mr. Renshawe?"

It was not a pleasant task, but Gervase made the best of it, hoping that Mrs. Hedgecock would refrain from using knives if she felt annoyed, but she took the story with astonishing calmness.

"Victor did not steal the jewels," she said with a shrug of her big shoulders. "The girl Jasmine was in love with him and gave him the jewels to raise money so that they could marry. She has no morals, that one, and no feelings of goodness for any one. Victor told me. He was frightened. He has never done such a thing; but Jasmine, she is bold and full of passion for Victor, and she is a sly, wicked creature and made him agree. But he told me and said, what can he do? That he will be caught and go to jail and lose his job and be ruined because of what she has done. So *I*"—she leaned across the table and tapped it significant-ly—"*I*, Mr. Renshawe, I say, we will say it was this stranger. No one can tell who he is. He has gone away. We will give the idea that he is the one who is the thief, and people will talk about it and not think of anything else, and if there is a second burglary it will give more to talk about and not only at The Place. So I went to the Priory the evening they went to the ball at Totter-ford. I knew where the jewel-case used to be kept, and I picked it up quickly and came away. I knew my way round the house in the dark, and it was easy for me. And that is the truth."

"My God!" groaned Joe. "That's a nice story for us to tell Mr. Renshawe, our new landlord. It's a fine finish up that this stranger chap that you put the blame on turns out to be the new owner of all this blinking village. Him being a Renshawe, that's how he spotted Victor's cuff-links and got a clue to all the trouble. Now where'll I be? Lord, why did I marry a foreigner and breed trouble like this?"

"There will be no trouble," retorted his wife, "if you let me settle it all. I will talk to you to-morrow, Mr. Renshawe, and I will talk to Jasmine's mother and tell her what a bad daugh-ter she is and how she leads my good son into doing wrong to please her. She will not want to spread *that* story, and I will talk nicely to young Mrs. Renshawe, who is always my good friend, and *she* will talk to our landlord. If he is in love with her, as I have heard, he will be in a good mood and he will laugh and say no more. I will give him the brooches—they are upstairs—and I will tell Victor to send back the sleeve-links; he took a fancy to them, silly boy!—and no harm to any one, after all."

"Louisa, this has been a night of surprises for me," said Joe heavily; "but you've been the biggest of the lot—and then some!"

"It is certainly complicated," agreed Gervase, "but as it seems to be a strictly family affair all round, I expect we can get it hushed up somehow. Mrs. Hedgecock seems to hold all the cards."

"We don't want scandal in Much Dithering," said Joe Hedgecock, "not more than what we've had. The Honourable don't hold with it and never did; and she's right, God bless her!"

CHAPTER THIRTY-ONE

THE Honourable Augusta awaited her guests with a feeling of grim amusement. She was relieved at discovering that her late husband's successor was such an entirely reasonable, not to say accommodating, person. The peculiar circumstances of his appearance on the scene and the numerous complications connected with the affair tickled her long-dormant sense of humour, and she decided to get a little fun out of it and to clear up the mysterious excursions and alarms.

That Jocelyn should have so suddenly developed character enough to conduct a secret love affair was quite astonishing. In fact, Jocelyn's behaviour lately had been exceedingly remarkable, what with the Murchison-Bellaby young man and the Tidmarsh complications, and now turning out to be engaged to Gervase Renshawe. Certainly for a young woman who had hitherto resembled a stained-glass window in the gentle insipidity of her personality, Jocelyn had managed to steer a fairly successful course amid the rapids of the past few weeks. The Honourable Augusta felt a new respect for her daughter-in-law and had no patience with the agonised twitterings of Miss Pallfrey, whose tender heart ached for the shattering of the romantic hopes she had fostered in Colonel Tidmarsh's bosom.

The party assembled at eight o'clock. The vicar was naturally pleased and excited at meeting the new owner of the Ditherings, about whom there had been so much speculation. Mrs.

Pomfret was struggling with so many emotions that she was even more incoherent than usual. Miss Pallfrey was chilly and disapproving, Colonel Tidmarsh astonished at having received what in Much Dithering amounted to a "royal command "to be present at dinner at the Priory. He was filled with anticipation of something momentous. Could it be that Jocelyn had changed her mind, and that this was a formal indication on the part of the Honourable Mrs. Renshawe that he was to be received as an accepted suitor?

There was certainly an atmosphere of expectancy in the group round the fire in the big drawing-room that was quite brilliantly lit this evening and had an unusual air of warmth and gaiety. The Honourable Augusta was impressive in black velvet with some fine diamond ornaments. (What a good thing the thief had not been able to lay his hands on them, thought Ambrose.) Clearly it was an occasion, and the perceptible quiver of excitement that animated the group suggested that his entrance was a matter of intense interest to every one. Ambrose realised that at once, and he felt a glow of importance as he bowed over his hostess's hand, a hand, he noticed, that plainly indicated the personality of its owner, strong, short-fingered, roughened with work. It might almost have been described as "horny." There was no nonsense about it. It was distinctly ruthless, and its firm uncompromising grip had something almost intimidating about it that robbed Ambrose of some of his complacency. It was the hand of a person who would not shrink from hurting an adversary, and suddenly Ambrose felt that she considered him that, and that the atmosphere in the large pale room was unfriendly. It was a nasty feeling, quite inexplicable, for every one greeted him with their usual friendliness. He glanced at Miss Pallfrey, a drooping figure that disturbingly suggested that tragedy was the keynote of the situation. Like the Honourable Augusta, she was wearing black velvet, but in her case it had the aspect of trappings of woe. Yes, Miss Pallfrey was mourning for something; that was obvious. (Oddly enough Mrs. Pomfret also wore black velvet, well worn and rusty, which somehow managed to convey an impression of unquenchable cheerfulness.)

"Well, Colonel Tidmarsh," said the Honourable Augusta, "I expect you are wondering why you have been bidden to attend my party to-night, so I must explain that it is in the nature of a celebration, and I felt that every one who was connected with the interesting events that have led to the climax should be present."

Ambrose bowed, feeling grateful at the charming manner in which the Honourable Augusta was expressing herself.

"Now you," she went on, "I believe, are already acquainted with my nephew. He tells me he made your acquaintance some years ago in India, so you are here in the guise of an old friend; and of course you are also acquainted with my daughter-in-law, so you have a double interest in the happy announcement I have to make this evening."

"Augusta!" Miss Pallfrey raised her voice protestingly, but the Honourable Augusta waved her aside.

"That announcement is the engagement of Jocelyn, with my full approbation, to—"

She paused dramatically as Mellowes opened the door and announced:—"Mrs. Renshawe, madam, and Mr. Renshawe."

"Ah!" said Mrs. Pomfret. "How very dramatic, and how beautifully staged! Jocelyn, you took your cue at the exact moment. How seldom that happens!"

"But dear me, dear me!" exclaimed the vicar. "I had no idea— why, we have been entertaining an angel unawares! My dear sir, I haven't forgotten your munificence in the matter of that five pounds you gave my wife for the Organ Fund at Christmas. My dear sir, my dear Mr. Renshawe—" He shook Gervase by the hand with great warmth, while Ambrose stood glaring with horrified disbelief.

Gervase nodded coolly. "So here you are, Tidmarsh—in at the death, after all. Well, you'll admit I've given every one a good run for their money, haven't I?"

"Mr. Blythe," stuttered Ambrose, "I don't understand this masquerade. I don't know what you are doing in this house. Every one here knows you for what you really are."

"Exactly," agreed Gervase blandly. "It is all rather astonishing, isn't it? I was sure you'd be surprised."

"And I was sure, Colonel Tidmarsh," put in the Honourable Augusta firmly, "that, as you appeared to have a completely wrong idea about the recent events that have been causing so much excitement and gossip in the village, you would be glad to know that all the peculiar stories about my husband's nephew are completely untrue. I am sure you will be the first to offer your old friend your congratulations and welcome his home-coming to the Priory."

Ambrose was completely stunned. This climax had taken him entirely by surprise, and he had no words for the moment. He looked at Jocelyn with a sense of being outside a door that had been firmly closed. This was so unexpected, so inexplicable. He had never realised that she had ever given Gervase a thought seriously, or that Gervase had had an opportunity of paying her court. She stood beside Gervase now, lovely in her happy serenity. To-night she was different. There was a suggestion of completeness, an air of having found something in life that she had hitherto lacked, a glowing warmth in her eyes and whole aspect that came of the knowledge of loving and being loved by the one man in the world for her. That Gervase should be this one man struck Ambrose as a strangely bitter circumstance, and his feelings were far from being congratulatory or welcom-ing. However, he put aside his gloomy thoughts as far as he was able and did his best to rise to the occasion under the grimly approving eye of his hostess, who was obviously determined to establish a friendly *rapprochement* and ensure an atmos-phere of peace and goodwill. He held out his hand to Jocelyn and murmured his congratulations with as much grace as he could achieve and allowed Gervase to shake his limp fingers in a hearty grip that caused him acute pain.

"That's really nice of you," said Gervase cheerfully. "Jocelyn and I thank you very much indeed for your good wishes."

"A nice spirit," murmured the vicar. "Our new Lord of the Manor is a man of nice feelings, an inestimable blessing. We are *all* to be congratulated."

"It is a matter of great pleasure to me," said the Honourable Augusta, "that Jocelyn will after all follow me at the Priory. She was brought up with that idea and, as every one knows, it was her original destiny and is now rather strangely to be realised. As you say, Vicar, every one is to be congratulated. Now I see Mellowes coming to tell us that dinner is ready. Gervase, will you take Jocelyn? Vicar, your arm, if you please; and Colonel Tidmarsh must be gallant and escort a lady on either arm."

Mellowes, with an air of importance, opened the double doors wide, and Gervase led Jocelyn through. Miss Pallfrey's long pale hand trembled a little as she took Colonel Tidmarsh's arm, and he laid a kindly reassuring hand on it and pressed it gently as he led her away, forgetful of Mrs. Pomfret, who gave a hoot of merriment as she followed them from the room.

"Two's company!" she chuckled. "Who am *I* to spoil the mating of elderly turtle-doves when love is in the air? As Shakespeare says: 'If it were done when 'tis done, then 'twere well it were done quickly,' or words to that effect."

"My dear," murmured the vicar reprovingly, "it isn't kind to jest on such a delicate matter."

The Honourable Augusta stood at the head of the table and looked down its length to where Gervase faced her. "Say Grace, Vicar. The fatted calf is killed, for the Prodigal is returned. I feel that Providence has been kind to the Ditherings."

THE END

FURROWED MIDDLEBROW